The Edge of Pleasure

The Edge of Pleasure

Philippa Stockley

A Harvest Original

Harcourt, Inc.

Orlando Austin New York San Diego Toronto London

www.HarcourtBooks.com

First published in Great Britain as a paperback original by Abacus in 2002

Library of Congress Cataloging-in-Publication Data
Stockley, Philippa.
The edge of pleasure/Philippa Stockley.—1st Harvest ed.
p. cm.
"A Harvest Original."
First published in Great Britain by Abacus in 2002.
1. Artists—Fiction. 2. London (England)—Fiction. 3. Self-destructive behavior—
Fiction. 4. Triangles (Interpersonal relations)—Fiction. I. Title.
PR6119.T65E34 2006
823'.914—dc22 2005023774
ISBN-13: 978-0-15-603210-0 ISBN-10: 0-15-603210-4

Text set in AGaramond

Printed in the United States of America
First U.S. edition 2006
A C E G I K J H F D B

For my father and mother

In the middle of the night you wake up. You start to cry. What's happening to me? Oh, my life, oh, my youth . . . There's some wine left in the bottle. You drink it. The clock ticks. Sleep . . .

From *Good Morning, Midnight,* 1939, by Jean Rhys

Prologue

On his forty-second birthday, Gilver Memmer woke up and realised he had slept for over ten years.

He lay and stared at the ceiling where a blade of light struck in from carelessly closed curtains. Beyond this pure flash, the ceiling was patched yellow. A cobweb made a wavering M near one corner. There was a dried-blood smudge near the other, where he had once thrown a cricket ball. He had been meaning to paint over it.

The room was not large. Dark curtains, too long and with missing rings, puddled on to piles of books. Bent into thick folds the heavy brocade was snagged. Fine coiled wires that might have sprung from a dainty watch poked out among the pulls, miniature priapisms stuck with yellow silk-fluff.

An old and very fine mahogany chest of drawers occupied a third of the wall opposite the bed, its ringed top piled with books, a burnt lamp, two empty whisky bottles, a mug and an evening jacket from the night before. Heaped clothes took up most of the floor. What floorboards showed were thickly dusty. Dust muddled the shaft of light, the only pretty thing in the room, apart from four cheap Dürer prints under dull glass. Not one hung straight.

Gilver felt around on the floor next to the bed until his fingers met a bottle with a weight of whisky in it, and a cup. He rolled over enough to pour some and groped for a cigarette.

Crooking his head uncomfortably in his elbow he looked

at the girl next to him. She had her mouth open and appeared dead. There were a lot of amalgam fillings at the back, yet she could not be more than twenty-five. They had met at a party the night before. He offered to take her home, staring down her cardigan, wondering if she would sleep with him. Lydia had seized his elbow as they staggered into a cab and wasted no time kissing him. He banged on the driver's window. At his flat they went straight to bed. He was not sure if he had made love to her, then remembered he had tried and failed. She didn't seem bothered either way and went to sleep without further embraces. Did he know her name? He thought not.

When she woke Gilver made a cup of tea. She left shortly afterwards, picking up and putting down a few books, turning them over in her hands and replacing them anyhow. This was annoying but he said nothing. Although he wanted to fuck her when she was sitting up drinking tea, making no attempt at conversation, with the duvet bunched under her armpits, it didn't seem a good idea. It would certainly have made her more difficult to get rid of.

When the street door slammed Gilver drank the last finger of Scotch and got out of bed. He wandered round his untidy living room and then went slowly up to the studio.

Gilver Memmer was a painter. At least, that's what everybody said who cared to remember. A brilliant painter, that was the general opinion, but he hadn't shown for so long, no one could think when they had last seen his work. He was still alive, though, wasn't he? A rumour had gone round that he was in a clinic; someone suggested he was dead, which had some currency for a while – it was almost more comfortable that way than the other. A name that was once on everyone's lips was heard less often or dismissed with a shrug of the shoulders, a strange look – there but for the grace of God; a slightly embarrassed laugh, twitched eyebrows. Then nothing.

PART ONE

GILVER

I

Gilver had been precociously talented. When he was a very young child, everyone admired his skill, his ability to draw straight lines without a ruler. A painting he did (in powder paint) of a red horse when he was four aroused considerable admiration. At ten, a drawing of a cast of the Venus de Milo, the spoils from a school coach trip to a London museum, led to the opportunity to lift up Kate Seddon's pleated skirt and have a good feel.

This early connection between possession of artistic skill and the granting of sexual favours was not lost on him. With a thick mop of golden hair and a physique that soon added muscles to gangling height, his manhood was swift.

By the time he went to the Ruskin, where he spent a great deal of time drinking and fucking interspersed with briefer periods painting and drawing, he easily consolidated the reputation of genius. The mantle was waiting. In the absence of other takers, Gilver slipped it on as if it had been put ready.

At Oxford he took up rowing to build the muscles in his legs and arms, creating a leonine body and staying power to get through exams easily without limiting his social life.

When, later, he arrived in London, after a few months' travelling on his own version of the Grand Tour, he was smugly ensconced in his talent. Everyone thought him talented and it was true, after all. He knew everybody who mattered, as far as he could tell, and everyone wanted to introduce him to everyone else.

Gilver shared a flat with his friends Harry and Max in Cornwall Gardens. They had been at Oxford together, having made friends at the Wine and Cheese Society, an excellent place to get outrageously drunk and debate cricket and girls. Gilver was the most handsome, standing a few inches over Max's clean, rich looks and a clear head over Harry, who didn't seem to mind being laughingly excused as an intellectual misfit. When there were girls around they headed straight for Gilver, who over the years benignly passed a couple on to Max. He got away with it every time. Easiness; the impression that his skin fitted so well it had been tailor-made, along with a grinning generosity and devil-may-care attitude were alluring to young women and forgivable to young men. When Max called him a lucky bastard, which he frequently did, Gilver only grinned wider, showing good teeth with a slight space at the front. He called it his Solzhenitsyn smile, although he was not absolutely sure how to spell it. No one knew how true Max's words were but they all – particularly Gilver – seemed delighted. It was logical to move in together when they headed for London. They were used to each other and there were no arguments – in Waitrose, at least.

Gilver had the best room, which was big enough to paint in. Even though the flat was at the top of the stuccoed building it didn't stop him painting large canvases that had to be manhandled down the stairs with difficulty. His first one-man show took place when he was only a year out of Oxford and it was a tremendous success. There was a piece in *Harpers* and photos in *Tatler*. A girl he had a fling with wrote him up as a bright young thing. The *Evening Standard* called him a young Turk. The show sold out. He was invited everywhere.

He had always valued his paintings very high on the

inverted principle that no one believed you could be any good unless the price said so. In consequence, by the time he was twenty-five he was extremely wealthy with a wardrobe to demonstrate it, and moved out of Cornwall Gardens to a place of his own.

Gilver rather favoured Savile Row tailoring with a supervised twist: he had thirty suits, all skilfully hand-piqued, set off by the occasional gleam of nacre or gold in the lining, an eccentric number of buttons on the sleeve or a viciously narrow cuff to the trouser. His touches were usually but not always subtle. For the boudoir, as well as gentlemanly cashmeres in soft browns and restrained Paisleys, there was a particularly handsome dressing-gown of Thai silk brocade in imperial purple and crimson, cut from an ancient Ottoman pattern book he found in the Victoria and Albert library.

Then there were fifteen pairs of handmade shoes on custom-built trees, several pairs of kid boots, two of patent pumps, two of embroidered Kurdish slippers. Four hand-stitched cashmere evening suits each with a different rever and tone suited various kinds of parties; there were more than fifty day shirts in every weight, weave and colour, and eight evening ones, all identical. He had myriad ties in the most magnificent silks, some of them specially made for him in a pleasing jacquard called the Memmer Ripple by a small Lyon company, woven in minute thread-dyed batches. Link and stud boxes had their own compartments in his wardrobe as did a peculiar long sharkskin box containing ten pairs of evening gloves he never wore, as well as yellow suede, pigskin, and a spectacular black pair with sealskin turnbacks that always looked dashing. Covert coats; sweeping black, charcoal and loden overcoats; breeches; Tattersall shirts, and a curious range of waistcoats (because he did not approve of them) by no means completed the town wardrobe.

Three French armoires housed this booty in a rented mews house between South Kensington and Knightsbridge. He took over the lease of the garage beneath for a considerable amount of money and turned it into a studio, connected internally by a spiral stair. Its double doors were handy for the massive works he produced.

In his twenty-eighth year a New York gallery offered him the biggest exhibition so far, a one-man show on the scale of a retrospective. Gilver rose to the challenge, unruffled by his youth, marshalling twenty canvases of enormous proportion. These were rolled and flown to New York where new stretchers were being made to his specifications.

The SoHo exhibition marked a turning point. Success was guaranteed. The paintings, moody and authoritative sweeps of the most expensive pigments, were deemed superb. His vigour in painting was relentless. Unfortunately Shira, the young assistant who primed the canvases in between rushing up and down the spiral staircase for frenzied sex, misheard his recipe instructions. As the paintings were restretched in New York they cracked one after the other. Only the feeblest survived unscathed. The rest reticulated like the backs of leaves. One or two inexplicably oozed.

The exhibition was cancelled but not before the American critics got hold of it, gleefully ripping the golden boy of British painting limb from limb. He was excoriated as a lazy charlatan, an example of the failure of Old World art. For no apparent reason the *New Yorker* was especially virulent. Despite the fact that his American backer demanded the repayment of huge sums of money, and a contract with the Museum of Modern

Art to buy one of his works was cancelled, Gilver's reputation at home was undented.

If anything, being spurned by American Philistines for what was probably – he decided – their own fault, only lent an extra burnish to his halo. He was fêted now not only for being handsome and extraordinarily talented but for being misunderstood. Before, the mere fact of his brilliance meant he could have anyone he wanted, anywhere and at any time (although he understood, albeit dimly, that there might be one or two exceptions); now, the apparent setback made women hurl themselves at him to cosset and nurture his wounded pride.

Gilver had a magnificent time. He threw parties attended by twenty or so of the loveliest models, actresses and television presenters intermixed with young male writers and musicians conspicuously less good-looking than him – so many girls, he couldn't remember their names. He painted the front of the house a colour that would make a useful backdrop tone for newspaper photographs and adjusted the porch lighting to minimise glare.

A year went by in which he did not paint a single thing. The New York disaster shook him, although he never mentioned this to anybody. Whether he painted or not, it made no difference. He was invited to the same glamorous and influential dinner parties and dances. His name was on the list of gallery openings, magazine launches, literary events, fashion shows. He was invited to country-house weekends and summers and winters abroad.

If anything, having more time on his hands made him even more of a success: he was insatiably sociable. He understood the responsibilities of polite behaviour, diligently dispatching charming thank-you notes and courteous acceptances on a pleasingly small and masculine paper from Smythsons. The handsome face and body set off by rigorously updated clothes made him that rare thing: a gorgeous, lone, enigmatic male.

Gilver further enhanced his standing over the next decade with a string of judiciously chosen liaisons. Before he was thirty the knowledge that he could have any woman he pleased made him enthusiastically – if circumspectly – promiscuous, but he had grown wiser. Choice made him discriminating. Moreover, as his peers began to settle down, he confined his attentions to unmarried women, thus gaining the liking and respect – only pleasantly tinged with envy – of influential husbands. 'Memmer's a good man' and 'Memmer's sound', exclusively masculine phrases, served as his passport to clubs and committees, judging panels and men-only drinking jaunts where important decisions got made, some reaching as far as Westminster.

He spent a delirious two years with a recently widowed Austrian countess, three with the scion of a publishing house, six months with a very boring but world-famous model who went by a one-syllable name, two years with the heiress to a vast fortune in olive oil and one with an unwilling art student, whom he introduced to techniques that availed her nothing outside his bedroom.

During all this time he painted little of any significance but was always ready, if asked, to toss off a sketch on a napkin, an envelope or a piece of paper that happened to be lying around. On the Croisette, at a shooting party in Argyll, fishing on the Laerdal, at a modernist house-party in Lewes, curled up by a fire in Gstaad or even at the Crush Bar, he was always delighted to oblige. His handsome demeanour, the strong brown hand carelessly, faultlessly using whatever pencil or pen was given him to its best advantage, his total absorption interrupted by a sudden, penetrating glance . . . Gilver won hearts with no effort at all.

These paltry sketches on their stained, crumpled or lipstick-smudged ground were immediately slapped behind bevelled glass and costly frames and prominently placed in the best drawing rooms and the loveliest bedrooms the length and breadth of the country.

II

Before the New York débâcle Gilver had made enormous sums of money. His paintings sold for many thousands each and with every sale he raised the price a few notches. It increased their desirability. He was soon into tens of thousands. Aston Martin gave him a car to be seen around town in. Fashion designers dressed him for nothing.

He had done some sketches for two big advertising companies that ended up on sky-high billboards, one in Seville and the other in Woking. It was his hand doing a bit of cursory painting in the film *A Brush With Angelika*, a ribald inconsequential tale that won the Berlin Film Festival and was a cult classic at Cannes. It was at the première for *A Brush With Angelika* that he met Eugenia, the Austrian countess, who sailed into the reception impossibly late in an unlined dress of cherry chiffon that lent her unknickered bottom something of a monkey on heat. Gilver sized up the man on her arm, a sallow, wizened afterthought who turned out to be her husband, at a glance. Nevertheless their affair started later.

While his parties before the show in New York were extravagant, they had also been profitable. Vodka distilleries and wine importers were not only delighted to supply the liquor but to leave Gilver with an extensive cellar. He owned some spectacular clarets and ports and had bought cases of forty-year-old whisky at a notable wine auction. Since he now painted very little and for months at a stretch not at all, a large section of the old garage, his studio, was carefully partitioned off into temperature-controlled cellarage. Gilver often went there to admire the darkly promising bottles and remove a couple for use.

The importance of drinking elegantly was a habit refined at Oxford. Even on the rare days he did not have company and stayed at home, he drank the best part of a decent bottle of claret at luncheon and at dinner. Plain-sided massy decanters held port, whisky and brandy. The freezer was stocked with four sorts of vodka. Curious Brazilian, Tunisian and Cuban liqueurs catered to the strongest stomachs.

In the decade after New York he paid scant attention to money. It was enough to know there was loads of it. He felt, correctly, that worrying about money was the only thing that might give him indigestion.

The cobbled street Gilver lived in was very pretty, turning off a wealthy row of terraced houses in powder blue, white, lemon and pink, with immaculate railings and stoops. Low-fronted antique and jewellery shops, a very good bakery and an excellent vintner and delicatessen supplied many daily needs.

He had accounts in most of the local shops which he used frequently on first-name terms.

One late September Friday morning, Gilver went for a stroll along the street, pausing to make a note of a rare cigarette case finished in undamaged *guilloché* enamel, luminous rose. The air was clean and sharp, the sky above the flat-topped houses a fresh blue. Even though there were few trees, a particular sparkle on the well-brushed pavements and a lively note in the air made this day the first of a glorious autumn. Gilver breathed deeply, catching delicious perfume from the warm rye in white paper tucked under his arm.

The maid came early on Fridays and did not reappear until Monday morning. He had established this somewhat unsatisfactory arrangement because the privacy gained by fending for himself over the weekend outweighed the irritation of making his own bed. Which he rarely did. There always seemed to be manicured hands eager to do it, fussing with the corners as if their owners were in training to be nurses at the Front. It amused him to play hapless bachelor with whoever spent the weekend. A little homely cooking and mess-making, if it wasn't carried too far, added zest.

The Countess, Eugenia – he thought how much she would have liked the cigarette case, her grandmother had been Russian – derived great pleasure from making omelettes for breakfast. They were rather lavishly mixed with bits of shell, but she fed them to him in bed saying they were good for stamina. They made violent love afterwards, sometimes until she begged him to stop, which he made a point of ignoring, fucking her harder. He disliked eggs and found her lack of understanding on this point – although he never explained – a reason for punishment. Eugenia loved it.

Rye bread was also one of her favourites. He wondered if he was missing her and decided to phone later in the day. She had married again and was living in London and Vienna by turns. Her second husband, a banker, bored her. Sometimes she rang up to talk about it at length. Gilver taunted her by pointing out that she did not even have the excuse of having gone from the sublime to the ridiculous, but when she was genuinely upset he was supportive, sympathising about the hours and often days she had not expected to spend alone. He agreed that it was completely unacceptable and who did Anders (half Norwegian) think she was? But for one reason or another he was only rarely able to meet: perhaps for an early, very public supper, or for lunch in a bustling restaurant they favoured, where everyone could see you but only lip-readers were privy to your conversation.

He liked his past mistresses, especially Eugenia whom he also, perhaps dangerously, considered a friend. They operated in the same way and were physically similar on passing inspection, with the same absentmindedness concerning conventional behaviour. While he had never yet considered taking a mistress back he was happy to let them toy with the possibility.

The mews was calm. The cobbles felt good under his fine leather soles. A slight edge of discomfort created the need to walk carefully to prevent actual pain.

His orange double drawing room was a bath of light, heightening the blue beyond the window panes. A letter had come while he was walking and lay on the breakfast table by the window where it had been put by the maid. He pulled a knife-blade through the envelope, thinking of Eugenia, and sat down to read.

The letter told him that the lease on his house had come up. Gilver read with astonishment that there wasn't enough money to renew it. He sat looking at the paper for some time, the acrid smell of Polish bread still in his nostrils.

He was thirty-nine, unbelievably handsome and popular, and looking at a piece of paper that while not quite announcing bankruptcy did not mince words about its close proximity.

Gilver understood that no one connected with him closely could ever be allowed to suspect what had happened. Even though things might change, he needed a breathing space to reinvent himself. The one intolerable thing would be the loss of face associated with poverty. It was a nuisance that he had split up only two weeks before with the young art student, Deborah. When he had met her she was smarting under the condition her parents made that she finish her two-year course before marrying the man she had in mind, a penniless scoundrel. Gilver never admitted that he knew her suitor Damian quite well and even rather liked him. He was clever, ambitious, and had prospects. However, in several sessions of comforting an unconsolable Deborah and listening with his gravest demeanour to bilious rants against her mother and father, Gilver found that her feelings for her former lover couldn't have been all that significant. After little persuasion she turned her attention to him.

Her trust fund was massive and included a property port-folio, which now, he thought wryly, would have come in handy.

On reflection it was good timing that Deborah had gone,

after a childish outburst over wanting to put some of her things in one of his wardrobes. How often, even in the middle of adversity, some detail worked in your favour. He didn't intend her to know about his setback unless it turned to his advantage.

III

After taking in the fateful letter's contents at a glance, Gilver poured a large brandy and sat back to think. The drawing-room walls shimmered in the playful noon light like the inside of a blood orange.

He went through a mental list of the hundreds of people he knew. Surely one of them must be useful.

He could borrow money easily, of course. He only had to pick up the phone. Eugenia, whom he intended to call anyway, would lend however much he wanted without question. But borrowing money was something he never did. It was distasteful, gave the lender a hold over you: Gilver liked to keep that in his own hands.

His friends and acquaintances were in powerful positions. Those near his own age were editors of magazines, political analysts, vice presidents of banks, gallery owners, playwrights. A large proportion of them were simply rich and always had been. Money seeped from his contact book. If he added up what that book was worth it would pay off a national debt somewhere, let alone address his paltry needs.

If only there was some way to siphon off the minuscule

amount wanting, a little from everyone, nobody would even feel the difference. For a moment, while he poured a third brandy, it was as if he had had a revelation and discovered some important financial fact no one else knew. Why, by redistributing wealth intelligently, how many problems could be solved!

Outside the window it was blissfully sunny. The rowan tree opposite was laden with berries sparkling rich coral in the sun, its clusters heavy and ripe. Nothing outside was diminished, yet the heat from the sun didn't seem to reach him. He shivered. His glass was empty. He refilled it. Systematically going through groups of people in the organised Rolodex that was his mind, he trawled through a Rothschild party the summer before. In a chance conversation next to a trestle heaped with great bowls of strawberries and gilt jugs of cream, fat Lucy Cavender, who had married Max in a coup that took everyone's breath away, told Gilver that Harry had not only come out but given up on physics and taken a course in interior design.

'Isn't it amazing?' she asked, her eyes completely round like blue marbles dropped into a bowl of dough, helping herself to another pint of strawberries. Gilver squeezed the chicken-flesh of her upper arm, which made her go pink and tell him everything.

Ignoring the concern of all the people around him, Harry did up the flat he was living in and sold it for double. He had done the same thing repeatedly. Those who once laughed at him now sought his advice.

Harry must surely know somewhere much cheaper Gilver could move to. Harry would be only too pleased to hear from him. Harry would fall over himself to help.

*   *   *

19

All thoughts of Eugenia temporarily discarded, Gilver rang Harry up. It wasn't difficult to find him. He recalled Lucy's whispering snicker that Harry had given himself a grand-sounding name and started a business. Gilver wasted no time calling. He put it to Harry, whom he hadn't seen or thought about for years, that he wanted a place to use as a second studio, somewhere with a bit of life, somewhere Bohemian. Knightsbridge was too stuffy. He invented a couple next door with a dog that barked and disturbed him when he was trying to work. He found nothing deceitful in this.

Over the phone the edge of pleasure in his old friend's voice was palpable. Like a spaniel, Gilver thought, jumping up to lick my face after all this time.

Gilver had known Harry longer than any other of his male acquaintances. They had been at the same dilapidated school in Surrey, where Harry had always been in awe of the older boy. Years after, Harry was proud, if he got the chance, to say that they had been 'at school together', a way of putting it that would not have crossed the other's mind – a coincidence, in Gilver's estimation, conferring no advantage. Harry pitched up at Oxford the year after Gilver. He had trouble getting used to the shortened name his friend had acquired at the Ruskin and sometimes still named him Ogilvy in full.

Harry was bright, a scholarship boy. They had that in common. But where Gilver had always been unquestioningly confident, tarred early with the brush of genius, Harry was shy. No one really understood why Harry was shy and even when he came out in his mid-twenties, when he and Gilver had already lost touch, it didn't necessarily explain it. Harry was still shy. If anything he was shyer than ever. But Gilver knew why Harry was like this, at least with him.

There are some people preoccupied with their own vanity on the momentous scale of Gilver Memmer who never take any notice of anyone else. They plough along on a crest of self-importance to die as ignorant of the world as they came in, impervious to the feelings of others as a hog to mud. Gilver, on the other hand, however busy he was with his own interests and possibly when most absorbed by them, knew the secrets of another soul through the merest touch or the fraction of an unguarded glance. It was as if his skin was covered not with fine hairs but millions of tiny aerials.

By the time they had spent three days sharing a flat together, Gilver knew that what he had assumed was hero-worship from the ugly little tot at school and well-founded admiration at Oxford was, in fact, love. Harry was devoted to him. Memories of Harry staggering along the nettle-choked path from the main school building to one of the Nissen huts housing the library, trying to pull up his socks while he carried Gilver's books, came back to him. At the time he assumed it was normal – Harry was a junior, after all.

At Cornwall Gardens it was Harry who insisted Gilver should have the best room, despite a brief struggle from Max; Harry who packed his paintings and made corner protectors for them when Gilver couldn't be bothered and was enjoying a bottle of wine or a draining-board shag in the kitchen. It was Harry who – Gilver now remembered – retouched the banisters whenever Gilver, pretty well hurling a canvas down the stairs in his impatience to have done with it, scraped the paint off, back to the wood. Harry with his little pots of paint that he got from God knew where and unskilfully blended.

Gilver had been able to make him go crimson simply by bending over the pot into which Harry peered, holding up a squirrel-hair brush to see if he had got the colour right (which he had not), and saying, 'Hmmm,' under his breath, close enough to ruffle the hairs on Harry's forearm. Gilver knew instinctively that Harry would never do anything except adore from a distance. Even Harry didn't seem to understand what was happening to him, or didn't want to.

Harry's parents had given up their cramped flat in Putney and gone back to Swansea, as soon as Harry gained his degree. They had stretched themselves putting their only son through school, and were very religious, in a way that brooked no dissent. Although he had eliminated any trace of accent he once had, in itself a grievance to his mother and source of contempt to his father, Harry could no more go to them and say he was a faggot than he could have announced a decision not to support the national side.

It was this natural bent for loyalty, love and honour that Gilver now manipulated.

IV

A week later Harry called and said come straight over. He had found something that might do, although he was already lamenting its disgusting condition. Gilver forced a laugh and suggested they see it anyway. 'It's more Ladbroke Grove than Notting Hill.' There was an apologetic twinge in Harry's voice. The distinction meant nothing to Gilver. They sounded equally hateful. Even when they arrived at the depressing, once-white terrace with its flaking pillars, in one of the worst bits off Ladbroke Grove, he still felt blank.

The flat Harry had found was at the top. It had been squatted for a couple of years, Harry said, and was in a pretty bad state. He went first, worrying over his shoulder about the difficulty of getting materials and canvases up and down the stairs.

'I'm working on some smaller pieces,' Gilver lied glibly, 'so it suits me fine. Don't worry, Harry.'

Had Harry always been such a worrier? No wonder his hair was falling out. Gilver, it was true, had receded slightly at the temples and had a little grey, which he hid with a product marketed at women – Burnished Gold, it was called, and ridiculously simple to use – but he rarely worried about anything. Someone could always be found to make things better.

After struggling for a while with the new key they got inside. Gilver was taken aback. Did people really live like this? Although Harry had already explained that the flat had been squatted, nothing in his limited experience of ordinary life prepared Gilver for what met them.

The door led into an apology of a hall. Off this gave a bedroom, a cupboard, a tiny bathroom with a rank smell and a small sitting room with a sort of kitchenette bar in the corner.

Gilver's heart sank. He couldn't live here and it certainly wouldn't sustain its fictitious purpose. Irritation was in danger of giving way to anger. The whole point of the exercise was that he was supposed to be looking for a second studio. How could Harry be so stupid? He held his tongue with difficulty.

Harry caught Gilver's look. 'I know, it's pretty terrible.'

While Gilver lounged gingerly on a filthy window-sill, patting imaginary dust off his thighs with the back of a pair of kid gloves and wishing he was somewhere else, Harry stood in the middle of the tiny sitting room – or whatever it was supposed to be – and took notes.

He wasn't bad-looking although distinctly short to Gilver's mind, perhaps five foot six. Curling mousy hair, now worn on the collar, and small round glasses made of the sort of astronaut metal that springs back. He was sporting an unstructured tweed coat and soft blue shirt, and his feet seemed to be shod in plimsolls.

Watching Harry toss back his head till his remaining ringlets caught the light and frown at the artex ceiling, Gilver mused that this was a different person altogether from the one he once knew. At school, and at Oxford when they shared a flat, Harry was a nervous swot. To correct rather peering short sight he wore heavy black-framed glasses, which were always smeared. They gave him a scholarly but unattractive air. Tailored suits, badly chosen, completed the impression of an aspiring bank manager with short legs.

Harry had read physics, because he was good at it, and got a double first. His father was dissatisfied even then and felt Harry should try for the civil service rather than mess around with Bunsen burners. He thought a dependable career important. Gilver did not waste time speculating on what Harry's father would think now but returned to the trying inspection of the flat.

Never in his wildest imagination had he conceived anything so squalid. A passing glance at the cooking arrangements revealed an ancient stove smothered in congealed grease on which sat a couple of aluminium saucepans, coated in glutinous khaki. The tiled splashbacks and meagre work-surface were covered in runnels of the same pus-like brown stuff. An unbelievable stench came from an open black rubbish bag spilling on to the patch of linoleum behind the counter.

In the rest of the room a stained double mattress and blue sleeping-bag lay on the swirling floral carpet, with a pair of broken dumbbells and a video recorder that must have have been dished in with a crowbar. Small plastic bags, empty beer bottles and cans, items of clothing, a wooden parrot and some rubber-wear magazines were randomly scattered. A small two-seater sofa, half of whose seat had been burnt and gave off a vile smell, stood on its end in one corner, serving as a table for a smoked-glass mug with mould in the bottom and a paper plate of dried chips. Whatever colour the walls had once been they were now ochre, turning to black round the door handles, as if the previous occupants had swung from room to room.

Harry glanced over to where Gilver sat motionless. 'Oh, God, Ogilvy, I'm sorry, this isn't all of it. Come and look.' They picked their way back into the hall. Harry opened the cupboard opposite the front door, which Gilver had assumed housed brooms. A staircase led straight up, unlit by the broken bulb dangling from a rudimentary flex. 'The loft was being extended before the squatters took over. It's a decent space. Come and see.'

Gilver followed with no feelings whatsoever, except disgust when his merino coat caught on something sticky on one of the narrow walls. The staircase rapidly lightened. At the top was a large room, almost completely bare except for two more single mattresses and two folding chairs, one with a pair of dirty jeans draped over the back. Rucked dark grey carpet covered most of the floor of a room about twenty-five feet long and twenty deep, with dormer windows right along the street side and an off-centre skylight.

It was cold. He could see his breath. The roof was imperfectly insulated and beams gaped across half the ceiling. The rest was clumsily boarded over. Against one wall a stack of chipboard, presumably intended to finish the job, still rested. Perhaps the skylight had posed Neanderthal woodwork an insurmountable problem.

'It's rough.' Harry waved his arms in uncoordinated circles, peering anxiously at Gilver with a strange expression of embarrassment. 'But you've got a good light. I know the rest is disgusting, it's not what you're used to, but . . .'

Gilver sat on the jeanless chair. 'You're a good friend, Harry. It's fine. Let's go and have a drink.'

V

They got blisteringly drunk in a pub off Ladbroke Grove, near the new studio, as Harry enthusiastically called it. Gilver turned down his friend's offer to do the place up. Harry was well-intentioned but it was intolerable to admit he couldn't afford it.

At first Harry was full of grandiose schemes, but Gilver squashed them. Harry's less fancy ideas included a steel shower room, panels of glass that turned opaque at the touch of a button, slate floors heated from underneath and something called intelligent lighting. It sounded like a load of expensive crap to Gilver, who preferred things hewn from a château, the more scutcheons the better.

'You're very kind,' Gilver purred, deliberately touching Harry's knee for a millisecond. Harry blushed scarlet. 'And very clever.' Harry went puce. 'I can never thank you enough for finding me the studio. I've been aching to work somewhere new for ages. One gets so stale, don't you think?'

Harry was pink with the pleasure of being appealed to and looked like a happy raccoon. He had not been accustomed, since Oxford, to getting blind drunk. The life of a physicist had been rather more straitlaced. Even in his new incarnation he worked more than ten hours a day and had little time for the glamorous social life people inferred.

'I've got my own team,' Gilver said, 'and they've helped me so much I think I'll use them. You don't mind, do you, Harry? I don't want anything done, really, except a good clean. I rather like the idea of the struggling artist. And that's quite a garret.'

Harry looked aghast. 'But you've never struggled in your life, Ogilvy. You don't know how to struggle. You've always been so successful. Everyone says so.' He beamed, flushed, over his beer.

'Well, I said I like the idea!' Gilver laughed. He hoped it didn't sound hollow. 'Maybe I should give it a go. I was always moved by that story of the sculptor in Paris putting his only blanket round his maquette on a cold night so it didn't crack as the temperature fell.'

'What happened?'

'He was found frozen to death.'

They both considered their drinks.

'Ogilvy, is everything all right?'

The question was surprising. Surely he didn't sound desperate? 'Harry, your imagination's too vivid. It's probably why you're such an astonishing success with this new business.'

'Oh,' demurred Harry, blushing again, 'I don't think so.' He looked pleased, his question forgotten. Gilver saw he had regained control. He consolidated it by asking Harry about his new ventures. After a hesitant start, glancing at Gilver to see if he was really interested (he never had been), Harry told him about his new life. He knew it was a surprise, but he loved it. He'd never admitted he liked that sort of thing, women's stuff they always called it.

'Love life?' Gilver interrupted breezily, maliciously. He knew Harry was out. He also knew that Harry didn't know that that fat-arsed butterball Cavender had told him so, or that she'd mocked him as pretentious.

Harry looked at his beer again. 'There is someone.' He hesitated, a smile starting.

For a moment Gilver had the loathsome impression Harry was actually going to come out with it and tell him a load of stuff he simply had no wish to know. For heaven's sake, surely there were limits, however drunk Harry was.

Something had to be done. He rose to his feet. 'Bet she's a cracker, Hal, you devil. I'm having a party in a fortnight, you must come. Bring your new girl.'

He patted Harry's shoulder firmly as he rose, forcing him back into his seat, and left the table; but not before he had seen the expression of misery that Harry, too slow in ducking his head, couldn't hide.

* * *

It was a long walk home. He had sold his Aston Martin through a private dealership a few days before, which was a damn nuisance. However, the speedy transaction raised enough cash for the deposit on the new flat, which was rented, and enough over to throw a party at the mews. Walking through the dark streets he started planning a triumphant event to put everybody off the scent of his financial disaster; a party shining so bright that no one would guess it was his last – at least for the moment. Gilver shivered. He had three weeks before his Knightsbridge lease ran out and then he would have to go and live in that ramshackle pigsty. The thought of what must be done in such a short time made his head, already swimming with blended whisky, reel. He hadn't worked hard for so long he had forgotten how. He had known once. For the past ten years, he thought, walking fast, he had let people do things for him, carry him along, tell him he was marvellous, welcome him without question. If he wanted something he took it. If there was a struggle he won. If it was a question of money he paid without thinking. For ten years he had traded on a reputation earned so easily such a long time before, and for ten years the money he seldom thought about had held out.

What had he been thinking?

Three years before, when he noticed that his once endless funds had suddenly – it seemed – shrunk to what he con-sidered pygmy proportions, he had been persuaded to invest the bulk of what was left. He was not then, in fact, poor. But he had felt a hint of it. That was tantamount to the same thing.

Gilver always knew better than anyone else what was best, even on subjects about which he knew absolutely nothing.

Despite being strongly advised to take on a solid mixed port-folio, he invested in just two stocks he fancied the sound of, a two-to-one split of his capital. It was the system he used at the tracks and it never failed. The gist of the second paragraph of the hateful letter was that the chief of these stocks was wiped out. The other had dived so far you needed a snorkel.

Until now, his stance of immutable certainty had always served him well. That the world does not like a ditherer he discovered young. Once it was men of action who won the day and got the girl, by going to war, leading armadas and battalions, raping and pillaging where need or whim demanded. In the modern world, since there were no territories to go and steal legitimately and piracy was considered illegal, there were other ways to get the same effect. It seemed to him that by invoking the shadow of the sword you could still appear to live by it: by acting as a leader of men, men followed; by giving an opinion with no leeway for discussion, your opinion was accepted.

It had been the same with his paintings. He knew they were good – that could not be gainsaid. The point was that he wasted no time in telling people they were good and worth a lot of money and those same people told other people the same thing, as if by rote. Like a pyramid sell, or one of those hideous letter things people talked about, his reputation made itself from his one little squeak in the wilderness. The message went from mouth to mouth, wallet to wallet, drawing room to drawing room. Once it started it rolled on and on, gaining momentum, weight and value as it went. He could no more have stopped it than James Mason could have stopped the polystyrene boulder in *Journey to the Centre of the Earth.*

Gilver pulled his coat round him. There was a snap in the air, it was midnight.

What would those same people think when they found he had scarcely a penny? He had worked out, on the back of an envelope, that there was enough left to pay the rent on this new place for a few years, with the sort of pittance left over that he would have felt guilty giving to an itinerant gardener. That was more or less the size of it, upfront. Which lists would he stay on, which doors would slam shut?

VI

The new flat was cleared of large pieces of furniture and carpet the next day. Gilver's team, two jobbing white-van men called John and Steve, turned up at lunchtime with a largish truck and threw things into the back as if they were weightless. Gilver noticed that the elder, Steve, did not seem remotely bothered by the state of the flat, or by trips up and down the stairs. John, a muscled South African from Johannesburg, tramped to and fro in knee-length shorts with carpenter's pockets, and army boots, keeping a running commentary on their progress. 'I've seen much worse than this,' he said conversationally. 'This is pretty ordinary. The thing is, when people have to leave a place in a hurry they just don't care. I've clocked some shockers, you wouldn't believe.'

Gilver gave them a bit of extra cash to take up the carpets. He imagined it was a difficult job, having watched when the

31

specially woven, border-edged stair carpet was painstakingly fitted in the mews.

John positioned himself in the doorway of the sitting room with Gilver hovering uselessly behind, said, 'Hold your breath!', bent over and pulled up the entire carpet with one great ripping flourish.

Dust filled the room as the vanquished thing lay there, its swirls bunched in rigid peaks.

John folded his arms and watched it, waiting for signs of life. 'There might be the odd tack, there might not,' he explained contemptuously. 'Rubbish like this generally just lies there, like an old tart. You don't need to hold it down.'

He went off whistling and Gilver heard him tramping over-head, rolling the grey carpet, which shortly appeared in a flaccid log-dive down the stairs from the studio room, straight out of the front door of the flat. 'Handy that.' Steve pointed to the way the doors to the flat and the attic were exactly aligned. They listened to John thud-thudding the carpet down the communal stairs to the street door, an abbreviated 'Fuck' rising up at every turning. 'Whoever designed that had a bit of common sense.'

Gilver asked why.

'You'd be surprised, but let's say those doors were just a couple of inches out of kilter with each other, you wouldn't believe how much trouble you'd have getting something like a sofa or a carpet up here. It's steep, see, and there's very little room to manoeuvre from the stairs outside to the stairs in. That was a good job.'

Gilver mulled this over.

'What about the fridge and cooker? Want us to clear those?'

How do you tell? he wondered, not exactly panicking, but feeling unfamiliarly uncertain.

Both his new friends were quick with an opinion. The fridge was rubbish and had to go, one whiff was enough, he'd never get rid of that, those bastards must have had a dead body in it. The cooker was in surprisingly good nick; it just needed a bloody good clean. They'd hardly used the oven, look, too bloody lazy probably, everything had been done on top. Like cavemen. Good as new with a bit of elbow grease. You'd be daft to throw that out.

They manhandled the fridge down the stairs.

When the sound of the truck faded from the street, Gilver sat in the living room on one of the folding chairs.

If possible things looked worse than before. Light was trying to get through the filth crusted on the window. The grey-brown dust-covered floorboards had bits of newspaper from the 1970s, which had been used as underlay, scattered all over them. One had a yellow photograph of Picasso. 'Death of an Immortal', crowed the headline. Gilver crumpled the frail paper and tossed it over the kitchen bar.

Luckily he'd had the foresight, given the temperature of the flat, to tuck a hip flask into his overcoat. He took a few decent pulls before ordering a fridge from John Lewis. At least that was easy. A couple more calls, to get a land-line installed and the electricity and gas reconnected, were less satisfactory. It was incredible to discover that he must be there throughout the next day in order to wait for workmen to arrive.

Impassive voices patched through from Delhi or the Outer Hebrides asked, 'Morning or afternoon, Mr Mommet?' When he demanded a more specific appointment the voices were incredulous. These were very rapid response times, he was getting preferential treatment. Gilver agreed to be there without further discussion.

The flat was depressing. He had to begin cleaning it up. Where did you start a job like that? He had never lived anywhere in London that wasn't immaculate down to the smallest detail. Even the old place in Cornwall Gardens, which until now he fondly recalled in the same light as an outpost of Artistic, was nothing like it. It belonged to Max's uncle, the biographer Piers Cavender, who had moved to Tuscany after his seventh book.

The boys had thought some of the decor a bit retro. There was a baggy old dark-brown corduroy sofa, and a chair that looked like a scooped-out egg hanging from a cord in the ceiling. But there was also a maid who came every day and polished the encaustic tiles in the hall and the stone stair-treads. The two deep-blue Murano glass chandeliers in the drawing room, casting a baleful light on a de Laszlo portrait of Piers's mother Lady Anchor-Cavender, were at least sparkling clean.

In his walk the night before he had passed a row of hardware shops. He thought he could remember the way back, it wasn't far.

Gilver found the street without difficulty, off Portobello Road. The market stalls were in full swing. He crossed an intersection where he was nearly mown down by a rubbish cart and saved himself by pressing against the side of a great green bin on wheels from which a foul smell leaked.

It struck him for the first time that his very smart coat and handmade shoes were inappropriate to the task in hand. The toe of his right shoe was badly scraped and a frond of cabbage stalk clung to the sole. Putting this impediment gingerly aside he went into the shop that sold paint. There were a few people, some of them builders, asking for things. At least, he thought grimly, this is something I understand.

Scanning the shelves behind the counter he noticed a female customer giving him a sideways glance. Never one to waste time he smiled broadly. 'Haven't got a clue what to get,' he lied. 'Do you know this shop well?'

The man behind the counter in a white overcoat had seen it all before.

Gilver and his new acquaintance stepped back from the counter in unison. She was rather short, with chestnut-brown hair that corkscrewed and spiralled below her shoulders, held back with a hard-twisted spotty cotton handkerchief. Bits of hair had come out from their binding and played round her face. She wore a red jersey with a loose, flopping-over neck, and jeans with carpenter's pockets. The style looked much better on her than on John.

She was pretty.

'What are you looking for?' she asked, in a frankly appreciative way.

'I've just taken on a completely hideous flat and it needs a damn good clean and a coat of paint. You look as if you might know what to get. Forgive me if I'm wrong.' He made himself appear anxious as he said the last.

She threw some hair back from her face. It didn't get far but stuck on the shoulder of her sweater. He restrained the impulse to unstick it, just allowing his hand to move perceptibly in that direction.

The movement didn't go unnoticed. The girl blushed. 'I had to do the same thing in my flat last year,' she said. 'It's not that bad when you get started, if you use the right stuff.' She told him what she had used and then looked slightly shy.

There were several people serving. Gilver bought all the things she indicated, including buckets, rubber gloves, sponges and mysterious hanks of dishcloth material, while she attended to her own purchase, a cotton dustsheet.

'Are you doing some decorating too?' He didn't feel like letting her go.

She said she wanted it to put over a sofa, they were a good bargain for that.

They walked out of the shop together.

'You've been really helpful.' Gilver meant it, watching her corkscrew curls turn rich red in the sunshine. 'May I buy you a coffee?'

They found a café where there was room to sit outside on spindly metal chairs and watch passers-by.

Alice said she worked at a newspaper in Canary Wharf. She seemed embarrassed, waiting for approval, trying not to make it sound much. She told him she'd written a couple of plays, which had been put on at fringe theatres, years ago, but didn't want to write plays any more. She didn't like the way the characters were reinterpreted by the actors and the directors. She didn't like – she hesitated – losing control.

He looked at her obliquely and she faltered before picking up the thread of what she was saying.

She wanted to try writing a film instead. 'Like everyone else these days.' She laughed, glancing at him and fingering her hair.

'Can you make a living at that?' He surprised himself by asking such a question. He would not have dreamed of asking the people he normally mixed with if they made a living or how they did it. A question you just didn't ask.

Alice wasn't offended. She seemed charmed by his interest and answered at once. She worked three days a week at the newspaper, doing something called sub-editing. This sounded very grand, but she pointed out that it just meant correcting everyone else's mistakes so they didn't end up in the paper. At least, that was how she put it. She smiled a lot.

'Do you like doing that?'

'It pays the bills.' The smile again. She glanced out of the window. 'And it's easy work, the people are nice, it keeps your brain alive. Yes, I think I do. It could be worse. I'm lucky to have a job like that.'

He didn't want her to ask him what he did. He had no idea how he would answer. They were at the end of their coffee and he offered her another cup, knowing she would refuse; he also knew she liked him but wouldn't do anything about it.

'I wish you could see the flat,' Gilver said, 'and tell me where to start. It all seems so daunting.'

'Have you really got to do it all by yourself?' The question was a good one. It had a lot of answers in it.

She was busy, he was aware, summing up his coat, his hair-cut, his shoes, his voice, his ring hand. She felt he didn't fit, but her manner indicated that she wasn't afraid of him, that she'd decided he was safe. He liked watching women do that, although he had never met one who decided against him.

'Yes, I really have. But I don't think I can bear to start until tomorrow. I'm not dressed right.'

This was cunning. She seemed relieved.

'I could give you a hand – if you want.'

'Are you serious? It would be wonderful. But I don't think it will be much fun. There's no heating. There isn't even a kettle.'

'I'll bring a kettle,' she said. 'I've got a spare one. House-warming present!'

He gave her the address wondering, as he walked back, at her simplicity. A kettle as a house-warming present! What a peculiar thought. Hardly what he was accustomed to.

When Gilver got home there was a message on the answer-phone from Eugenia. Anders was a bastard and had gone to Copenhagen, leaving her in the lurch with a pair of tickets for an opening night at the Royal Court. It was an experimental thing, only an hour long. Please, darling, would he come?

He listened again to her voice. There was something unusual in it, maybe a little unhappiness. Eugenia was so ebullient, so *Prussian*, even when she was complaining – especially when she was complaining – that something must be the matter.

The curtain was due to go up in forty minutes. He texted 'yes' so he didn't have to waste a moment on conversation and stripped off on the way to the shower, discarding the memory of auburn curls.

VII

Over dinner in a fish restaurant near Brompton Cross, Gilver got a proper look at Eugenia.

On the surface she was magnificent. Her hair, a lustrous and professionally messed-up shoulder length of dark honey colours, some of them natural, gleamed. Fine-boned hands, finished one end in shards of blood-black varnish and the other sapphire *pavé* cuffs, ripped apart a very large crab with unerring violence. She was sheathed in black leather so cruelly and accurately tailored that her breasts challenged him like nose cones of rockets. When she struck one of the crab's claws unnecessarily hard with the hinged end of the crackers and bits of claw splashed into his fingerbowl, a table-game Dam Busters, Gilver was shocked.

'So, are you going to tell me about it?' he teased, discreetly wafting another bottle of indifferent Pouilly-Fuissé towards their table.

Eugenia put down the crackers she was gripping. 'What's to tell?' She gave a defiant look. 'That bastard has gone off to spend the weekend with someone else.'

'Are you sure?'

'Darling.' Her expression was reproving, her mind obviously made up. 'He used an expression a few times this week I've only ever heard that cunt use.'

'What phrase?'

She leaned over the table and whispered.

'Yes, I see,' Gilver said thoughtfully.

'*And* he packed his own bag.'

This was more shocking. Anders was the most pompous,

lazy piece of trash Gilver knew. His only attractive quality was extreme wealth. If he had another it was waiting to be noticed.

'I saw the lawyer today,' Eugenia continued, drinking a glass of wine straight off with a faint grimace. 'I don't think I would have minded so much if it was another woman, but this is impossible.'

Gilver refilled their glasses and took Eugenia's hand gently over the cloth. Her returning grip scratched him.

They dropped into a basement bar quite far up the King's Road and took a tawdry Moroccan banquette in an alcove. Flammable-looking organdie curtains, of some synthetic material in garish oranges and sugared greens, added a pleasantly vulgar touch. Eugenia was almost lying on the banquette drinking her second brandy, her legs, in a short leather skirt, slightly apart so that Gilver would have been able to see her knickers had she worn any.

He leaned forward, running the flat of his hand hard up her leg from the knee, and gripped her flesh where his hand met her skirt. 'I'll take you home now.'

Gilver hadn't exactly forgotten what it was like to have sex with Eugenia, he had just tried not to think about it. He had especially tried not to imagine Anders doing it; that rather soft-bellied body, his too-big mouth, the mud-coloured eyes.

He told himself they were both completely plastered and this interlude didn't count: Anders was a two-timing shit whom Eugenia was going to divorce anyway. It was an emergency.

He felt angry at what she had told him and fucked her

with all the energy he could muster, in the particular ways she used to let him. He had her on the hall floor from behind, as soon as the front door was shut, ripping her split skirt apart as he pushed it up. He sodomised her in the bedroom. When she cried out he couldn't tell if it was from pleasure or pain.

Eugenia turned away and Gilver curled round her like a carapace and slept, holding her sharp-clawed hands captive in his own. Her face was wet from crying, but over Anders or him there was no way of telling.

When Alice got home she undid the cotton dustsheet and arranged it on her sofa. It wasn't exactly great but it would do. The sofa was dirty on the arms and this gave it a new lease of life. It was one of many economies she had taught herself, pretending she really didn't mind. Her flat was in a basement of a curving terrace that must once have been beautiful. It was small. She had two rooms. The sitting room at the front, catching the last of the afternoon light in a golden gust, had the sofa, two chairs, an unstable round gate-leg table that sat four and a wall floor-to-ceiling with books.

The bedroom just managed to contain an ironwork bed and a chest of drawers; there was no room for a wardrobe, her clothes hung in an alcove in the hall. She had bought an old ecclesiastical robe from a second-hand shop in Munster Road and pieced it back into a cloth that hung over the rail. Its rich metal threadwork, although tarnished, was extremely fine. 'French,' the man who sold it to her had said disparagingly.

The rest of the flat was poorly partitioned into a tiny kitchen giving on to a dank lightwell and a poky bathroom. She had painted everything off-white when she moved in, covering up damp patches as much as possible. A ripe smell came from the lightwell in summer. She coloured the little kitchen deep yellow.

After arranging the sofa she went into the kitchen. There wasn't space for a table, but her collections of coloured glasses, majolica bowls and a row of cup-hooks with fragile Sèvres cups in pure gilt made the small room seem to glow.

She had bought ten irises on the way back from the coffee with Gilver and put them in a celadon vase, letting them spill into their own arrangement. They looked like a detail in a Japanese print, some tightly furled, a couple already opening deep purple petals like yawning yellow-tongued dragons.

Stroking their whippy green blades Alice thought about Gilver. To be exact, she thought about the coat he had worn, brown with a softly tied belt; about the dark green polo-neck sweater underneath, setting off the golden skin of his neck; about his shoes with their shiny tassels, one a bit scuffed, and the peppermint socks. She saw his eyes, which were the colour of topaz, or tiger's eye; his wrists, strong and planed off with a muscular breadth quite unlike her own; she thought about his dark gold hair going to brown at the nape.

He was a fair bit older than her, maybe thirty-seven or so; there were fine lines on the natural tan of his face, and from the sides of his nose to his mouth. While he was, without doubt, the most handsome man she had ever seen, he looked as if he had lived in ways she would never know about and perhaps known things she did not care to.

Just before they left he had glanced cursorily at the bill and put a careless handful of coins on the table. She saw how his face would age. She saw, too, that there was exhaustion in him, perhaps cruelty. Then he looked up. His face transformed with a wide grin, sweeping away the nonsense she was thinking. Alice saw there was a gap between his front teeth, something she had once read was useful for hulling sunflower seeds. It was such an interesting thought that she had tried it, but it made her gums hurt.

'You look as though you've just seen a monster!' His accusation was playful. 'Have you?'

Alice knew she had gone crimson, feeling the blood under her skin. She shook her head, smiling back.

His smile was infectious. He had invaded her somehow, she felt helpless and couldn't tell what she thought.

'I'm not sure what monsters look like these days,' she countered.

'I hope you never find out.' Gilver helped her up, handing her the package she had stowed under the rusty table with a grace that almost caused her pain.

Alice thought about him like a patchwork, hardly daring to put the pieces together. Each piece gave her a feeling of such visceral pleasure that she felt dizzy in the shop. She would not think of him as a whole in case the sum was disappointing, or too much to bear.

She made some pasta for supper and started rereading *Tess of the D'Urbervilles*, imagining herself as Tess, dancing in a white dress with a scrap of red ribbon in her hair, longing for the boy who dances with someone else.

But the afternoon intruded, distracting her.

She took the book to bed and continued for a while, wondering about the next day, how it would be to see him again.

Putting the book down and stretching out, Alice wondered if it really was possible to fall in love at first sight, feeling her heart beat faster at the mere thought of tomorrow.

She turned the light out at eleven and lay under fresh-smelling linen, clasping her hands to herself in the dark.

VIII

For a few moments when Alice woke, looking at the ceiling, she knew she felt happy but didn't remember why. Then the smile that had curved her mouth all night came back. She sat up and hugged the duvet. They had not discussed a time for her to go to the flat. Even though the thought had crossed her mind at the time it had seemed pushy to say so. Now she regretted it. It bothered her that they hadn't exchanged phone numbers, which might have been useful. At the very least, surely it was normal.

She also thought that the idea of going to a strange man's flat would fill her mother with horror. Alice, too, would advise a girlfriend against such a thing. You might disappear without trace! Who would know? If only she had told someone, but it was too late now.

There was a message on the answering machine, left by her oldest friend Juliette the day before. Unusually, Alice hadn't wanted to talk to her about meeting the most handsome man in the world, in case it broke the spell or – worse – set some sort of jinx. Now she regretted not calling. On the other hand, if he was a murderer that was her fate. She hoped he was not:

she wanted to see him so much she almost didn't care if he cut her into ribbons and wore her as a favour on his hat. It would have been a spectacular reincarnation.

Nevertheless, eating breakfast, she puzzled over what to do and finally called Juliette at work at a quarter to ten. Alice had the strange sensation, while the phone rang and she waited for Juliette to pick up, that she was going to confession, or seeking absolution, or a mixture of both. Why she should feel guilty she had no idea.

Juliette worked on a small fashion magazine called *Flame*, a repackaged import from the States. She was much more successful than Alice, as she wasted no time in reminding her friend at regular intervals, although surprisingly narrow-minded. This same closely focused attitude made her efficient at pursuing a career.

Alice and Juliette had met at university. Brighter than Juliette, but so accustomed to it she put no value on her cleverness, Alice was dazzled by her new friend's social ease and striking looks, as if Juliette had arrived with a dance card already full. It pleased Juliette to have a friend who was pretty without being threatening, always ready to put down her books and come out to a party when Juliette rolled up, knocking imperiously at her door after someone more interesting had let her down. Alice set her off rather well, Juliette thought, and didn't seem to mind that when men looked with the beginnings of interest in her direction, Juliette had a knack of making their eyes slide over to her and stay put.

In fact Alice did sometimes mind, and sat thinking about how it happened late into the night. There had been a Canadian rower called Michael, whom Juliette dismissed out

45

of hand as a fool and a half-wit, until she noticed him gazing fondly at Alice one warm summer picnic. The next time they met, bumping into him on a stroll up the high street to buy Juliette a dress, Juliette knew everything about rowing and commended Alice's admirer lengthily on his physique (he was wearing training shorts), telling him he was misused as number two and should be number four. She offered to introduce him to the first eight's trainer, with whom she was Very Good Friends and – coincidentally – having dinner the next evening.

Even so, Alice never wanted to be sure how she got stood up for the dance Michael had promised to take her to and tried not to think about it, making herself decide it was fate.

She started spending less time with Juliette and concentrated on getting a first.

After university they saw each other less frequently, but the friendship continued, on the same pattern, by default. When Juliette needed something she called Alice and always managed to make the favour she sought seem an honour. Juliette had stumbled early on the secret that once you got someone to do something for you, they would do it again. It was interesting. Its deployment accreted power. She slightly despised the people who were most useful to her. Over time, Alice had been the most useful of all.

Juliette was associate editor on *Flame* and had worked on magazines since leaving university, working her way up with inexorable determination. She said that if she wasn't editor of one of what she called darkly 'the big three' in due course, heads would roll. She said it often, with relish. Everyone seemed to think it would happen. Except Alice, who wondered, feeling horribly disloyal, why the least visionary people always succeeded.

When she heard Alice speak Juliette made busy noises. She had a knack of this even when flicking paperclips at the framed photograph of her ex-husband Paul.

'Why didn't you call me last night?' As usual her voice was challenging, preoccupied.

'I'm sorry. I met this man . . .' Alice tailed off, already wishing she hadn't rung up.

'Aha! Are you hung-over?' Juliette's interest was up. She sounded suspicious. 'Don't tell me you . . . ?'

'No!' Alice had never got accustomed to Juliette's scorn over her shyness with men, nor her veiled inference that Alice didn't because she couldn't. 'But I'm fine. Anyway, that's why I didn't call.' Alice had lied. She wasn't sure why. It wasn't a very big lie.

'What's his name?'

'It's a weird name. Gilver. He's really—'

'*Not* Gilver Memmer?'

What was the implication in Juliette's question? Disbelief? How On Earth had a Girl Like Alice met a Man Like That? It was a strange tone. Alice couldn't place it. 'I think so . . . I think that was his name,' Alice lied again. Something coming from Juliette made her cautious.

'Where did you meet him?'

Alice heard herself say she had met him at a drinks party – only briefly. And, no, she didn't think she would see him again. They hadn't exchanged phone numbers. It was almost a relief to utter the truth.

'Good Lord, Gilver Memmer. He used to be so handsome. Is he still?'

The inquisition was becoming tiring. 'He was pretty good-looking.' Alice waited. She didn't have to wait long.

'Gilver Memmer used to be one of the most eligible men in London. I haven't heard about him for years. Christ, Alice, where have you been? He was an amazingly talented painter, he must have made a packet, he had these shows . . .' Juliette had a brief aside with someone in the office. 'Put it there,' she snapped, 'no, *there*.' She came back into range. 'Who was he with?'

Alice felt uncomfortable. 'Oh, some girl,' she started, faintly. A cock crowed in the background.

Juliette snorted. 'Rich, young and gorgeous, I bet.'

'Yes, she was,' said Alice. 'Anyway, I just rang to say sorry about last night.'

'Yup.' Juliette dismissed her, already calling up the cuttings on Gilver Memmer on the electronic library. 'Let's have a drink next week some time.'

IX

Alice only had access to an electronic cuttings library at work, and had a feeling that her friend might take such a course now. Juliette's skill in pivoting the relevant *Debrett*, *Who's Who* or *International Gazetteer* down from a high shelf behind her head without looking was a byword among her peers and source of amusement to her rivals.

With what Victorian authors called the weaker sex's charming habit of inconstancy, Alice, irritated by Juliette's characteristic gazumping, let herself forget that finding out about Gilver had been the true purpose of the call. Nevertheless, the conversation had achieved its aim. He was well-known – evidently not a menace to society. Her fanciful notion of dismemberment was unlikely to happen at his hands. She would not end her days as a titfer.

Thus fortified, she set out to the address Gilver had given, an old kettle rooted out from beneath the sink under one arm.

It was another magical morning. Light rain had fallen during the night and just dried from the pavements, leaving only a small damp blemish here and there on fast-whitening slabs. In luxurious privet hedges, on a late-flowering fuchsia and an over-arching white rose, wetness still sparkled like diamonds *tremblants* among the deeper foliage.

On the market stalls, piles of late purple plums shone through their dull bloom and pomegranates jumbled with shaved ribbons of glittering red plastic spilled from wooden boxes. Alice took a short cut between the barrows, deftly skirting a municipal garbage truck, wondering where all this splendour ended up, how much was trodden underfoot, or left to rot in some dark place. She bought a paper bag of almost black figs, oozing tears of colourless liquid, and a handful of riper purple anemones in a twist of pink paper.

The oppressive terrace of vast houses to which Gilver had given her direction ran, unlike her own, straight as a die. His side was in shadow and the grey porch appeared to hold traces of decay in its recess. A presentiment of gloom cushioned Alice when she rang the bell and there was no answer.

She rang again, to be certain, then stood in the street scanning down its length in both directions. As far as the eye could see it was deserted. No elegant figure with bright hair loped towards her, an eventuality she hadn't considered.

She put the bag, flowers and kettle on the cracked balustrade next to the door and crossed over to the sunny side of the street. There was a clean enough set of steps to sit on, at an angle from Gilver's but giving an uninterrupted view. The frantic beating of her heart slowed while she considered what to do next.

It was almost a quarter to eleven. Alice decided to wait until the hour, reasoning with herself that they had not, after all, specified a time for their second meeting.

Gilver woke with a start and a slight headache. Eugenia's luxurious marital bed was unfamiliar. He wallowed in a tangle of her scented monogrammed sheets for a few moments, idly noting, as his large body crushed the crisp embroideries, that the monogram was hers alone. Anders was already written out of her laundry basket.

She was not beside him and the pillow was cold. It was no surprise. Eugenia, never sexually enthusiastic in the mornings, went early to a nearby gym to perform what she dubbed her *German* callisthenics, with an arch look that made Gilver laugh.

Gilver couldn't see much of the room in which his recent adultery had taken place, but it felt thick with stuff, padded. The heavily draped windows shut out all but a wavering red trace of light. Gilver peered at his Rado and saw with astonishment that it was ten o'clock.

In the pleasure of waking his situation escaped him. Now the memory of his predicament returned; he remembered what he had to do. Then he remembered the meeting he had arranged with Alice. A nice girl, he thought, transposing an image of her on to a particularly pungent moment from the night before.

Gilver spent an efficient amount of time on this fantasy. Shortly afterwards he let himself out of the house without leaving a note – it had never been his way – and made a passing cab take him home and tick while he threw on a change of clothing.

At a quarter past eleven, when Alice had told herself several times that she should go home, a cab pulled up on the shaded side. She watched Gilver, carrying a canvas kitbag, pay it off and spring up the steps. He stopped to examine her offering, placed mutely to one side. Scooped up the flowers with both hands, put his nose to them, and laid them back down.

Her heart thudded unreasonably in her chest. 'This is foolish,' she rebuked herself, rising in silence from the sunny step, almost decided to slip away. In a confusion of feeling she hoped he would go straight into the house without seeing her. 'If he does,' she reasoned, 'it will be the end of it, and that is how things are meant to be.'

At this precise moment Gilver turned, glanced briefly in the direction he had come and at once caught sight of her. His smile illuminated Alice's heart.

That's it, then, she thought, a strange hammering in her throat. There's no turning back.

The flat did not strike the same terror or hopelessness into Alice that it inflicted on Gilver.

Where he was sunk in gloom, she saw possibilities. While the lower floor was perhaps slightly smaller than her own place – although this could have been settled by tossing a coin – the attic was a revelation. When Gilver showed it to her she did not repress an exclamation of pleasure and paced it out as if it must contain fresh delights at every turn.

He watched her moving around. She craned out of the row of windows, which opened, she pointed out, without difficulty – as if this was a novelty. Apparently if you leaned out as far as you could, you could see the flat-topped tower of All Saints. Gilver sensed he would not do that in a hurry, but kept the thought to himself.

She stared with apparent satisfaction into the roof eaves, wondering aloud if the skylight would open and frowned slightly at the part that was patched over.

The dreary kitchen did not infect her with his dismay and she summarised the state of the cooker much as the removal men had done, drawing in her breath at one point and asking if he had any bleach. She trod systematically along the boards as if she were tightrope-walking, to test for loose ones, she explained; and tried the taps in the kitchen sink and bathroom basin.

While Gilver observed her he was unaware that she occupied herself deliberately. Her knowledge of his reputation, slender though it was, still felt awkward, almost as if she had spied on him. She did not want there to be a lull into which conversation might fall too soon.

Alice was keen to learn how he would present himself and hoped he would not keep her in suspense; but felt that, if she were forced to be first to ask a personal question, something unmendable might break, or she might say something that let him know she had – against her will – been talking about him. If only she was not burdened with that; if only she had not rung Juliette. Trying the taps, she realised that what he said or did not say and how it squared with the unbidden information from Juliette would create the foundation of their relationship. Whatever that turned out to be.

While Gilver followed her efficient movements around his new flat she watched him covertly.

He was dressed in a pair of jeans that could hardly be called old and a grey sweater that, despite being practical in colour, was evidently cashmere. The only sensible note in his get-up was a pair of deck shoes.

Alice decided to let Gilver speak when he was ready, though she was dying to ask questions. If she had not talked to Juliette, she would not feel awkward now. It was almost as if, in some subtle way, she had betrayed him. What fool said knowledge was power? Knowledge could be a curse.

There was a constraint which she did not like but saw no easy way of overcoming. While she understood what was causing it on her side, she felt it from him, too.

The preliminary inspection complete, Alice announced more cheerfully than she felt that they should start. She would begin in the kitchen. This seemed to fill Gilver with relief. Since he remained standing still, she told him to go and sweep the attic room. Puffs of dust had lazed around their feet up there. The cheap timbers of the recently revealed floor provided the only fresh smell.

'Is there a broom?' Gilver asked doubtfully, in the same tone that says Nanny knows best.

Alice looked at him, amazed, before laughing. 'Go and buy one,' she ordered, seeing that she would have to take control if anything was to get done. 'You know where the shop is.'

She dispatched Gilver with an additional list of requirements, including a few groceries, and set to work.

Once back from the shops, furnished with outline instructions, Gilver worked hard cleaning the attic while Alice stormed the kitchen. She was relieved to find no sign of cockroaches, despite such heavy traces of recent squalor.

They broke off at two for a sandwich and a bottle of wine. Gilver ate his standing, just as she did, from a piece of clean newspaper spread on the kitchen counter; but between bites he looked at the prepackaged item with suspicion.

He was more at home with the wine, having chosen something so shockingly expensive Alice would only have bought it for a dinner party. They drank out of the smoked-glass mugs. Alice had found more of them in the one dismal wall cupboard and scalded them aggressively. Poisonous-looking discs of mould floated out. They sold them on the market for fifty pence each, they were unbreakable.

'So, what do you think?' Gilver asked after the rapid meal, sprawling – as far as it was possible – on one of the folding chairs he had insisted on bringing down from upstairs.

'I think it's a good space.' Alice was being truthful. Taken as a whole it was twice the size of her own flat. She would have given a lot for a big light room like the one upstairs, and said so.

Her remarks met a look on Gilver's face that suggested she must be teasing him, a look he quickly rearranged when he caught no answering expression.

Relaxed by the wine Alice decided to find out what she

wanted to know. 'The room upstairs would make a wonderful studio.'

Gilver looked at his mug and then at her. The pause horrified her. Perhaps she had already said too much.

'I used to be a painter,' he said, simply.

The phrase hung for a moment in the air. Alice wished again that she had never rung Juliette. To hide momentary confusion she also searched her wine, in case it inspired her. There was something in the tone of his voice that was unbearable, final.

'With a room like that you can paint again, if you want.' Terrified she had really gone too far she glanced at Gilver, who was frowning at the encrusted window, now thrown wide open.

He turned back, the frown softened. 'Yes, you're right.'

She smiled in relief and asked if there was any more wine. Gilver tilted the empty bottle. 'I drink faster than you, sorry. Let's have a drink at the end of the day, though.'

Alice had to go back to her job after the weekend, but they got a lot done. Gilver put his back into it. They talked little, and only about what they were doing. It felt as if they had known each other for years rather than three days, which was illogical, but in her happiness she tried not to analyse it. Yet the thought came that the brief biography she had given him so easily in the café was for him, for now, sufficient; he did not seem interested in knowing more. This absence of curiosity was perturbing. When they finished, late in the evening now the electricity was connected, Alice refused Gilver's offer to go for a drink and went straight home.

On the second evening, Sunday, aware that she would be at work for the next few days, she felt nervous. She was tired after two days' cleaning without pause and needed to go home to prepare for her real job, but that wasn't the reason. It was as if the connection with her everyday life had snapped, as if she had not been to the office for years and might never go there again. She wished she could come back in the morning. Around nine thirty Alice hoped Gilver would repeat the offer of a drink. Surely he would, they had worked so hard. When she had refused the night before, saying she was too tired, he had patted her shoulder with a gentleness that shocked her and said, maybe tomorrow. He didn't seem to mind.

They were winding up, tying a couple of rubbish bags. The moment she dreaded came.

'You've been such a great help, you know.' Gilver straightened, pushing strands of hair from his face.

Alice tensed. Something was wrong, she felt dismissed. 'There's still an awful lot to do,' she parried. It was painfully true. There seemed a great deal more to do, now they were doing it, than there had at first. It had been the same in her own flat.

'Yes, I know, but I think if I just carry on I'll get there.'

Alice felt her heart, hard and small, die. In approaching agony she tried again. 'I'd like to come back on Thursday. I love doing this sort of thing.'

There. She had said it. She retied her rubbish bag unnecessarily with a complicated knot.

'You're very sweet. Why don't you give me your phone number? I'll give you a call in the next day or so.'

*   *   *

56

Alice got home, somehow, and ran herself a hot bath. She drank a large whisky then got in and lay fuming.

How was it that there were patterns of conversation, so a man could throw you off like that? Why was her volition nothing and why hadn't she asked a direct question – at least forcing an answer there and then? She had helped him so freely, surely she deserved something in return.

It was not so much that she didn't want to admit how much she liked Gilver or how much she wanted to see him again, it was that she felt duped, or as if she had fallen into a ready-made trap. It was how she had been brought up to behave – she was a *nice* girl.

Alice got into bed depressed, almost pleased that the pillows were in a squashed huddle from the night before and leaving them as a perverse punishment, a sort of hair shirt.

Unhappiness and anxiety, mixed with whisky and the genuine exertions of the day, made her fall asleep. She slept well, dreaming – contrary to romantic expectation – of absolutely nothing.

X

Monstrously egotistic though Gilver was, he had not dismissed Alice intentionally. He simply did not know what his intentions were and wanted to have a quiet drink on his own.

He liked her. What little of her nature had penetrated the self-absorption and self-interest in which he was steeped seemed pleasant enough. His immediate reaction to her, a pretty girl, had refined itself after two days working side by side.

She was – undoubtedly – pretty. Attributes he noticed at once – her hair, her expressive face, her able, small hands with pared-back fingernails and no adornments – gave her the quality of a quiet field animal, which was pleasant, and to which he was not accustomed. Added to these superficial effects were the quiet assurance with which she moved, her vigour and cheerfulness.

Even from his depths of selfishness he knew she was helping him, giving him more than the sum of her actual contribution. If she had not been so spontaneously enthusiastic, if she had not, as it were, grasped the nettle, he would still in all likelihood be sitting immobile with a bottle to hand. Which, now she had gone, he was. Lit only by the filthy orange glare from the street-lamp outside, he had been drinking for an hour. In the strange phosphorescent light, his face took on the semblance of a gargoyle. Its contours, which despite some traces of age many still called classically handsome, were viciously distorted. The angle of the street-lamp and the severity of its chemical beam conspired to plunge one side of his head into a glimmering black and the other a flattened orange. He had taken on the evil appearance of a mask in a Greek tragedy. On the orange side the eye socket was profoundly black, while a glimmer came from the orb in darkness. His ear-lobe on that side stuck out curiously, like a velvet handle.

Gilver knew Alice wanted to see him again. He wouldn't have minded seeing her, but felt little beyond that. She was nice – but there were so many nice women. He had had so many of them, knew them to be so readily available, that one more seemed neither here nor there. Could he be bothered to start something with someone new? It didn't seem worth the trouble.

He poured a large measure and settled for a while to work out what needed to be done in the forthcoming week. If it didn't go well, he decided generously, he would call. He had her number. She would like that.

It wasn't unreasonable to call her if he changed his mind and needed help getting something done. She probably did like a change, stuck in an office three days a week doing something that sounded very boring. He chose to take her words, that she liked this sort of work, at face value, not considering that she might have been being charming or generous, and might have pursued this line of thought, even to the point of wondering if there was anything more in it for Alice than charity, when his mobile rang.

On seeing it was Eugenia, calling from her own mobile rather than the phone at home, Gilver toyed with diverting the call.

He couldn't be arsed to get involved with Eugenia again and was slightly cross that he had broken his golden rule and slept with a married woman. Of course it was all her fault. That was glaringly obvious. She had set the evening up with one thing in mind and it had happened. In fact, in his own estimation, he had been rather obliging. An old-fashioned courtesy. Like in *Zorba the Greek*, where a man who refuses to pleasure a woman who offers herself is not a gentleman. (The reduction of an entire novel into the one phrase that suited his own life was not a habit exclusive to Gilver Memmer, although he was particularly good at it.) His behaviour had been faultless: there was the proof.

Much as he liked Eugenia, much as she was without doubt his favourite ex, they were not going to start all that again. When she found out how his fortunes had changed – as she must if he went on seeing her – he doubted she would want it either. Eugenia loved luxury, cleanliness, order, service. She especially liked the importance of her title and wealth – both very important in her own estimation – celebrated daily. This celebration could take many forms, but one of the invariables was that huge sums of money were spent on her and vast amounts of expensive attention paid. She had even less time for impoverishment than he did.

As a further courtesy, however, and knowing she would call again later if he didn't answer now, he picked up.

She was drunk.

Anders had come home an hour earlier and they had had a row.

'I said I wasn't going to live with a queer and he said he wasn't going to live with a whore,' she screamed down the line, pronouncing whore with a great whoofing sound.

'Why did he call you a whore?' Gilver kept his voice level. This seemed the important question. Sod Eugenia.

'I told him two could salsa!' Blurred but triumphant.

'Is that all?'

'What do you mean, "is that all", darling? Isn't it a great deal? I told him to get out.' She was very excited.

'Did he?'

'No, he didn't. He said he was tired and going to bed, so I drove round to yours and you were out.'

Thank God, Gilver thought. Anders was a jealous bastard, with that Scandinavian perseverance that meant that, once roused out of his perpetual torpor, he would strap on metaphorical skis and trudge for hours in pursuit of his prey. This was why, even though Anders had less imagination than a piece of cardboard, he had risen in the bank. And it was also the reason Gilver did not wish to meddle with him, particularly over Anders' wife.

'Where are you now?'

Eugenia had gone to Sally Ann, her current best friend, who had three dress shops in Mayfair – one of a clutch whose pecking order changed regularly.

Gilver was satisfied Anders didn't know anything concrete, they had just had a slanging match. It wasn't the first. 'Sleep,' he advised soothingly. 'Don't do anything rash. It'll seem different in the morning.'

'You're damn right it'll be different in the morning,' Eugenia extemporised after him. 'I'll divorce him in the morning.'

XI

The fortnight before the date set for his party at the mews, Gilver had never worked so hard in his life, becoming an intimate of the decorating-supply shops, on nodding terms with the staff. He spent three more days cleaning, for which he bought a very good ladder and some workmen's overalls, and nearly took the skin off his hands and arms with caustic chemicals. The wiring was found to be in a decent state of repair, but he had a modern circuit board and new face-plates installed.

By calling John and Steve he found someone to come and replaster the artex ceilings in the bedroom and sitting room. A luxury, but you couldn't have a hangover under that swirling miasma and Gilver had recently got into the habit of waking with a whisky head.

A handyman from Steve's inexhaustible list changed the nasty surface of the kitchen bar for a solid piece of second-hand oiled teak and put up plain slatted blinds on every window except the bedroom. There, Gilver had a strong pole fitted, ready for the priceless Venetian cloth-of-silver brocades that currently added lustre to his drawing room. Everything else he scrubbed, bleached, scraped, sanded and polished, surprised that these techniques taught themselves, at how fast he improved.

By the middle of the second week he had finished painting the walls white. This, after all, he knew how to do. The final two days went on staining and sealing the floorboards, to the approval of Steve, who came round unexpectedly on the last morning to retrieve a sander.

'You've worked hard,' he said, taking keen stock. 'I wasn't sure you'd be able to do it, that first day.' He bent to examine the walls more closely. 'One coat. Nice job. If you ever need a bit of spare as a painter I'll put you in my book.'

It would have been reasonable after working like a navvy during the day to go home and do nothing. Certainly, for the first few days Gilver was shocked to find he ached all over, despite considering himself reasonably fit. But there was a party to organise and, even though he could do it with his eyes shut, he spent the evenings in a haze, writing out names on thick pasteboard and having prolonged discussions with his caterer and decorator, the tantalus never far from his elbow and his gold and malachite cigarette case always open.

Moreover, although surely no tom-toms pulsed yet across the jaded society that passed for his closest friends, there seemed more bleeps on his machine each evening than he had ever known.

Ruthlessly he cancelled dinner invitations, benefits for the Royal Ballet and for what sounded like Distressed Fruit Bats, openings at both Tates and at Hamilton's, and drinks at several clubs. Sacrificed next were inevitable requests to be a walker at galleries and afternoon teas for those numerous women to whom the adornment of a handsome man, his arm firmly clutched, is worth at least one eye-tuck.

A rogue phone call from Deborah – in alarmingly poor taste, and made after midnight – got wiped without answer. When Harry rang he pretended to be out and called back on the answerphone the next day, leaving a brief memo about the party, to which he felt certain Harry would not respond.

The one person who didn't call was Eugenia. She had huffed off to Germany for a quick cure and to buy herself a fun BMW. 'A cheering advance replacement for Anders' old wreck, my love,' she had sung. 'Do you want me to get you one while I'm at it?' She promised, without being asked, that she would be back in time for his party.

To Alice, Gilver did not give a thought.

On the night of the party, cars parked the length of the mews, spilling into nearby streets, bumpers and bonnets gleaming nose to tail. Behind the sheaves of immaculate windscreens dark winnowed figures waited patiently to transport their charges home at dawn.

Gilver's house blazed with hundreds of candles tiered round wired pillars, looping up in helicoid blurs of flame like Trajan's column, or fiery complex molecules. Two feet from the ceiling and throwing up flickering heat reflected on some burning lake, rows of nightlights necklaced the walls. The thick scent of white hyacinths spilling waxy out of eighteenth-century soup tureens almost stifled breathing in the still-warm early October air.

In the drawing room, which spanned the first floor, musicians played without pause and champagne circulated in lazy arabesques. Magnificent gilded mirrors held every glint from silk, bare skin and jewels in their seamed and foxed depths. They caught the cross-current of bright glances, pinpoints from the corners of eyes, copper wires of hair flying aloof from expensive coiffeurs and returned every one tarnished and distorted.

In the tiny kitchen large bins held countless empty bottles plunging belly-up in their black depths. Pounds of caviar had been eaten. The shark-toothed cans gnashed in a heap on the floor. Clean-picked lobsters loomed through green plastic sacks that bulged refulgent like the buttocks of a Rubens beauty.

Gilver sat on the stairs leading down to the narrow hall, escaping the noise and crush, an empty bottle next to him and another crooked in his lap. The front door stood wide. He gulped the welcome air. It was one o'clock in the morning. The confusion of noise and heat had given him a headache. He had little idea, and cared less, who half these people were. Many he dimly recognised from other parties, from magazines. Those whom he knew had been announced; others had drifted in, nodding at someone, giving their coat to someone else. Now they were all dancing upstairs. Some were on the sofas, some – he had no idea who – had dispersed to other parts of the house.

On the bottom step below him a young couple he had observed meeting were kissing each other. The boy had his hand up the girl's transparent sequined fishnet dress, between her legs, while his right squeezed the back of her neck until his fingers left a mark.

The girl got up suddenly and stumbled towards the front door, yanking her dress over her knees as she buckled forward.

'Is she going to be all right?' Gilver, feeling avuncular, clambered gently to the bottom step and gazed out in the same direction as the boy. A dim splatter that might have been a cat pewling up grass-balls came to them.

The boy turned to look at him, leaving off sniffing at his left hand. He looked about nineteen. 'Her name's Tara,' he said, by way of introduction. 'She *said* she'd be sick if I kept doing that. Boring party, isn't it? Is there anything in that bottle?'

Gilver divided what was left. 'What do you do?' he asked the boy, whose name was Giles.

'Do?' Giles was puzzled. 'I don't do anything. I'm at school. What about you?'

Gilver smiled. 'I don't do anything either. I don't know what I do any more.'

He suddenly felt tired and wanted to confide in someone. Giles was paying him no heed, staring off into the black street waiting for Tara to come back. The vomiting noises stopped.

'It's my birthday today,' Gilver told him.

He had caught Giles's interest again. 'Birthdays are great. But they're special, you know. If it was my birthday I wouldn't spend it at this old queen's party.'

Tara reappeared in the porch. The front of her dress was wet, stuck to her thin chest. Her breastbone stood out through the gauze. She came wobbling across the marble.

'Do I know you?'

She presented her hand like a bird keeling for a dive. 'My name's Tara.' Her accent was profoundly suburban.

'Gilver,' Gilver said.

Giles tried this on. 'That's the same name as the bloke having the party. My mum's upstairs, she said so.'

'Ah,' said Gilver, 'I think you must be my godson. I expect you should go and dry Tara's dress off before she catches cold. Use the bathroom on the second floor.'

A bottle of wine later, he went out into the quiet of the mews for a smoke, crossing to the other side to lean against the warm brick wall under the rowan tree. Berries squelched beneath his patent feet. A figure dislodged itself from the shadow and moved aside companionably.

'Gilver,' asked Anders quietly, dropping his cigarette and twisting it out with his toe, 'is Eugenia inside?'

'She didn't turn up. How long have you been out here?'

'Oh, I don't know. Half an hour maybe. I thought if Eugenia was here I'd take her home.'

'Yes.' Gilver was noncommittal.

Anders lit another cigarette. In the flare his mouth made a downturned line, the fleshy lips thin-drawn, hard away from the nose. 'She wants to divorce me, you know.'

66

'Yes, she told me.'

'Did she tell you why?'

'She said you were having an affair.'

'It's not true.' Anders spoke very softly. 'I think *she* may be. Or maybe she's just bored. You know Eugenia.' There was a peculiar dull quality in Anders' voice. 'I don't think she ever got over you.'

Before Gilver could find a convincing way to refute this, a loud cracking noise came from the house.

'Jesus Christ,' observed Anders slowly, gesturing at the second floor with his cigarette. A flame leaped from the exploded black window, sucked back and shot out again. After a hair's-breadth of silence, the alarm went off. People started to scream.

The commotion caused by the fire lasted several hours. No one was hurt, but most of the second floor had burned out before the firemen gained control.

In the crisp dawn, smoke hazed and drifted gently from the charred fabrics and furnishings in Gilver's bedroom, dressing room and study. Little bits of what once might have been taffeta, lace or paper twirled on the breeze, like wrappings from after-dinner Amaretti cast up to tell the future, drifted a short way along the mews and landed on cobbles, where they were ground underfoot.

Gilver's entire wardrobe was destroyed; his collection of books from the Library of Baron de —; his personal letters including all his love-letters, and his four rare Dürer engravings.

The cause of the fire, though undoubtedly unattended candles, was not clear. In a rather taxing breakfast interview with the police, Gilver suggested that a romantic couple might have taken one of the Trajan columns into his bedroom to illuminate their gropings and then left. If so, the delicate wire structure would have melted into the rubble that had been his bedroom floor, once covered with Chinese silk rugs. Or perhaps the guilty pair, whoever they were, had simply taken one candle, and placed it too near the silk gauze portières.

'Was it sensible to leave your bedroom open, sir?' One of the policemen – the least ugly one – asked.

They had given Gilver a mug of tea, two gingernuts and what he believed was a custard cream. These delicacies were untouched in front of him on a saucer on the table.

'I never shut my bedroom door, Officer.'

The policeman gave him a look.

'I don't like shut doors, especially at parties.'

'You shut the door to your studio. We found it locked, sir.' The man was quick to point it out.

'Yes, I know.' Gilver was tiring. 'That's true, forgive me. But I did that because the spiral staircase might be dangerous if someone was drunk, and because my work is stored down there. I have never considered my bedroom intrinsically dangerous.' Intrinsic was close to the knuckle, but he was past caring.

'So it would be dangerous to leave an unattended staircase but not unattended candles?'

'There weren't any candles on the second floor, except in the hall and bathroom, where everything is stone.' Gilver had said this before, now he repeated it. He knew he had to go through this vile process and that he had to keep his temper, however many times they went over the same ground, however many times he caught the insinuation that he might not be telling the truth.

Gilver was allowed to leave. They would call if they needed him.

XII

Alice met Juliette at Black's in Soho. Her friend was lounging on a heap of cushions and had ordered a bottle.

It was pouring. The window-panes, runnelled with water, were quite black, save where rain threaded brilliants down their lengths, now dull, now scintillating in the flare of a headlamp. Alice shook specks of water from her hair, dark with wet, and sat down.

'So, have you heard the news?' The other's brown eyes were alive with an evil spark.

Alice had not. She was bent over, organising her things around her, and paid little attention. The next words brought her up fast.

'Gilver Memmer's house caught fire. There's been talk that it might have been Foul Play.' She looked challengingly at Alice as if to say, 'There! That's the sort of exciting life *he* leads.'

Alice did not understand. Her mind turned instantly to the place she had worked on for a weekend. She still smarted from the memory, even though it was weeks ago. It certainly wasn't a house, by any stretch of the imagination.

'His house?' She was all incomprehension.

'Yes, his house! He used to have fabulous parties and he was having one the Friday before last when the whole place went up in a blaze. Don't you read the newspapers?'

Juliette's exaggeration of the extent of the fire was not her only embellishment. It had only, in fact, been a small single column – 'Forgotten Painter's Blaze of Publicity' – near the back of *The Times*. Juliette billed it as if it had been a front-page splash with a half-page picture. Dramatic inflation was, after all, her bread and butter.

'Was he hurt?' Alice still couldn't square the notion of a house where fabulous parties had been held on a regular basis with the place she had seen. She felt there was some mistake. Perhaps, after all, the man she had met was a weirdo, an imposter, not this notorious painter at all. It was a nasty thought.

'Nobody was hurt.' Juliette clearly judged this considera-tion a tiresome irrelevance. It would have been much more interesting, she implied, had everyone burned to a crisp. 'No, they all got out, it was only the top floor that went. But he lost loads of valuable things and only stuff like paintings was insured. Can You Believe That?'

Alice could easily believe that. She had no insurance what-soever.

When Juliette explained, repeating the column word for word, what had been lost, Alice was amazed. 'Such a pity,' she remarked sorrowfully. 'He seemed so nice. It must have been a terrible blow to lose his library.'

Juliette looked as if she was seeing Alice for the first time and not getting her money's worth. 'Bugger the books! You can get more books. It was the clothes! Christ, his wardrobe, he was famous for it. He had the most amazing things, all hand-made.' Juliette went off into a reverie in which the number and value of Memmer's garments were tripled and most of them hand-stitched by nuns. 'But the thing is,' she leaned over, spilling Petit Beaujolais on a plump lemon cushion where it sucked along the fibres like a birthmark, 'they think he was trying to destroy his own paintings!'

'Who thinks?' Alice was still floundering.

'Everybody. Everyone's saying so.' Juliette, in the habit of speaking for forty thousand readers, expanded easily to global range. 'He'd lost it. You know, he hadn't painted for years, he's losing his looks . . . so he had some sort of mad fit, like Rochester, and torched the house.'

'Rochester didn't set fire to the house,' Alice offered.

'For Christ's sake, Alice, that's so not the point. I mean he went barking mad and started a bonfire, a kind of *auto da fé*. But it didn't work.' She took a breath and leaned back again. 'What do you think?'

'I just feel sorry for him.' Alice wished she was anywhere but here, confronting Juliette's face sparkling with ill-will. 'He seemed a nice man, when I met him.' She chose her words with care, taking care too that her tone was matter-of-fact.

'Well.' Juliette was disappointed. 'Anyway, he's left the house empty and no one knows where he's gone. Or cares,' she added unkindly.

Her conversational centrepiece concluded, there was little left to discuss. They managed to linger for an hour, Juliette revived by means of a running commentary on those who came in and out. Some of her remarks were clearly audible to the objects of her scrutiny.

This tasteless activity gave Alice the chance to pursue her

own thoughts, not required to contribute to her friend's social critique.

She went home wrapped in these musings, getting soaked again in the process.

There was nothing to be done. As far as Alice could see, her meeting Gilver Memmer had been one of those events that cross paths with your own life and fizzle out. She had met someone, she thought wistfully, whom she really liked. Now he was gone: probably abroad; he must have lost a lot of money. If she was in the same position she'd run away too. If only to escape the prurient interest of people like Juliette, who hadn't even met you but would say the foullest things just to spice up their own lives.

XIII

Over the next two years, Alice's life changed little on the surface. Late that winter she acquired a bruisy red kitten called Baxter, who died of some hateful kitten disease. All his fur fell out. The vet said there were too many kittens anyway. This made her terribly sad for a long time, she wept over nothing at all.

The following summer she started an evening course in creative writing, wondering if it would do her any good, hoping she might meet some nice people. By this she meant a boyfriend – more specifically, someone to take her mind off Gilver – although she would not have admitted it. The course did not yield romance and winter came round again. At the paper's New Year party a recently hired journalist, Charles, offered her a cocktail sausage then asked her out for dinner a few times. They slid drily into a relationship, which suited Alice up to a point. It took away most of the fact that she was lonely. As an unforeseen sideline, prompted by her new boyfriend and spurred by the irritation she had felt at the writing course, she published a few articles on this and that, a sort of writing she found facile. Posing few challenges it bored her, but brought in a little money. It also served, by its irksome smallness, to remind her that her life seemed to be running on a system of diminishing gears and strengthened her resolve to produce something better. Meanwhile Charles continued to come and make clumsy love to her, snore next to her and tell her she was a poppet.

He bought her a saucepan with a recycled red ribbon round the box, because one morning she had burned the milk using the wrong sort of pan. He exclaimed first at the bitter taste in his coffee, making a wry *moue*, which would have been funny if it had not been so unattractive. He went on to lecture her about non-stick surfaces until she lost patience and told him he should be working on a consumer magazine. Perhaps he could start one up called *What?*. It was his favourite word, after all.

They did not speak for several days, which was rather agreeable. Alice felt that Charles had no idea, really, what she did, beyond the fact of seeing her immobile in front of a computer screen in the news room. Perhaps he thought she was simply shiftless, untalented, only able to get three days' work a week. He never asked what she did with the rest of her life, what her ambitions were, and she never told him what she had done. However, he questioned her doggedly on her day's activities

73

if he saw her in the evening. During these sessions he nodded benignly, patronisingly, not reacting to anything she said. Even the time she told him she had been held at gunpoint for two hours in the top cabin of the Wheel.

She remembered that Gilver Memmer had asked what she did the first time she met him, had even seemed interested in her reply. She put aside the fact that he had asked nothing subsequently. It still put him one step ahead of the game.

Charles and Alice did not live together. She never invited him to stay more than one night – God forbid – although he had asked her, and she only escaped on a technicality. He spent the night a couple of times a week. Charles's own flat in Baron's Court was gloomy, with the seventies wallpaper that must have been there when he bought it. 'It's groovy now,' he said irritatingly, looking sideways at the large biscuit and avocado lozenges sidling up the walls, faintly glossy. 'You can wipe it clean.' He demonstrated.

Alice made her hatred of the decor a reason not to go there. She said it depressed her, which neatly sidestepped the real issue, that Charles depressed her. She knew that if she had any gumption she would ditch him, but she was not ready to be alone again.

To be fair, she had no idea what Charles did when he was not with her. On the evenings when he had not seen her during the day, he rang, unless he planned to come round. In those cases he was economical and sent a text message. For the rest of the uncharted time she hoped he was having frenzied bondage parties wearing a leather mask and nipple clamps. Anything to stop him being as dreary and predictable as he actually was. Alice reckoned that if he *was* having an affair they must have sex in front of the television, since

Charles's conversation mainly comprised a review of the night before's viewing. But, then, he could have memorised this from the back page of the paper and still spent the preceding night in delirious passion with at least one other human being.

Either way, as summer came and went again and nothing happened to remind Alice that she was alive, her anxiety and depression deepened. She felt an urgent need to make changes somehow, or peter out. On the days and nights when Charles was not there and she did not have a social engagement, Alice reread Shakespeare, line by line.

September turned into October and the days were particularly beautiful, stretched out, slow. The great bird of summer, which strictly speaking had already gone, beat its wings once more in a last rehearsal for the long cold flight across the globe. Early evening was particularly lovely. Thick gilded light poured into her sitting room in a slow stream where she lay reading, dust motes sometimes catching in a hail of red-gold glitter that held her spellbound. Much of the time she simply sat, book to one side, lost in dreams whose jewel-like colours were brighter than her own. Then, her thoughts often turned to Gilver. There had been little talk of him since her evening with Juliette. She had heard his name mentioned once more, a year ago, by someone at a party who had followed the events after the fire with keen interest, as you would a drama on television. She didn't know them well enough to ask further questions and then they were gone, leaving her with a few fragments that made her more dissatisfied than before.

Alice had not realised that Gilver had apparently gone back into the building to try to rescue some papers, but failed.

Unlike Rochester, however, he came to no harm; he was not disfigured in any physical way. But her source hinted that something had snapped. He had disappeared. There was a hint of something odd: disgrace, adultery, financial ruin, social ruin . . . Annoyingly, these gloating hints that might have provided a clue to the truth were unsubstantial. Alice heard nothing to back any of them up. Only the suggestion of disgrace, of failure, lingered. The ashy taste after a fire.

The one certain thing she heard was that he had indeed gone abroad, somewhere in the South – Italy, she fancied – to put it behind him. Perhaps he was abroad still; perhaps he had given up the flat she had helped with. At any rate, wherever he was, she did not see him again.

Even though her own life had, in its dreary and halting way, moved on, this brief romantic interlude was the one that stayed alive in her memory, perhaps because it was unfulfilled. The memory of him as she had first seen him, in the plain surroundings of the paint shop, was as vivid as ever.

It had been a day like this, basking in the rags of late summer with glorious light streaming into the shop. She felt she would never forget the tall man who entered: his bearing, the quality of his face that had attracted her so much, the tiger-light glancing from his eyes. She had never seen anyone so handsome, so attractive to her.

Alice knew that all this was one-sided: she had fallen in love that day in the most dangerous way.

But how could you punish yourself for falling prey to a *coup de foudre*? Especially when you held it up against the bungling, well-meaning, lamentable specimen of manhood who happened to be your boyfriend? Wasn't this knowledge of a higher state of grace, a more intense feeling held secret and close to your heart, the only thing that made it possible to accept real life without despair? The hope that, after all, there was beauty that made your heart explode with insane beatings; beauty that made you tremble and imprisoned you for the rest of your life?

Plato thought so, Alice defended herself against an invisible interlocutor; Plato said it was ennobling.

She made herself sufficiently guilty that she went out to buy a decent bottle of wine for Charles's supper.

XIV

The past two years had not been easy for Gilver either.

For countless numbers of the human race, time has a habit of passing almost unawares. It slips day by day from our grasp, filled with the tasks of ordinary daily life. The relentless burden of making a living, affording a home, raising children, is sufficient to dull those bright enthusiasms of youth for fame or achievement. One chip at a time their lustre dims, so that the great block of shining marble from which we thought our own monument would raise itself is scraped and chiselled away, little by little. Such a slow process, so nearly insensible: so unerring that there comes a day when one turns to contemplate the great memorial and finds a pebble.

Gilver Memmer had started out with a rare gift, of which he was fully aware. But flamboyant early success had lulled him into the secure impression that it would continue for ever, whether he flexed his powerful artistic muscles or not. Society's demands had never been irksome but they had, nevertheless, been great. He had been seduced by the temporary pleasures of good living, the empty rewards of reckless amusement. A constant kaleidoscope of diversions, a comfortable sense of belonging to the right crowd and of being admired by what he fancied were the right people, sustained him without the need to work for himself. In return he was required to be a pretty lapdog: well-dressed, charming, entertaining. He had been all of these things so he was always in demand.

That society is capricious he knew well, in the abstract. It was, after all, the theme of so much of that in which he was steeped and on which he could converse so entertainingly. It captivated him at the theatre, held him spellbound when he sat, countless times, in some enchanted place in Italy, Greece or Spain, a sun-splashed book negligently open in his hand. While he laughed at or pondered the tragedy of characters in fiction, created surely for his amusement, he did not profit by them, did not apply the warning to himself.

As time passed, Gilver's place in society, so seemingly secure, altered. The changes came on imperceptibly, stealthily crept up, so that he was unaware. In the early years after his success, he was known for what he really was and his talent genuinely admired. But as younger people hurled themselves into the maw of the cavalcade in which he moved, scrambling to greater prominence and influence in it, they did not know him and had never seen what he could do. To them, Gilver Memmer was a handsome, elegant social fixture. A rich older dandy, a desirable man-about-town. He was always monied, always correct, very generous. They liked him but had no interest in his well-being or his soul. Their energies were directed to their own advancement or their own descent into obscurity.

Gilver Memmer had been a painter. That is what people said. That was all.

Before the fire he had planned, vague though those plans were, to throw a memorable party at the mews, pack up the house and slip away as quietly as possible to the flat Harry had found him; to his new life – whatever it proved to be – and new circumstances. He had been determined to leave no wake, no trace, no forwarding address; no means by which he might be unearthed and, once exposed like a mole routed from its hideaway, mocked.

The double shock of reduced circumstances and the fire had been so sudden, absorbing Gilver in making arrangements, that he could think of nothing beyond his immediate situation. Despite almost enjoying the hard physical work of transforming the vile flat into somewhere habitable he did not let himself contemplate what it would mean, day to day, to live there. How he actually planned to adjust to a different way of life, how to think about supporting himself, had hardly occurred to him. If he wondered about it at all, when his back was breaking with the effort of bullying the recalcitrant flat into something tolerable, he put it from his mind. He would come back to that later, he told himself, when he had leisure to contemplate it and when it became a reality that must be addressed.

There was the faint glimmer of hope, too, that a miracle

might happen, that circumstances and fortune might reverse again as they had so recently done and he would wake from this horrid dream. Life had always been so kind to him. Why should this happy state not go on? So, Gilver made minimal preparations, putting off what must be done because he had no way of telling what that was.

The fire changed things completely. It made his fancied transition from one state to another, which, in order to contemplate at all, he had managed to invest with a threadbare romance, quite different. It threw him into the tasteless glare of publicity and brought him, with a thump, face to face with how he appeared to an indifferent world.

He did not see the column in *The Times* but it was drawn to his attention. Even a hermit, secure in a mountain cave, will discover a well-wisher eager to scramble up the rocks, cheerfully hallooing, waving news of fresh discomfiture. The headline alone sickened him.

There had been little time to dwell on it. Only a few days were left before the date set to evacuate the house, and though he felt certain in the circumstances that it was possible to arrange a little leeway, he had no wish to try.

The fire officers had advised against going up to the second floor, which was cordoned off. They said the structure was stable; but the entire building stank offensively and its insurers still had to complete their report. A glimpse snatched from the stairway when Gilver went back to pack had been more than enough.

Convinced there had been no foul play after all, the police had finally left him alone. Their job was done. Despite his carelessness in insuring so few possessions, the building was covered against fire and all other matters would be drearily

resolved by his lawyers over time. He would receive something eventually: the Dürers were one of the few insured things
and were worth a great deal. But it was small comfort for the
loss of so many other lovely things and it was the loveliness,
lost for ever, that he mourned most.

In the middle of the week following the fateful party Gilver
sat in his stinking drawing room, its intricate plastered ceiling completely black, packing the last of his things gently into
boxes. He wanted to do this himself and had dismissed his
maid. Her mournful offers to help and woebegone expression
defeated him after only one morning, although the offer of a
bed in her own home in Putney, to escape the creeping smell
of smoke, was profoundly touching. He gave her a delicate
box inlaid with jasper and she left.

The doorbell rang. He peered out of the sooty window,
but his visitor stood too close to the porch, shielded from a
patter of rain. Gilver was tempted to ignore the bell and carry
on. He had seen no one since the disaster, although many of
his friends had rung up and some had tried to call round. He
had not answered the phone or the door and notes that had
been thrust through the letter-box lay untouched in the hall.

The bell rang again while Gilver still looked gloomily down.
Harry stepped out suddenly from his concealment. 'Gilver!'
Harry, glancing up, perceived Gilver, ghostly at the window.
Behind the coating of soot on the pane he appeared deadly
white.

Gilver went and let him in.

Harry displayed skill in wrapping. For a while, after his face
had run through a repertoire of shock, dismay and horror,

they settled silently to padding Gilver's splendid china and glass in reams of tissue paper. While this was going on Gilver glanced at Harry's face and was annoyed by the signs of real concern displayed there.

When it was time for a break, Gilver stretched. He fetched the port decanter and unwrapped two glasses Harry had just lovingly nested, so they might drink. It had already struck him, looking down at the visitor's imploring expression, that Harry might prove useful in fabricating the structure of his new life as the world would see it. This was the only reason Gilver had opened the door.

By the time he left an hour later Harry was convinced he was a life-saver.

'It's amazing,' Gilver said, 'the timing . . . how you found me the other place, the studio, like that. Otherwise I would have nowhere to go.'

His friend looked surprised. 'What are you talking about? You can't *live* there! The damage here can be fixed in a few months, then you can come back. You could travel or something while the mess is sorted out. Have my place in Oxford. There are loads of places you might go. And while you were away, I could . . .' He was already planning dramatic renovations, leather floors, that sort of thing.

Gilver interrupted the reverie. 'I don't know what I did to deserve such a good friend, Hal. But I can't come back here.' He approximated a look of wistful grief. 'Too many sad memories. I'm giving up the lease.'

Harry tried to persuade him out of it. Gilver stuck firm, with difficulty. At one point, Harry was damned if he couldn't see a tear starting in Gilver's eye. Nothing came of it, though.

Gilver managed, with a heroic struggle of will, to pull himself together. 'Too many memories,' he repeated sadly.

Having got Harry practically weeping, Gilver charged the other glass again. He tried not to sound brisk in his impatience to get shot of the little sniveller. 'There's one thing I want to ask you. As a dear friend.' Harry was rapt, coiled in his palm. 'I want to disappear for a bit and concentrate on my work. I can't help wondering, Harry, if this fire hasn't been a sign from God.' He warmed to his theme. 'I've got too dissipated, too accustomed to an easy life. You remember that conversation we had about the starving artist, the garret?'

Harry nodded.

'I want to give it a go. No, I'm serious. Nothing you could say will make me change my mind. I've wasted too much time and this seems to me like a big chance.' He forced a stoic countenance. 'And that's quite a garret.' If he went on like this much longer he would give himself a standing ovation.

'I don't want our friends' (how Harry longed to be included) 'to know about it. I don't think they'd understand, they—'

'But they would! Of course they would!' Harry broke in, his face glowing with pride.

'Don't interrupt, Harry,' Gilver almost snapped, just regaining possession of his martyred tone. 'So I want to disappear for a few years and get on with it. You must promise me to keep it secret.'

'But what shall I say? You know people will ask.' Harry was struggling, visibly, between love for his friend and concern about telling the truth. He had always been a stickler for facts. A tendency that was tiresome at the best of times and a distinct fag now.

'Tell them I've gone travelling. Tell them I've become a recluse. Tell them I've gone mad and become a monk. Just, for God's sake, don't tell them where I am. Honestly Harry, you'll think of something. I'm relying on you.'

Gilver more or less shovelled him down the stairs, once he was certain that Harry was really very drunk and inclined, hopefully, to forget that he had been rudely treated.

Christ, the effort! After a brief detour to the cellar, Gilver went back upstairs cracking open another bottle on the way. Still, if any foot-soldier could be persuaded to lay down his life completely pointlessly, that man was Harry.

XV

When his things were ready they were packed in plain cases and moved without ceremony to the new flat. The caravan lumbered off with John and Steve at the helm.

It was an irony of fortune to Gilver, wearily waving the van on its way, that so much had been destroyed: there was no space in his forthcoming life for many of his possessions. Of his furniture he selected the small, simpler pieces. Others – the grand piano, a superb five-seater sofa, a set of pretty Louis Quinze chairs, all but one of the great mirrors – were collected with alacrity by an auction house he had once frequented. His vast French bed, scene of so many battles and conquests, the armoires, a library table that, rumour had it, once belonged to a distant cousin of Napoleon, had all burned.

The day after the fire he bought a pair of Gap jeans, two T-shirts and a black sweater. Aside from the practical matter of having no clothes, it struck him as time to adopt a more low-key look. A pair of deck shoes he kept in the studio, along with some old work trousers and a thick pea jacket, and his coat, left downstairs on the night of the party, comprised the sum total of his current wardrobe. His *Sartor* would most probably never be *Resartus* again, unless in the shape of the smoke-perfumed evening suit he had worn that night, now rolled round a cardboard tube and thrust in a bin-bag with its shirt, tie, pumps and Edwardian chalcedony and enamel studs, and slung in the back of the van with the rest.

Clearing the studio downstairs at the mews proved the most difficult job of all. A number of long-forgotten paintings stood against one wall, loosely covered in a piece of spare canvas. He had not seen their faces for years and spent time looking at the way they were done, marvelling at his own work, the technical skill. It was almost strange that he had made these things: they seemed so far from him. He did not know if he could paint like that now if he tried. He didn't know if he wanted to, either. Looking them over he found them shallow. He'd been good with colour, that was certain, and knew how to make an effect, strike a mood. Bold, daring, romantic . . . you could dream your own thoughts in front of them, at best, or match the decor at worst – something he had seen done more than once and, reconciling it against the huge sum involved, shrugged it off.

But otherwise what were they? Had they ever meant anything to him or anyone else? Worse, he couldn't remember which way up two of them went until he looked at the back again. He'd been in the habit of painting something like a benchmark or a convict's arrow there, to help with hanging. That he now needed it himself said something. Perhaps he was just tired. There were not many in the stack, only five: he had always sold well. He slashed these unceremoniously from their stretchers with a Stanley knife, past caring about the damage. If only they too had gone in the fire, or that he might have the courage to destroy them. Stubbornly, with some pale sense that it was foolish to spoil his own work past redemption, he laid them carefully, one on top of another until they resembled a large *mille-feuille*, and rolled them up.

Sifting through the rest of his materials, discarding what was dried out or useless, took several hours: drawings; boxes of crayons and papers; the battered tin case of paints and leather bag of brushes: all the paraphernalia of painting still belonging like a desiccated shadow to a man who doesn't paint.

In the dust behind the stretchers, among a miscellany of champagne corks and pieces of charcoal, a card belonging to the owner of the New York gallery came to light.

Jerry Grisher
Grisher Gallery, SoHo

Gilver turned it to and fro for a while then threw it out with the rest. He drank steadily while doing all of this and by the end of the day recognised that he was extremely pissed. It helped dull the blow, soften memories. It didn't matter. The next day he was leaving for good and then he could sleep off a bad head – for ever, if he wanted. This self-pitying mood put him in such danger of being maudlin that he drank a further half-bottle and fell asleep, his head resting on the rolled canvases.

Despite his own concerns, Gilver worried that he had not heard from Eugenia, who had promised to be back for his party the previous week. She generally did what she said she was going to.

When he arrived at the new flat, the sight of packing cases, boxes and bags left anyhow depressed him so much that he urgently wanted to talk to someone. He thought of that girl, Alice, but God knew where he had put the scrap of paper with her phone number. It seemed too much effort to hunt for it. He called Eugenia.

She was in the apartment she kept in Vienna, at Schönbrunn. Three enormous interconnecting white rooms with splendid Versailles parquet and double-height double doors. Her bolt-hole, she called it, without a trace of irony. She hadn't heard about the fire. No, she hadn't spoken to Anders. Gilver did not mention that Anders had come that night to fetch his wife home. As he told her about the party, Gilver marvelled again how well things had turned out. Because of the fire he did not have to explain why he had moved and sensed that he could use it, if necessary, to throw up all sorts of ongoing obfuscations.

Eugenia was shocked but efficient. 'Come here right now,' she ordered. 'You can't hang around there. I don't care where you've moved to, sort it out later. You've had a shock, I'll put you up.'

He didn't feel like arguing. Let her be masterful. It suited his current aimless, black mood well.

Three days later, his affairs in some sort of order, Gilver flew to Vienna.

XVI

They spent late autumn and winter moving restlessly, hilariously, drunkenly and expensively around Europe, plotting erratic trajectories between Vienna, Paris, Geneva, Zurich, Berlin and Vienna again; from one house-party or dance to the next; a wobbly gyroscopic etch over their personal map. Rather like the old days, but with one big difference: Eugenia was pregnant.

She discovered she was expecting a week after he arrived. They had got back at nine from a couple of days in the country and eaten simply at home. Eugenia wasn't very hungry and sat quietly by the fire in the middle reception room. Her lust for sociability had always turned to occasional bouts of introspection that Gilver left to run their course. So he thought little of it and went to a pleasant, mock-rustic bar with wooden beams and thick cream sauces a street away to get drunk on Austrian beer with a truck driver from Berne. When he let himself back in Eugenia was sleeping.

The next day, walking round the gardens at Schönbrunn, they trudged up to the folly and lake, from where magnificent sweeps curled down to the yellow palace below. It was mid-afternoon and there was no one else in sight. Icy air raced round them, a cold late October. On the water a swan and cygnet pitted their necks against the blast. They sat easily, leaning together for warmth.

'Fuck, fuck, fuck, fuck,' Eugenia began.

'What?' Gilver knew what she was like when she was ranting.

'I am with child.' The archaism, in any other context, would have made him smile.

'Is it mine or his?'

She stared off into the distance where cloud masses, pink and blue, were daubed on the sky. 'Who can say, sweetheart?' She shrugged wryly. 'Yours, his . . .'

Gilver's arrogance faltered momentarily. 'You mean there's someone else?'

'*Liebling*!' Her gloved hand covered his on the stone bench and gave it a squeeze. 'Gorgeous though you are – and you always are, you know, to me – a girl has to keep herself amused.'

'But who?'

She reproved him with one look. 'A tasteless enquiry, my heart, which will not bear fruit. Let's just give the poor little darling a sporting chance. Best of three, though, I promise you.'

'Will you keep it?'

Eugenia looked pleased with herself. 'Oh, *ja*! The timing is so good I can't believe it. I get the child I want, the father gets nothing to do with it – whoever he is.' She shot him a teasing look. 'I don't care, you know, who shall be the father. You all have your qualities and you all have failings. Here we believe that children's characters are more the product of socio-logical conditioning than physiological factors. It will be brought up according to tradition and decorum and it will be fabulous.'

'But what if it looks like—'

'It will look like me,' Eugenia said firmly, 'however much that costs.'

In January they went to the *Opera Bal*. Despite complaining that her waistline had seriously let her down, Eugenia dressed in a crinoline of black hooped net, layer upon layer, so wide and complicated by bands of glistening ribbon that it diverted attention; a trick she repeated with a plunging bodice that drew the eye to her enlarged bust. When Gilver came from the dressing room she was fastening her grandmother's sapphire collar with its heavy pendants and needed help with the matching cuffs. A parure of astounding value.

'Do you think it's worth it for this?' he asked, smiling at her and clicking the tongue of her right bracelet safely home.

They always laughed about the Opera Ball. It was a scrum, no one took it seriously. Eugenia had sometimes gone when she was younger. 'Oh, why not.' She was in excellent spirits. 'A couple dropped out of Alexander's party. I didn't want to let him down, he's bringing some new people. Maybe it's my last chance to dance for a while.'

Gilver stepped back and looked doubtfully where her skirt brushed the floor.

'Will you be able to dance in that? Is it a good idea?'

Eugenia laughed. 'My mother says I waltzed in the womb. Anyway, it'll be so packed I'll be carried along. Stop worrying and give me some wine.'

It was her affair, she was probably right. They drank pink champagne until the car turned up.

The lobby was crowded with people fighting to get to the cloakroom. Gilver repressed a sigh and stood in line with their coats while Eugenia went upstairs to find the party. He couldn't bear the idea of another evening with dull strangers, a polyglot group flown in for the event, like so many other evenings these past months. He was tiring of the whole game: small-talk with people you didn't know and wouldn't see again, a froth of vapidity. He used to like it, but since the fire he found himself thinking about things more than he ever had. He wondered if he was losing his sense of humour.

Gilver fought his way upstairs, getting lost in stuffy corridors and side bars, pushing past a gaggle of young women in shiny cream satin dresses huddled on an ornate landing. Round faces already flushed, they resembled sacrificial swaddled pigs and snorted and giggled as the handsome man went grimly through.

Eventually he found their mismatched party cramped round a table high up on the hooped balcony, looking down on the dance floor below. Hot, perfumed air rising from banks of flowers and moss was suffocating. Gilver bore the introductions, exchanged a word with Alexander, whom he had met years ago, and merely acknowledged the rest. It had been a mistake to come. If Eugenia hadn't needed an escort he would have let her come alone.

Champagne and red wine was plentiful on the table – you had to go and fetch your own, he was told, but Alexander had stocked up. Gilver drank two coupes straight off, watching Eugenia catch up on news. Sitting between Alexander and an over-well-turned-out man from Geneva she was more animated than he'd noticed for a while. He wondered if she was becoming bored with him, too.

The opening of the ball provided momentary diversion. A stiff swatch of young men led in escorting the piglets, full of anticipation, still painfully inept at waltzing, despite their lessons, the girls proud of their ungainly dresses and long gloves. When they left, after what seemed an age, the floor opened and was crowded in moments.

Gilver wandered off to find a bar and propped himself up on a velveteen stool. It was going to be a long evening. From here he could hear the music, which was pleasant at least.

As the night wore on he danced, as a formality, with the other two women at the table. One was Alexander's wife Molly, sweetly unremarkable; the other single and too narrowly dressed, it transpired, for the polka. Neither had much to say, nor could he hear over the music, the stamp and swish. He observed how few of the younger couples could actually dance. There was a great deal of bumping, giggling, treading on other people's feet. They all seemed to be enjoying it. Older couples, some of the men with a ribbon in their buttonhole, moved with neat, disapproving dignity.

Around two, Gilver went unsteadily back to the table. No one was there. After some time, picked out by a flash of blue wrist, he spotted Eugenia dancing with the surgeon from Geneva. Alone, he helped himself to champagne and smoked. An endless stream milled past, glancing curiously in his direction.

Gilver felt something like despair. Surely they could leave soon. Some time later Eugenia demanded he come and dance. She was drunk too, swaying and rather damp. The surgeon had brought her conspicuously back to the table and left making smug apologies: he had a clinic in a few hours, needed a steady hand. He hoped they would meet again. Gilver didn't like him but kept his mouth in a parting smile.

'Come on,' Eugenia urged, trying to pull him up.

On the floor the dancing had changed to formal sets, with complete lack of order or understanding. Gilver allowed her to lead him down and took his place in a worse crush than before. Everyone was drunk and the older dancers had prudently retired. He saw himself among them all with horror, no better than maypole dancers tipsy on cider, and held on to Eugenia while they whirled and passed. Perhaps it was a gavotte or some ancient imperial thing; it didn't really matter since no one knew how to do it or seemed to care.

Gilver's head started spinning in the heat and noise. Beads of sweat slipped down inside his tight borrowed collar.

A complicated series of steps was coming up: hands, linked arms, bows, exchanges and turns. Diagonally across the set a big man in another couple was drunkenly showing off and spun Eugenia too early and too fast towards Gilver. He saw with alarm that she was a little off-centre, her movements clumsy. Turning his own partner as neatly as he could in an attempt to get her out of harm's way, he trod on the trailing froth of Eugenia's dress as she almost hurtled past him. She lurched sideways, caught by her pinioned skirt, tried to get a bearing, lost her balance and sat down hard without warning on the slippery chalked floor like a great black marshmallow.

Near Gilver's elbow a woman tittered.

Dancers in the immediate vicinity tried to step back, to make room for Eugenia, whose ripped skirt was still pinned down by passing feet.

'Did you see that? The brute tripped her, I saw. Completely drunk, how ghastly.' A male voice behind him.

Gilver bent to Eugenia in the gap widening round them, desperate to get her up.

'Who is it, d'you know?' A woman's voice, different from before.

'Gilver Memmer. *Frightful* heel. Lost everything, you remember. *Kept.*'

Gilver finally lifted Eugenia, pale with mortification at the accident. He was sure she hadn't heard anything and tried to move her in the opposite direction to the voices, but she wanted to go that way, the quickest route off the floor.

Shielding her as much as possible from inevitable expressions of concern he tried covertly to work out who had spoken, thankful that Eugenia was oblivious to everything except getting away.

The man Gilver sought was moving off. At this distance it was impossible to be certain, but he looked exactly like Eugenia's first husband.

Gilver escorted her, shaken but fast recovering, into the courtyard. Snowflakes seeded the black air, not yet settling. The cold was a relief. He beckoned a cab and put her carefully inside, ignoring her protestations not to be so silly, she was fine.

They rode home in silence.

The stay in Europe threw Gilver's financial calculations into disarray. True, Eugenia proved spectacularly generous. But there were still enormous expenses to be met, costly fripperies to buy: they had always spent twice as much on everything as was necessary. Although Gilver had given Eugenia a whitewashed account of his reduced circumstances, her grasp was vague. People who had inherited a *Schloss*, he now saw, never understood much about money.

Immediately after the shock at the ball he would have liked to escape back to London, but realised a day later that he wasn't ready. The business at the dance troubled him more than he cared to acknowledge. Whether it had been Eugenia's husband or not, it was someone who knew him, and the jeering voice had been unbearable. It would be worse in London, the chance of bumping into someone bent on malice far greater than here. He did not feel up to facing that yet. Besides, he had promised all along to stay for the baby. So he was relieved when Eugenia announced at supper her wish to go home to Innsbruck and wait for the lying-in. They would never need to go out, she enthused, they could walk in the grounds, there was a stream, they could fish. She had had enough excitement. Gilver told her she was sensible.

Before the ball and before removing to Innsbruck they had behaved pretty much as ex-lovers, even brother and sister — one of Eugenia's more interesting fancies. As the birth approached she became increasingly withdrawn, which suited Gilver and gave him time to think. Watching her sometimes, happy in piles of baby magazines, unaware of his glance, he wondered about the pregnancy. Whoever the third man was, if he even existed, Gilver never discovered. He suspected it was a bluff designed by Eugenia to make it impossible for anyone to start asserting a paternal attitude. She took complete responsibility for the child.

When the infant was born, screaming, in a vaulted *salon* converted into a state-of-the-art hospital (an effect marred by Rococo murals all over the ceiling), Gilver studied it hopefully in case it resembled him. Carolina disabused him of this notion, with a black straggle of hair offsetting a tomato face and boot-button eyes.

Even her mother seemed perplexed, turning the prune-complexioned baby this way and that to catch the light. 'You know, darling, I'm not even sure she is *mine*. If anything she looks like my first husband.'

Gilver held his tongue.

He went back to London two months later. The morning before leaving he made a small, tender pencil sketch of mother and child. Eugenia loved it. 'You have been a good friend to me,' she said, looking softer than usual. 'By doing this, you make Carolina a little bit yours. When she is older I will tell her what a great painter you once were.' She beamed before turning to the insistent clasp of her child's tiny knuckle on her breast, not seeing Gilver's almost comic spasm as he tried to wipe horror away.

Absorbed in her daughter, Eugenia had no further need of him, although it was not unkindly expressed. She was being aggressively courted long-distance by the plastic surgeon (practices: Geneva and California) from the Opera Ball, whom she courted back as a bulwark against the future.

Anyway, Gilver could not afford to stay.

XVII

The return to a flat he didn't want to be in, after almost a year's absence, struck Gilver, clinking his third double on the small plane, as akin to an out-of-body experience.

Unlocking the door, he was relieved that it had not been tampered with. Inside, his new home greeted him forlornly, with a closed-up, cardboard smell. A bed had been delivered before he left. The dusty, homely wooden structure crouched in the bedroom. There was also a fine mahogany chest of drawers that once added grace to his drawing room, its top badly scratched from the move. He didn't care.

Putting the rest in order involved a series of mechanical tasks, which he carried out as best he could. Aimlessly, he unpacked glasses from dull paper; inexpertly hung the too-long drawing-room curtains in his bedroom, astounded by their weight. Left bundled up for so many months their crushed volumes unloosed a distinct smell of smoke. The precious cloth-of-silver stuff was damaged in the folds, some of its frail metal strands torn.

These depressing activities kept his mind from his prospects, bleaker since the time abroad.

There wasn't much money left. His time with Eugenia had bitten a huge hole in his calculations. All he could count on immediately, beyond an amount set aside for rent, was the proceeds from the auction of his goods. To his relief, when the relevant envelope turned up among piles of junk mail and rubbish in the padlocked box assigned to his flat, it was more than he anticipated. If he lived carefully there was enough for a year or so. He supposed that he could look about for something to do, some teaching perhaps.

It took several days to make the place bearable. During this period the phone never rang. He might have been washed ashore on an ugly desert island.

Sorting out the upstairs studio, with one of the eight-foot mirrors from his old drawing room with its four golden eagles – one newly decapitated – hunting cheerfully for dust-balls at the top, took another day. After trying to work out how to hang it in its immense frame he saw it was impossible to manage alone. He leaned it against a wall, manhandled a small chaise longue up the narrow stairs, flung a length of sky-blue silk over its splotched upholstery and put it in front.

Everything he did, everything he touched, brought back memories that taunted him. If only he could escape.

When he came to the sad roll of hacked paintings, damaged almost beyond repair by his own hand, it was too much. Gilver drank a great deal as fast as possible. Empty bottles piled up at an alarming rate. He did not remember eating, although he supposed he must have. He had not shaved, or changed his clothes. Replacing one horror with another was a sort of palliative.

Yet whatever he did to it, the flat stood in woeful contrast to the life he knew he must forget. The inadequacy of his possessions reinforced the sensation. Twenty-two rare gold-rimmed Bohemian wine glasses and a dinner service of French porcelain did not make up for a lack of essential kitchen equipment. He might easily have sat and wept, when the sight of Alice's kettle pulled him up.

Now there was someone who had liked him, who had not been put off by this appalling place. He wondered where she was. Probably long gone. Married, even. A nice girl. It had not been a propitious time to meet. She had given him her phone number, a lifetime ago. He could not remember now whether it had been lost with all his papers at the house. It didn't really matter. If it turned up he would call her. Even that was a dreary, nearly painful thought and he put it aside.

During the following year Gilver did not adapt well to his new life, which he made worse by being reclusive. He made no attempt to find work, not knowing how to go about it. But he suspected that if he could not put actual distance between himself and the past, he should put the next best thing, time. With every month that passed, he reasoned, it should become less painful to meet people he had known when he was successful. So the logical thing was not to go out and risk a chance encounter.

To speed the passage of time he sought oblivion in the quickest way he knew. He drank.

Winter was the hardest. It snowed and sleeted constantly and the flat was cold. He read absentmindedly, trying to keep warm with a bar fire the former tenants left behind, and slept a lot. Meanwhile, bottles piled up. One of his infrequent excursions was to take out boxes-full. Their reproachful clank, however softly he left them on the pavement for the dust-carts, was a sound he came both to dread and find fascinating. In his muddled brain the bottles' green sheaths reminded him of Keats's Lamia, taunting him with their curves. The only curves now warmed by his grasp.

When the remains of his cellar were finally gone, with such scant pleasure, he made forays for liquor at a nearby store.

Summer revived him a little. Light came into the studio room, where he had not set foot for six months. One day he took an unsteady look around. On catching sight of himself in the mirror he stepped back, appalled. Surely he had not aged so much? He knew he had taken no care of his appearance: the vanity of dye to touch in grey at the temples was past, there were obvious grey strands throughout the gold of his head. More alarming was an indefinite change in his features and frame. Through staying indoors, drink and worry, his skin was dull. It looked pale and uneven; there was flesh where once his jaw had been taut. He had put on weight.

He pulled himself erect and looked from every angle. The image came back the same at each turn, mocking, refusing to respond to these feeble tricks.

That evening Gilver took more care than he had for a long time in shaving and dressing. He found a local bar, a strange, underground place where no one seemed interested in you or your business. Odd-looking characters roamed in and out. The scent of marijuana drifted over Formica tables and wooden settles.

Gilver brooded in a corner.

He returned several nights in a row, staking himself a place and forming meaningless acquaintanceships. On the fifth evening he managed to pick up a girl, who said, giggling, that he was the handsomest man she had ever met. He didn't care if she really thought so or not. He wanted someone to say it, whatever their real opinion. He took her back to his flat.

In this way Gilver got through the summer, striking up deliberately temporary friendships with like-minded women. There was a relief and comfort in it. It was better, he reasoned, as his forty-second birthday approached, to get drunk with someone else and have momentary oblivion in their indifferent embrace.

XVIII

Two of Gilver's dubious new friends at the bar, who introduced themselves as third-generation dotcom entrepreneurs, were going to have a launch party at a club in the dark hinterland at the top of Ladbroke Grove. They were in their early twenties. 'It's going to be a helluva do,' one of them emphasised over a bottle of vodka. Gilver repressed a smile at the deliberate vernacular. 'We've got so much drink lined up you wouldn't believe it, man. And the chicks!' Expanded with goodwill appropriate to the moment, he said he would turn up.

Waking next day, crushed on to the bed with a thousand tons of sand, the evening seemed an unlikely, distant prospect. After half a bottle of red wine his hangover assumed normal proportions.

Gilver stared out of the window at a uniformly grey street and chain-smoked. The following day would be his birthday, a prospect that terrified him. Its recollection brought memories that time had not even begun to dim: birthdays surrounded by crowds of glamorous friends in places that, in his mind's eye at least, consistently glittered. And the hateful party at the mews. His birthday was not an idea associated with celebration any more.

Nevertheless, waiting for it to come and go in a bar or at home was too dreadful to contemplate. He got out his dinner jacket. It had hung on the back of a door for two years. Perhaps with a press it would pass. Surely the party wasn't going to be all that smart, but he might as well make an effort.

* * *

Night came early. Rain had fallen steadily all afternoon. Now it had stopped; darkness and cold began to draw round the streets and houses like a damp blanket.

Alice, picking up her dry-cleaning, glanced out at the wet blackness. The market was flinging itself into carts and garbage trucks, impatient to be gone. Barrows hauled away to storage on lumbering wheels, the last string of lightbulbs was pulled off a stall and bundled into an old laundry bag.

She stepped out of the shop, hovering in the doorway to pick her best route home. Charles was not coming that evening. With relief she considered buying a bottle of wine and a chop and curling up with a book.

As she debated this a tall man passed unsteadily. There was something familiar about him, his build or the way his hair fell around his down-turned head. He was immersed in a heavy jacket. It looked like Gilver. Alice's heart jumped into her throat. Feeling foolish but not caring, she started to lunge after him. A voice called her back into the shop, saying she had forgotten her umbrella. Habit made her reply politely and go to pick it up. When she turned back he was gone.

It was time to get ready for the party. Losing courage, Gilver collected the pressed clothes from the dry-cleaners as the light began fading and went in search of a bracer before getting dressed. He felt a bit shaky, a few drinks would help. It was an extraordinary evening, after all, and extraordinary measures should be taken to get through it.

When Alice caught sight of him he had spent an hour and a half in a nearby pub and was carefully selecting the way home, paving slab by paving slab, as if he was solving a puzzle.

*   *   *

102

Thoughts of Gilver were still uppermost in Alice's mind when Charles rang. He always rang at about eight, despite being told repeatedly that this was when she liked to have supper. Her cutlets had reached the point of blistered perfection under the grill and she left the phone on answer, resentful that even this dumb intrusion interrupted a much more pleasant train of thought.

What was she still doing with such a buffoon anyway? Charles was well-meaning but dreary, completely predictable and a boring lover. It came to her that she couldn't face him lying next to her, stroking her back heavily after they had made love and informing her, 'That was nice,' in the self-satisfied, rather common voice, one more time. It was tempting to ring him back and say so.

Only recently, when she had bought him a really good bottle of wine because she had felt mean about something – she couldn't quite remember what, it was all so pointless – he had turned his nose up before tasting it and said he didn't like Spanish. Wiping out the industry of an entire country with one petty, ignorant remark. 'What about port? You like that! What about sherry? Your mother's pickled in it! What about that bottle of brandy at that stupid dinner party the other day? You practically licked the hostess saying how splendid it was!' Alice had wanted to scream.

She half hoped Charles would ring again. He sometimes did if she didn't answer – another irritating habit. What the hell were answering machines for? If he was that stupid she would give him a piece of her mind.

XIX

It was Thursday, Alice did not have to work again till Monday. Those days off in a row always filled her with excitement. Like skiving – something she had never done at school.

She slept badly. In her dream, Charles was a matador fighting a giant sheep that trampled him to death. The whole audience rose up in applause. She made a dress out of his stained and stamp-stencilled cape. Waking in a sweat, restless, she wandered round her flat unable to stop wondering if it really had been Gilver she had seen the previous night. After an hour of fruitless debate, Alice gave up the struggle and walked towards the street he had lived in two years before. She didn't care if it was crazy. He was probably out, anyway. It probably hadn't been him but someone a bit like him. That could happen.

This litany of nervous unreasonableness sustained her during the walk. She wasn't going to ring the bell, just stroll past.

As she reached the house its grimy front door opened. A girl came out. She had dark, disordered hair, shiny earrings. She was doing up the top button of her cardigan across voluminous breasts, shivering against the chill early-October air. Her clothes were evidently meant for the evening. Alice faltered and moved aside. The girl just brushed against her, rudely, and gave her one of those smiles women are so good at: a smile that says, 'I have just had sex and you haven't, you frigid old cow'. Alice shrank back. When the girl had gone she supported herself for a moment against the railings. Her mouth was dry. She was numb with something that tasted

104

like fear. This was absurd. There was no telling which flat the girl had come out of, but with the instinct some sensibilities are tortured by, Alice knew perfectly well.

She went home.

One Saturday lunchtime a month later, two weeks after she told Charles to get out and take his sodding saucepan with him, Alice went into the stationer's for a highlighter pen. As she put it through its paces on a small pad, someone came up behind.

'It's Alice, isn't it?' Gilver touched her arm with the box of charcoal he had just bought, to attract her attention. She thought the arm would fall off, molten and fused. Her face engulfed in flame and she stood burning.

'How lovely to see you.' Alice was confident she sounded normal, if a little prim.

They went to a nearby café. On the pavement beyond the window a woman slapped her child. Thin wailing penetrated the glass. Gilver ordered a bottle of wine. Alice watched him, her knees shaking under the table.

Something terrible had happened. It could only be a couple of years since they met – she did a rapid calculation – but he had aged noticeably. He was still beautiful: at least, she found him so. But he had coarsened, his face in particular. There was white in his hair, making it paler, and it was a little unkempt. His clothes were ordinary and not absolutely clean. On his fine hands the fingernails, previously manicured, had black rims. None of this would have mattered: she had aged too, everyone did. And compared with that oaf Charles, Gilver was still a god.

What perturbed her most was his expression: his eyes, the

turn of his well-shaped mouth. As if the light had gone out of him and he was far back inside himself where before he had sprung, beaming, to meet her. The lines leading from his nose and around his eyes were not from smiling. When he glanced familiarly at the wine list his mouth turned down into an almost haggard expression. It was an expression she had guessed at when she first met him, now it was real.

He asked after her pleasantly as if only a week had gone by. He said he had thought about her. This was true in part. Piercing winter sun struck in through the large window. Her hair, which he remembered as the finest thing about her, basked in its glow as if it was alive. She was unchanged, except for a faint expression of concern that brought tightness into her face.

'Are you all right?'

Alice seemed almost puzzled by his kind-sounding enquiry and shook herself. 'Oh, yes, quite. I'm sorry, I was surprised to see you . . . it was a nice surprise.' The shyness he remembered had not changed either. She had a way of looking at him, straight on but sideways, inexplicable concealment.

He gave her a generous glass of wine. His hand shook slightly as he poured. She noticed he drank his as if it was water and recharged the glass. Alice tasted a little of her own out of companionship. 'Have you done any painting?'

Gilver's mouth twisted. 'Not really. But I've started some drawings these past weeks. I'll show you some time, if you like.' He faltered, stopped.

There was a difficult silence that Alice struggled to fill. She would very much like, she said. Her enthusiasm vibrated through the smoky air.

Gilver marvelled at her. She seemed charged with electricity, scintillated in her plain clothes. Her skin glowed. He looked into her face and wondered if it was because of him. His life over the past few months had dulled him so much that he had lost his refined judgement. In the bars he had taken to frequenting, you said what you wanted and either got it or not. Transactions were swift. Repudiations were momentary delays. There was no need and no wish for finesse. Alice's mixture of withdrawal and fire unnerved him a little. Drawing-room behaviour that he had put behind him with everything else. He couldn't decide whether to find it tiresome or not. If it was going to be tiresome, this was the moment to leave.

'I should go.' It was Alice who spoke.

Her announcement unseated his half-formed intentions. Unaccustomed to being pre-empted, it determined him to make her stay. 'Shall we have another drink? Do you have time?' Turning on the smile he was once renowned for, he leaned over and lightly covered the back of Alice's warm hand with his own.

At his touch her face flushed. She knew he understood that she was lost. A group of East London men dressed in ponchos and ear-muffs came through the double doors and struck up a frenetic version of 'Bamboleo'. The spectacle of their garments relaxed the sudden tension.

'Would you like to have that drink at my place?' He knew what her answer would be.

Wrapped in her outdoor clothes, which included red woollen gloves, Alice wanted to skip along the pavement. She repressed the impulse. Walking beside her with long strides that had an unendurable plodding quality, he was silent, his chin on his collar. The icy greyness of the sky and street was stripped of sunshine by massing clouds. Against this backdrop he, too, looked grey. Not an ethereal grey, that he might once, she fancied, have held easily against the elements but a dense, worn, non-colour. Maybe he was sickening for something. The romance of the moment in the bar held up poorly against the street's bleakness. Step by step it was being stripped away.

By the time they reached his flat the glow had faded. Sitting on the steps was the girl with the big bosom and cardigan. Arms squeezed round her against the cold, her immense cleavage ran up to her chin. She took them both in at a glance, rising with a victorious, brief look at Alice. Only Alice, seeing her first, caught it. The girl turned her look to Gilver, who started towards her away from Alice's side.

Alice fell back a pace. As if in a nightmare, Gilver continued up the steps to greet the girl. Alice fled the way she had come, hearing Gilver calling her name as she reached the far end of the street. She did not turn or stop.

Once home she hurled herself into her sitting room and wept on the sofa. There was a message from Charles asking if he could see her. She rang back and said yes.

XX

'What the fuck are you doing here?' Although he spoke quietly, rage showed in Gilver's face. Lydia assumed an air of theatrical surprise. She could see Alice, stunned, behind him. Lydia threw her arms round him, so suddenly that it took him unaware, and engulfed him in a hug. The wind taken out of his sails by this unexpected manoeuvre he lost his footing and staggered. Limp as a rag doll she staggered with him. 'For Christ's sake,' he exploded, as he regained his balance, furiously trying to unmould her, 'what on earth are you doing here?' Not bothering to pay him a direct glance the girl observed round his shoulder the progress of Alice, disappearing down the street.

They had met a couple of times since she slept with him on his birthday. She was raucous and, in his opinion, difficult. He didn't want to have anything more to do with her but she appeared to have odd ideas: that the one uneventful night they had spent together constituted a promise of some sort, for one thing.

She relaxed her hold enough to toss her head back from the warmth of his breath, but still held him by his coated elbows. 'I just came to see you. Aren't you pleased?'

Gilver stared at her again before recalling Alice, utterly forgotten in Lydia's onslaught. He pulled free and whipped round. Aghast at Alice witnessing this shaming encounter, he was nevertheless not prepared to watch her vanish at the end of the road. Just stopping himself from cuffing Lydia, he stepped cursing on to the pavement, calling Alice's name. It was too late. She didn't hear.

Lydia laughed. He saw she was drunk. '*She* was here a few

weeks ago,' she jeered, triumphant. 'She's a wuss, isn't she?'

Gilver looked at her in disbelief. 'What do you mean, she was here? What crap is this?'

'You know.' Lydia exuded hissy white breath like a steam-train. 'That first morning, after we met. I was leaving and she was coming to see you. You *must* remember. She looks boring but she can't be that boring? Are all your friends as dreary as that?'

'Fuck off,' Gilver said, so icily that Lydia deflated. He took one step towards her and she slipped past him nervously. 'I told you, I don't want to see you. I mean it. Don't come back here.'

The moment Lydia had gone Gilver wandered around for an hour, past all the places that had anything to do with Alice, hoping she might materialise. He stood for a while in the stationer's, looking at the pad she had tried her pen on, and peered through the windows of the bar they had sat in. It was freezing cold, that tinge of sickly lemon in the darkening sky that threatens sleet. But still he walked, aimlessly, burning with fury against Lydia.

If what she had said was true – and he had no reason to disbelieve the accuracy of her tipsy venom – Alice had tried to find him. That was the only sensible explanation. She must have been thinking about him. He was touched. Now she was gone again and he still didn't know her number or where she lived. And it was all the fault of that stupid drunk bitch he had picked up because he felt bored. 'Lydia the lush,' he heard someone call her one night, when they met by chance in a pub. He had laughed, then.

As there was nothing to be done about it he went up to

his studio. He had not felt so angry for a long time. Large pieces of paper were tacked to the walls. The drawings, deep sooty images that might have been skin, water or sky, loomed out under the bright overhead light. Furiously Gilver pinned up another sheet and started trying to draw Alice's face the way it had looked in the bar. He was incensed and drew without thinking what he was doing, his hand flying to and fro across the paper with viperous noises. The charcoal crackled and wore back against the speed and weight of his arm. Small fragments snapped and flew from the surface.

He stepped back, flexing his blackened hand and looked at what he had drawn. It wasn't bad. She was there, at least. Despite the vehemence of his feeling, as the charcoal skidded over the paper, the drawing caught her gentleness and gave it back to him.

The violent work tired him, but his anger had softened.

Gilver noticed he was hungry and needed a drink. Two hours had gone by. He went to a little French restaurant. Grotty but reliable, it had the outstripping virtue of being cheap. The waiter showed him to a small table in the corner, half hidden from the rest of the room by a pillar with coat-hooks holding a nasty belted trench-coat with a check lining. Gilver ordered a bottle of red wine, to which he applied himself, reading betimes a small treatise on painting by Alberti.

He looked up from the page. More people had come in. By the door, an ugly thin man, who had been sitting alone when Gilver entered, was talking to the waiter over Alice's shoulder.

After the shock of seeing Alice Gilver experienced a surge of contradictory feelings. He could watch them from his vantage-point, although he could not hear what they said. He would not have been scrupulous about this if it had been possible. He wanted to hear their conversation. Alice had her back to him and it was her companion – who the hell was he? – who held Gilver's attention. Aside from the man's ugly, boorish face, there was little to make him memorable. In ordering their food he had an overbearing quality Gilver found offensive. There was some pantomime to-ing and fro-ing about the wine. The man tried to score a point over the waiter with a pompous remark. Gilver noted how the waiter curled his lip as he walked away from the table. Quite right, he thought, cheering inwardly, you don't need that sort of twit. Alice's back was rigid. It was obvious she didn't like her companion much.

Gilver took his plate of spaghetti as unobtrusively as possible, no longer hungry, and fiddled with a bit before returning to his ringside seat. The man leaned towards Alice possessively. He was trying to take control of the table. He was trying to get hold of her hand.

Hooked, Gilver drank his wine and signalled for more.

Alice wasn't having any of it. She sat very upright in her chair. She had taken away her hand. Gilver imagined it clenched in her lap.

Next, the man tried supplicating. He had an earnest expression. That didn't work. Now he looked cross. Go on this way, thought Gilver, and the curtain will come down in no time.

Over their coffee, however, the man seemed to be gaining. Women could be so pathetic. Carry on battering away long enough and they usually came round. Surely Alice would not give in so easily.

Gilver was pinned to his seat. The man tried for her hand

a second time. The move failed. He had run out of tactics and really did look angry; his face was liverish.

It was a dangerous moment, they were calling for the bill. Hurriedly, Gilver settled his, even though the spaghetti was practically untouched, half his wine left. He didn't want either.

Their table stood next to the door. As he approached, he heard the man in the iron mask say, 'Well, I can't understand why—' He broke off in amazement as Gilver stopped right behind Alice, so close his thighs brushed her hair.

Her companion looked up over her head in surprise. Gilver ignored him. Feeling someone so close to her, Alice turned, following the man's gaze.

'Alice!' Gilver said smoothly, aware that her thwarted lover could not see the look on her face. He bent over her, his hand on the back of her chair so it pressed into her shoulder, and looked straight into her eyes. 'It was so nice to bump into you. Please give me a call. Here's my number. I've lost yours.' He handed her a matchbook, putting it with soft force into her palm. She coloured.

As the door, which was right by the man's apoplectic back, swung to behind him he could hear the voice start an aggrieved interrogation.

XXI

Juliette, now the editor of a gossip magazine called *Rogue*, was having her Pimlico flat remodelled by Hal de Vere, interior designer to the stars. She thought his ideas tremendously exciting. Not only were the floors and walls concrete, 'classic simplicity', according to de Vere, perched on her aluminium Bengtsson chaise, but he had sourced the most extraordinary pieces to dot about. He was explaining an Anish Kapoor glass sculpture, two glass bendy balloons shaped like a penis and a doughnut, thrust into each other and resting on a red glass triangle.

'Marvellous,' Juliette pronounced, as he balanced the small sculpture on a wenge stool that would have supported a coffin.

Even after months hanging sliding glass panels and dangling stair-treads from high-tensile wires threaded with light filaments, they had not become close. In the bid for a heftier discount than the one she had already bullied him into giving her, Juliette made occasional stabs at sisterly intimacy. It would be rather cool to have a pet interior designer – let's face it, *the* interior designer – under her belt. She might be able to get a scoop on him, even though he was not very forthcoming.

Moving the sculpture infinitesimally this way and that for several hours under her expert direction had naturally exhausted him. There were shadows under the poor thing's eyes.

It would have pleased her if he had thrown a fit of the vapours, like a character from *La Cage aux Folles*. She liked to reduce everyone to a headline or a caption. Her ideas of what an interior decorator should look and behave like were limited and childish; she had got most of them from cheesy movies.

Juliette almost forced him to lie back and rest while she poured champagne, making sure he saw the label. 'So how did you start in the design business?' She felt a magazine feature coming on. No one had yet secured an in-depth interview with de Vere, which helped his exclusivity. If she was canny she might be able to get enough out of him without his noticing.

'I used to share a flat with a painter,' Hal was happy to explain, 'years and years ago. He was really talented, and did these things everyone liked. But what interested me most then was how it made doors open for him. At the time – I was very young – I thought it would be nice to live like that.'

Juliette stifled a yawn. 'Who was that?' She didn't give a shit about the painter. This wasn't going to work. Hal had a faraway look in his eyes. He was obviously dreaming about some faggotty romance.

'Gilver Memmer. I don't expect you've heard of him.'

Juliette put down her champagne. 'I've heard the name,' she said cautiously. 'Wasn't he insanely rich? Didn't he have lots of fabulous girlfriends and stuff? And then he went mad or something?'

'I don't think he went mad.' Hal, shocked at her dismissive comment, still couldn't help wanting to talk about Gilver. Even though he hadn't heard from him for two years, which stung more than he cared to admit. 'He became a socialite and stopped painting. It was tragic. He was a genius, you know. And then his house caught fire. No one's seen him for years.'

Sod Hal de Vere, the piece on him could wait, Juliette decided. This was much more interesting: she thrived on other people's failures. The story of Gilver Memmer had obsessed her for a long time. 'I wish I could have some of his paintings here.' They looked round the bald walls together. 'Wouldn't they look fantastic? You're a genius, Hal, as far as I'm concerned. You can get hold of anything. Do you think there's a chance?' She refilled his glass.

Despite her blandishments, so voracious was Juliette's interest that it jumped out of her throat like the lure of an angler fish. Hal woke up. She leaned forward, her eyes gimlets. 'Do you know where he is?'

Under her menacing aspect Hal remembered he was Harry Davy, and Gilver, whatever had become of him, however neglectful of Harry he had been, was once Harry's idol.

Juliette held her breath. De Vere was teetering on the edge of something. You could see his mind going round. She would never have considered that he was hovering on the edge of revulsion. 'To have Memmer paintings here *would* look fantastic,' he said, slowly, gazing at the floor. He said 'would look' in a voice devoid of colour. 'I'm sorry. I've no idea where he is.'

Back at his office after the grilling from Juliette, Harry was upset. Juliette was by no means his favourite client, although he was too polite to make distinctions. He tried to give her the home she wanted, to interpret her confusion of hackneyed ideas. What he took for her vulgar computing of what it would mean to get hold of some of his friend's paintings made her face look like a monitor on the stock exchange. It filled him with a mixture of horror and grief.

Her raking over of the past, flipping through the facts as she would through a tabloid to get to the spicy bits, disgusted and alarmed him. He was concerned that she would try to pursue the matter and track Gilver down. Harry was sure he could find Gilver, but he was worried that even if he didn't give Juliette any information she would have enough contacts and determination to find out what she wanted without him.

It was two years since Harry had acquiesced in Gilver's request to disappear. He was too sensitive, and loved Gilver too much, to go against him. Harry believed profoundly in artistic temperament. But he still wished they had kept in touch. He wondered from time to time how Gilver was doing, what he was painting. There was nobility in Harry's soul. He knew he had done a tremendous favour in finding Gilver the studio – for it was still just as a studio that Harry considered it – but he didn't feel that this kindness gave him any rights. He hoped Gilver would come to him one day. As time passed and that didn't happen, Harry was generous enough to accept it, without harbouring mean thoughts. He had no way of judging how rare this quality was: it came naturally. When he met people who made bargains with each other's gifts of friendship, he thought they were strange, anomalous.

So, even though it hurt that he hadn't heard anything for so long, he took it in good part. His own enterprise kept him busy, with little time for wishful thinking. The business had built to astronomical proportions. He had a team working for him and was highly regarded. After he changed his name things really took off – if something as silly as a fancy-sounding name made a difference.

He decided he should warn Gilver that someone was coming after him and tried to work out the best way to do it.

Juliette slammed the door behind Hal, who had been instantly relieved of his champagne, and flung herself into an armchair. She wasn't going to be led up a blind alley by a poncy little git like that who was, after all, her hireling. She got straight on the phone to Alice. So what if she hadn't given Alice a thought for ages? She'd been promoted, for God's sake, and was far too busy to keep up unimportant relationships. There was no point beating about the bush either.

'Alice,' Juliette barked, 'you remember ages ago you met that painter, Gilver Memmer? I need to find out where he is.'

'Why?' Alice had been sitting holding the matchbook when her phone rang.

'What do you mean, why?' This was too much. Why did she have to explain why she wanted to do anything? Who did Alice think she was? *She* was the editor of *Rogue*. 'I've just been speaking to my interior designer Hal de Vere' – Juliette made his name sound like a ski resort – 'and he says Memmer was the reason he got started. I must talk to Memmer about it. De Vere is really hot at the moment.'

In Alice's lap the scribble of pencil on the matchbook said, 'Please call, I want to see you.'

Unlike Juliette, Alice did think you had to keep up relationships. She thought her old friend was a manipulating cow and that since she had edited *Rogue* the magazine had gone superficial and downhill. Like *Hello!* with the 'H' missing.

'I only met him once,' she said. 'Someone told me he left the country.'

'Who?' Juliette shouted.

'I don't remember their name.'

Alice was shaken by Juliette's call. What was it about Gilver that exerted such a powerful fascination over everyone? That she felt the same was forgotten for the moment. She felt angry and protective.

Still holding the matchbook she re-experienced the sensation that had seared her as Gilver pressed it into her hand, made her want to rush out after him. Instead she had had to stay in the restaurant with a defeated, petulant Charles and tell him something or other – it didn't matter what, he knew it was all over. She did not want to consider whether she would have given in to him if Gilver hadn't appeared: she had only agreed to see him out of misery. If she had made that ghastly mistake and taken him back, if Gilver had not materialised to save her . . . the moment Gilver arrived it became unthinkable.

Alice shivered with longing. She picked up the phone, holding it for a moment as if it was him she touched, and rang the smudged number with trembling fingers.

'You said you wanted to see me.'

Alice didn't say who she was. She was only glad when Gilver answered straight away. His voice was deep. Had there been a colour attached to it, it would have been tawny brown. She thought she would faint, just sitting there knowing he was at the other end of the line, his mouth next to the receiver; his breath, which she could hear, so close.

'Yes, I want to see you. Can you come round now?'

'Right now?'

Alice felt as if she was falling, drugged, into a deep hole.

'Yes. Please come round right now.'

She threw on her coat and walked as fast as possible, as if her heart and head would blow up. She felt and saw nothing; she almost got run over, the faces of other pedestrians were a blur.

The moments in life when destiny is tangible are rare, if they come at all. For Alice, her surroundings and her body were a united haze. She could not have said who she was, what was going on around her, how long the journey took. But she moved towards one bright focus that drew her like a beacon, the only real thing she could see or feel.

The strength of her attraction was so great that, had she tried to stop her feet, it alone would have dragged her on.

XXII

Gilver waited impatiently for Alice to come. He even went to the window to look out for her, moments after she rang off, knowing this was absurd. He figured from what she said that it would take ten or fifteen minutes. To help pass the time he opened a bottle of white wine – he preferred red – and drank a glass.

Gilver had been thwarted once in relation to Alice, by the untimely irruption of Lydia. The second occasion so shortly after, forced to watch her with another man in the restaurant, made his feelings of liking intermixed with a certain amount of attraction change to desire. When he bent to speak to her, his hand shocked by the static from her hair, he was excited by her and held by her eyes.

He straightened the covering on the bed. Alice liked him too, he had been sure of it since they first met. Her speed in calling him now, the way she sounded, convinced him.

The bell rang. He heard her feet on the stairs.

He opened the door and gently kissed her welcome.

* * *

Once inside, Alice looked round out of curiosity. It seemed more or less the way she remembered. Although he had obviously done some work, it was still pretty basic, and rather grubby. The paintwork had been redone but was no longer fresh. She caught a glimpse of the bedroom. Wonderful curtains reminded her of her pieced-together cope; the rest of the room was a mess.

Reproaching herself for nosiness she followed him into the small living room where a bar fire introduced welcome heat. The relatively Spartan furnishings were all, nevertheless, things that had once been beautiful. A French writing table in one corner, piled with papers, old newspapers, a ball of garden twine and a jumper, took her breath away. She went to touch it. Marquetry inlay on the fronts of the curly Rococo drawers, of birds and flowers, was exquisite. Beneath the heaps of rubbish she could just make out that the miraculous pattern continued on the desk's top. She stroked the silky wood with her fingertips.

Gilver had gone into the kitchenette and was offering her a drink. There were marks on the back of his jeans where he must have rubbed his hands repeatedly, ingraining the cloth with what looked like coal dust. Her throat was constricted by shyness and made answering hard.

'Alice,' he tried again, 'what would you like?'

Alice knew what she wanted, but it was not the answer to the question he put.

He felt her confusion. It was touching and spilled over into him. He poured some of the wine with a hand not utterly steady. 'I drink too much.' He stayed behind the bar, looking at her. 'Do you think that's bad?'

She glimpsed a perturbing edge of anxiety. He was appealing

121

to her about something although she was not sure what. 'I don't know,' Alice hedged, wondering what he expected her to say. After all, she scarcely knew him. She recalled seeing him in the street, stumbling along the pavement. He had been oblivious to everything, including her. 'I don't know how much too much is,' she enlarged, cautious. It was the truth, as far as it went. She knew already that he drank. What was he trying to say?

'You're right. It's hard to tell. Maybe I don't.' He seemed cheered.

Now she was there, Alice didn't know what to do. She felt dejected. If she had been a man she would have made a pass, but standing in a duffel coat with someone a foot taller made that seem ridiculous. Mata Hari hadn't worn a duffel coat. Men made passes, not women. These thoughts made her toggles chains.

'You said you wanted me to come . . .' It was a better tack. Gilver, too, seemed less than sure of himself now she was finally here.

'I wanted to say sorry about yesterday. That girl – Lydia – she's a drinker. She's nothing to me. I was sorry you rushed off. Why did you?'

Alice sank on to the sofa, still trapped in her thick coat. 'Oh, I don't know.' Under her bright tone she was miserable, struggling.

Gilver was not a fool. He knew perfectly well why she had run off. It was cruel to try to make her say it. 'Come upstairs to the studio,' he suggested, offering his hand for her to get up, to take away her outdoor things. 'I didn't get the chance to show you the drawings the other day. Would you like to see them now?'

*　*　*

122

Ten large sheets of paper tacked to the walls, strongly marked with dark striations, light and shadow, stunned Alice. She had not known what to expect: she had never seen any of Gilver's paintings. If she had ever read about him, she had forgotten.

The vigorous charcoal abstracts suggesting schemed and scarred volumes were like nothing she had ever seen. The impression they gave of a violent mood was disturbing and somehow erotic. She wandered from one to another as she might in a gallery while useless words floated into her mind: brooding, cruel. A critic had used the first about her second play at the Tricycle theatre, a word that was almost anodyne these days. But she had not been called cruel. Power flowed like slow blood through these drawings; beauty with menace, a sensual warning. By standing in the middle of the room she was able to look round slowly and take them in as a set. They appeared better like that. She guessed that they had been done in a short space of time and were linked to each other, at least in style. Energy burned off the paper as if they were still warm. They appealed to her as they disturbed her, in a way that went beyond liking and perhaps was not liking at all. Since they were not of things but rather of an intensely personal mood, it seemed reckless to comment.

Anyway, how did you comment on abstract art? Was the question, 'Does it move you' enough? She could see that, from a technical point of view, they were highly controlled. No false starts, no attempts at erasure. Every line and each sparkling area of unmarked paper felt as though it was in the right place. Every savage-striped darkness dared you to look again, to wonder where it came from, where it might go.

All the time she looked, Gilver sat on the blue chaise. She was aware of his eyes following her.

Gilver was not as self-possessed, at this moment, as he had once been. Certainty about his ability as an artist had been undermined through inaction, even though the stubborn supposition of it was the only thing that made him recognise himself.

But sitting here in the middle of the day, with thin November light sifting through the skylight, he was nervous of Alice's appraisal, grateful for her taking the time at least to pretend to look, grateful that she kept her mouth shut and looked in silence. He saw her first reaction was almost to recoil, but she kept on, moving slowly from one drawing to the next. Her expression relaxed. When she took up a vantage-point in the middle of the room and looked round once more, Gilver found he had been holding his breath.

This demonstration of sensibility touched him. He recognised that she had that power, she woke something more complicated than mere liking. She considered things carefully; not just his work, but him. Perhaps she was like that with everything, but at the moment she was focused entirely on his drawings. It was almost as if she had a silent dialogue with them. The difference between looking and seeing – that was the time to speak. So Gilver waited.

However vulnerable these drawings were, able to be rubbed out or besmirched by the passage of a careless hand over their surface, they were still the first serious work he had done for a decade. And Alice was the first person he chose to show them to, maybe the only person. Although her reaction could not affect him in the long run, at that moment he felt as if he depended on it. He knew that her reception could throw him into despair again. He was so close to it still: these moments were precarious. He begged her, in his mind, to be gentle. When Alice turned to him at last she did not speak. Her eyes shone. She took a few steps, smiling, and stopped hesitantly a pace in front of him. Gilver rose, put his arms round her, and kissed her.

XXIII

After a long embrace in which time stopped, Alice disengaged herself. Only the warmth of Gilver's body pressed close, his arms holding her tight against him, was real. Suffocating from his kisses she felt she would faint, and struggled against the feeling to come to the surface. 'I should go,' she said gently.

A renewed attempt to convince her to stay, a battery from a much stronger force, did not dissuade her. Old-fashioned propriety made it hard to be doing this so suddenly, even though, in his arms, she was losing strength. 'I'm sorry, I can't, not now,' she pleaded. He kissed her forcefully again. Her senses were in uproar. She wanted him and felt afraid; ill at ease, too, from the morbid images on every side. She needed more time.

Gilver let go abruptly and sat down, leaving her standing. He picked up his glass and twisted its stem in the feeble light, not looking at her. 'All right,' he said, 'you're probably right. I'll show you out.'

Alice did not know what she expected, then. To be coerced, perhaps; a renewed attack under which she would have to submit. Nothing happened. He was remote.

'It was awfully nice of you to come,' he said politely at the door. 'I'll call tomorrow.'

Alone, Gilver could not believe what had happened either. He could not understand it in any way except that he had been, however gently, repulsed. He tried to think if it had happened before and knew it had not. He felt outraged. When he thought of all the women who—

After pacing his sitting room until night, anger gusting up through wounded pride, he flung out of the house without an overcoat and went to the underground bar. The smoke-filled main room's blatant offer of darkness and familiar unfamiliarity was soothing, enough to change rage into an unformed search for revenge. Lounge music was playing and there were a few other people.

Gilver got a half-bottle of Scotch for company. A couple of rapid glasses blotted the fury in his stomach. Alice could whistle for it.

On the other side of the room two young women and their friend made a noisy group. Their remarks amused and animated them, they vied for laughs. Snatches of tipsy conversation floated over. One of the girls, with a cut-off top that emphasised the full ball of her breast and nipple, her athletic stomach, wanted to go dancing. Their companion, in his mid-twenties, sweated in the heat. Good-looking, easy in his movements, leering at them like a pimp. They were not going anywhere, his expression said.

Gilver saw that he was buying drinks for both of them, filling glasses as fast as they emptied. They openly smoked a joint, passing the precious fragment from one long-fingered hand to the next. The man rolled these too, a pouch of grass held casually against his groin. Metal picked out his signet finger as he rolled deftly, watching.

The other woman, arms polished branches in the subdued light, glanced curiously in Gilver's direction, aware of his gaze, before returning to the conversation. She laughed louder, her head going back to show the flash of teeth, the gleam of her eyes; smoothing her dress over her body, fingering her hair. She looked at him repeatedly and he returned her look with increased interest.

He had seen her before, he felt sure, crossing the road near the off-licence at night-time. Wrists that appeared to have a double bend, hips moving with dislocated beauty.

They continued this private conversation until Gilver's bottle was suddenly empty. He saw that she noticed and looked at her harder, locking her eyes to his. She got up, stumbling against the man in the suede jacket, who cupped a haunch and hoisted her, talking all the time, a familiar solution. They laughed. She leaned over the table and said something to her friend before weaving across the room, not taking her eyes from his face. 'May I?' There was mockery in it.

Gilver glanced over to the others. With a scraping noise, the man turned to see what was going on, one arm negligently over the chair back. He watched slowly, without expression, returning just as slowly to the other young woman.

Gilver patted the wooden bench next to him and she sat down laughing, in a heap, as if the air suddenly rushed out. Covered in silky turquoise stuff that was not silk, her thigh a pad of meat against his leg. 'Buy me a drink,' she ordered, one hand hot on his arm, giving him a look he understood. 'My name's Esther, call me Star.'

*   *   *

For the next week Gilver saw her every evening. She came very late, usually drunk, her eyes huge, black. They drank and smoked. He did what he liked with her until he was almost sick of it, without caring if he pleased her or not. Sometimes he thought of Alice as he watched her under him. Then he made love furiously, out of spite. Star laughed. 'Anyone would think you hated someone,' she observed once, in the middle of the night, standing by the window, looking with satisfaction at the way her nipples caught the moonlight. Her skin shimmered and her belly was a plane of blue glass. 'Not me, though. You don't give a shit about me. Not to hate, anyway. Who is she?'

'Mind your own business and come here. Turn over.' Gilver hated questions.

Once she gave him a bonus for the hell of it. 'Toss a coin,' she said amicably, 'head or tail.' After a week he was bored but offered her some money to stay and pose for him. 'Double,' she said uncompromisingly when they got to the studio. 'It's fucking cold in here.'

She was naked except for one of his sweaters and wandered round the room, beetling her fingernails along the drawings.

Gilver watched with mounting impatience as she ran the back of her hand across a few more, slouching along next to them in a fair caricature of a model's walk. She had a good body. If she had bothered to hold it straight she could have been Nefertiti. It was an idea for a drawing. Along the backs of her athletic legs the muscles played, her high backside moving as though a hand squeezed it at each dawdling step.

Lost in his sweater her shoulder rubbed the next picture hard. It smudged.

'Take it off.' Her carelessness goaded him.

Star dawdled provokingly towards him. 'It's only a drawing. Anyway, you can't tell the difference.'

He bent her over the chaise longue and got a wry backwards look. She laughed at him.

Star turned this way and that in front of the mirror pulling at her rump, bending almost double to get a better view. 'There's a mark, you fuck. Come and look at this. A fucking *bruise*.'

'Don't exaggerate,' he said benignly, not moving. 'It'll wear off. What a fuss.'

Watching her gave him an idea. Pencil in hand Gilver waited for her to simmer down. He posed her giggling with her feet in a large bowl of warm water, his dress shirt held loosely round her waist. 'You are Susanna,' he encouraged her. 'Look sideways at yourself in the mirror and stand still, like that. It's better when you try to look cross. You're supposed to be terrified.'

'Yeah, right.'

He drew her, changing her pose, reheating the water round her feet, until his hand ached from holding the pencil so hard. Red streaks crossed the palm.

She was a good model, albeit petulant. The mark on her was fading by the time he finished. They said goodbye in fine humour. Gilver gave her a parting slap on the backside and Star belted out 'It's In His Kiss' on the way down.

XXIV

In his cottage garden Harry sat on a stone bench, scuffed brick warming his back. He had been trying all morning to write a note to Gilver. An espaliered apricot, bereft of fruit, kept him company against the wall, its leaves turning pale lemons and greens. Late autumn sun streamed down. The garden, full of wet grass long from happy neglect and three crabbed apple trees valiantly holding a few bright fruits like wormy trophies, gave him pleasure. In London, everything seemed dark and full of portent. People schemed against each other. You felt as if you were in a play where all the dialogue had to be smart-edged, a little mean.

He watched a group of sparrows twitting a starling that was trying to get the biggest crust of bread. They ganged up and mocked the bigger bird in peeved flurries, fluffing themselves out and making assertive runs and jumps, eyes glittering. They didn't stand a chance, he thought, but they were giving it a shot in case the bigger bird made a mistake, aimed the wrong way.

One sidled too close in a doomed flanking movement and the starling sailed off with the choice morsel. The sparrows returned to the absorbing task of sifting crumbs from damp green blades.

Harry's pen faltered over the sheet. He wasn't sure now what he was warning Gilver about. Perhaps he overestimated the importance of Juliette's interest: perhaps she had already forgotten. Surely she was one of those people who got fired up in the moment and then forgot, or moved to a new enthusiasm. He wished he believed it.

There was a muffled tap from a window laced with apricot and passiflora. From inside the cottage Jamie, his boyfriend, beckoned with a wooden spoon to come and eat.

Harry scribbled a note and sealed it. There was no point going into detail unless Gilver agreed to see him, anyway.

A warm scent of braised rabbit, thyme and shallot filled the kitchen. Jamie looked pointedly at the envelope in Harry's hand, where it cast a blue shadow on his thumb. 'You should leave him alone, you know, darling,' he said mildly. His face, a little flushed from hanging over the Rayburn, was gentle. Grease spattered his stripy top. 'He hasn't been in touch with you since you found him that studio. I think he's an ungrateful bastard. Don't you think he deserves what he gets?' He handed Harry wine in a chipped Georgian glass.

Harry sipped it and put the note on the sideboard. 'I just want to warn him.' Harry appealed to his lover. 'He seemed in such a mess last time I saw him, I couldn't bear it. You know, when someone has once been so much, or you have cared for them so much, and you can't stop thinking of them in that way. You can't stop caring. Do you think that's wrong?'

Jamie stroked his arm. He loved Harry. He was less keen on Hal de Vere. He loathed Gilver Memmer, whom he had no wish to meet. 'No, I don't. I think it's a very fine thing.'

'So—'

'But there are some people who think you're weak if you look out for them. I think there are some who despise you for it. And from what you've said he's probably one of them. He still thinks he's God's gift. It's such a joke! What has he ever done for you?'

Harry was distressed. 'Nothing,' he said truthfully. 'I don't know why I bother either. It's as if he infected me, when I was young, like some sort of poison. I can't get him out of my system. Even though I know you're right, I still have to go on. And the strange thing is that because I know he isn't great any more, isn't shining, I have to go on now out of something else – pity, maybe.'

Jamie dropped a big dollop of rabbit into a soup-plate and gave it to his friend. 'Well, you're kind, ducky, and that's a good thing. It's one of the reasons I love you. Eat up.'

Dear Ogilvy,
I need to talk to you. May I come and see you? Give me
a call.
Love, Harry

Gilver hadn't opened the blue envelope. He vaguely recognised the handwriting but couldn't place it. The sense that it was from someone he knew made him unwilling to read it. It had come the morning Star left. Out with the new, he thought, climbing the stairs to his flat. He put the letter on the spiralling heap on his writing table and went back up to look at the drawing of Star he was working on.

She was too thin to be a Biblical figure. He had always felt they should be plump, like the ones in Rubens and Rembrandt. But that was a silly prejudice, a distortion of fact. It was more likely that there were lots of thin people then, that the Dutch painters were the ones distorting the truth with their overblown models puffy from lounging around drinking hot chocolate, or stuffing themselves with milk and cheese. Whereas this rangy woman, he decided, could have lived for days on unleavened bread or manioc; quenched her thirst with thin ewes' milk, or brackish water with the tang of iron.

But Rembrandt's Susanna wouldn't leave his mind, however hard he shook her off. The vulnerability of that painting, the uncertain rendering of its subject, gave it a poignancy his hard-limbed creation could never have. Perception of superiority vanquished him.

He sat a long time in front of the drawing, tacked up in indirect light, charcoal and pencil. The tall figure, a white garment held clumsily round her not covering her nakedness so that her elbows jutted like bird's wings, looked in terror over her shoulder. Round her feet the shallow water was agitated, light striking the rills she made stumbling away from something. She had been in some sort of struggle: there were bleeding scratch-marks, bruises, on her thighs and bottom. Bathing in her own garden Susanna had felt happy and secure when the Elders tried to violate her. He wanted to show her escaping from them, fearful for her life, horrified at what they had meant to do to her, scared to death by what they would do next.

But the drawing wasn't working in black and white, wasn't alive enough. He needed colour: his only solution was to paint again.

XXV

When Juliette got hold of something, she liked the idea of being a terrier with her bloodied nose down a sett, jaws clamped, shaking her victim to death. She spent a considerable time after work going through the electronic library. Modern technology was definitely a marvel and as tenacious as she in its vast ability to hold on to potentially useful information.

There were fewer references to Gilver Memmer than she had hoped. She found some stuff on his early triumphs. There was one devoted entirely to him as a dandy, detailing his wardrobe and the tailors he favoured. Although she knew most of this she devoured it again anyway. One of the reasons she had divorced Paul – for want of any that made sense, apart from the fact that he bored her – was that he had no idea how to dress. He didn't see that it mattered and wore a particular jumper that once made her very nervous. She never forgave him, or for wearing three-quarter socks with suspenders.

In the photographs Gilver was gobsmackingly handsome, staring at the camera with a pleased arrogance out of eyes that sometimes caught the flash with a feral gleam. That was her kind of man. Self-assured, able to have anyone he wanted.

There was a piece about the New York failure. She put it to the bottom of the pile. Bloody Americans.

Many more society-column inches on him followed, his affairs and his parties. He popped up all over the place at charity benefits linked to various women. Juliette spent a lot of time on those, making notes. She read again the few reports of the fire at Gilver's house, the valuable things he had lost, before returning to the women. If you wanted to get to a man you went through the girls.

The most interesting one was the Austrian countess. Juliette felt she could go back to the others later. The olive-oil heiress would have been worth pursuing if she hadn't died years before. Juliette checked up on the countess who had recently been granted an uncontested divorce and remarried a multi-millionaire, a plastic surgeon. They had a daughter called Cara and were based in Geneva. Although she assumed the child belonged to the surgeon, Juliette went further, using every means at her disposal. The surgeon had no children. The child was Eugenia's, born when she was separated from her second husband. Juliette couldn't see that this was necessarily interesting, except as a type of modern morality. But in the name of thoroughness – a useful term to cover nosiness – Juliette carried on, widening her search to Austrian newspapers. It wasn't difficult to get the right database. She had contacts everywhere. Early next evening she found a snippet about the baptism of the infant in Innsbruck, which seemed irrelevant but she read it anyway, as it was all there was.

The child had been christened Carolina in a small family chapel. She had worn family robes of magnificent lace. The countess wore so-and-so. All this was deathly dull, parochial, and with her limited grasp of the language, Juliette couldn't be bothered with it. There followed a short list of those in attendance. Gilver Memmer's name was the last one.

Juliette sat back and looked at the screen for a while. The text was hard to read and her eyes were tired. She had to look again to make sure she wasn't imagining things.

What was he doing there?

The cutting was more than a year old. Although she continued scrolling for an hour it was the most recent reference she could find.

It was a simple matter to find a number for the surgeon's

practice, and hardly more taxing to get one for his apartment, in a smart part of Geneva. The town wasn't that big, after all.

She rang at once and got a rather harassed Eugenia at the other end of the line.

Juliette told her who she was. Eugenia knew the magazine. She had been in it, although before Juliette's time. Stuck out in the Genevan sticks she sometimes had trouble getting a copy. Could that be sorted out?

Juliette told her that she wanted to do a big series on Geniuses of our Time and she wanted to feature someone completely brilliant called Gilver Memmer. She thought Eugenia might know how to contact him; she had read somewhere that Eugenia had been his most important patron.

After a pause, Eugenia said she was going to the opera but was sure she still had the number somewhere, in one of her old books. But Juliette was far too kind! Gilver Memmer had simply been a very good friend. And they had lost touch in recent years.

On the London end Juliette tried to keep her face straight. She had never heard someone over-egg a pudding so loudly before. Juliette asked Eugenia when she had last seen him.

'Years ago, darling, absolutely years.'

They agreed how terribly handsome he was, how fabulous his parties had been, how he deserved to be written about in the most glowing terms. Eugenia found the number and had to fly. It was *centuries* out of date, but she wished Juliette luck.

They hoped to meet when she was in London. Yes, Juliette could get her into the show she wanted without a problem.

Juliette glanced at her notepad. It wasn't a Knightsbridge number. Of course it wasn't. She smirked at the lined paper as she might have done while twisting a Borghese ring over a rival's drinking cup.

XXVI

In London when the season hits full stride, tailbacks of red lights and oncoming streamers of white flash like cheerful bunting strung for the benefit of the privileged along the great thoroughfares of the city. Those elegant streets, flanked with decaying Georgian mansions miraculously restored by street-lighting, or by the mirrored funnels of grand stores, become the gateway to a private club, signalling dances and parties, the glint of champagne and the mating call of costly scents.

Harry was at a dinner in the dismal grandeur of the Dorchester, glumly waiting to get his award as interior designer of the year from the Prince of Wales. To his supreme irritation Juliette, whose hair was piled on her head like a spun-sugar Tower of Babel, sat at the same table, elbows territorially squared to the cloth. She looked as if she would tear it to pieces if it so much as wrinkled. Juliette glittered at him whenever she managed to catch his eye.

Harry knew she had arranged to be there on purpose. On his final visit to her completed apartment he inadvertently mentioned the award. Juliette looked nonplussed, before an expression he had got used to flicked into her eyes. A few days later she let him know, casually, while ringing up on a spurious enquiry about the fashionable height for door-handles – which she called door furniture – that she would be at the dinner too.

Worse than that, as he entered the ballroom what seemed like hours earlier, he saw her switching name cards under cover of searching for her own seat. She was now only three places away from him.

The horrid ritual of dining was almost over. There had been five courses of torture, proceeding with agonising slowness as the kitchens strove to serve everyone simultaneously. Harry picked at each tepid offering in increasing depression and drank as much as he could to offset the nervous trembling of his stomach. Wine glasses spun out from his plate in a messy constellation.

Most of the dinner he talked deliberately to the young woman on his left, a pleasant textile designer who had won a commendation in another category. She made things out of heat-treated felt and wore a strange garment of her own design that made her look like a yak-herder. He liked her, and was interested to hear how she worked. They made an arrangement for him to go and see her studio. She let him feel the texture of her jacket, which was indeed softer than you would expect.

The older woman on his right appeared to be made entirely out of lacquer. Her face, her hair, her nails, the backs of her hands, the strange pearlised surface of her breasts presented as if they were baked egg-whites, the odd sheeny stuff her garments were constructed from, all were brittle and glistening. She might have been a series of Chinese boxes reassembled into the simulacrum of a human form. Once Harry was sure he caught a glimpse of himself in her forehead. She must be a society figure. He knew enough of them to be familiar with the approximate lines they were written on. Her dress, with its shiny impression of incarceration, was the most astounding piece of engineering he had ever seen and he wondered if she had to remove it in a special pressurised chamber.

Now and again through the meal she tried to talk to him. At each fresh assault he was aware of the pale three-quarters of Juliette's face cocked across from the man in-between. Even though Juliette was talking animatedly to what Harry assumed was Chinese Box's husband, she was on full alert for him. She was practically sending semaphore messages. Under a rising tide of panic and an increasingly wide blend of intoxicating drinks, whose colours had progressed through the entire rainbow, he had nevertheless successfully evaded the shiny American's overtures by paying zealous attention to his left-hand acquaintance. They had had so many detailed discussions of the niceties of wool-combing and boiling that Harry, his head spinning, felt in a position to start up a business on his own.

He longed for the announcement of the award ceremony. Perhaps he could faint and be carried out.

The woman from New York was not easily dissuaded. She bided her time. When there was a slight interruption between Harry and the felt-maker as a waiter offered them madeira, she pounced. Her hand clasped Harry's jacket too firmly to be ignored.

She and Mr Grisher were art collectors and had a foundation. Mr de Vere must have heard of it.

Mr de Vere was just starting to say that he had not, lamentably, heard of it, when Juliette leaned across Mr Grisher. 'Oh, but you have, Hal!' Her face was flushed with alcohol.

Mr Grisher contemplated the unexpected arrival of her head and its sticky architecture on his chest with clement resilience.

'Mr Grisher has been telling me all about it. It was the Grisher Gallery that backed Gilver Memmer's New York exhibition!'

Someone tapped Harry gently on the shoulder. They were about to announce the awards. He might like to prepare himself to be presented to the Prince of Wales.

In a battery of applause and light Harry threaded back to the table as slowly as possible. The Prince had been very kind, a charmer, in fact, asking Harry if he thought young people should be consulted in the decoration of their home. Harry replied that that sort of thing was best left to the family concerned. His reward was one of those wry laughs that made the Prince popular and let you feel for a moment that he was your friend.

Even though Harry was touched, knowing he would call his mother the next day to tell her all about it, he took small comfort.

As he struggled through the sea of half-wrecked tables, flinching from good-natured arm-slaps, he could see ahead an involved knot comprising Mr Grisher and his two over-excited satellites huddled round a decanter of brandy and a slew of coffee cups. He straightened his shoulders and sat down in the space Mrs Grisher made for him between her and her husband by dint of a complicated series of clicks and ratchets.

'Now, Hal, you clever, talented boy,' the former scintillated, 'Jerry and I – you must call me Beverley, by the way – have had a fascinating talk with Juliette and it seems you know Gilver Memmer very well.'

Juliette was nodding and beaming. Her hair had taken on an alarming Pisan slant. Strands of it were glued to Jerry's lapel.

Jerry, who looked even older than Beverley and had a large, off-kilter face, thrust out his hand and enveloped Harry's in a firm shake. Of the party, Harry felt that he at least was amiable: perhaps a put-upon sort whom he would get on with.

They all looked expectantly at him.

'Well I did—' he started, lamely, knowing he wouldn't get away with leaving it at that and wishing he had heard from his friend. So far there had been no reply to the letter, sent a week ago. He didn't even know if Gilver still lived there.

'Oh, Hal knows him terribly well,' Juliette enthused, 'and I was saying Only The Other Day that I desperately wanted to get some Memmer paintings for my apartment. I'm sure he's due for a revival. I might do a big piece on him, which would *make* his career. But Hal is being ever so mysterious about him.' She gave Harry a challenging playground look that said, 'So there.'

On each flank the Grishers pivoted closer. Jerry, who – unlike his wife – did not smell as if he slept in a sarcophagus full of pot-pourri, was the more congenial at close range.

Harry knew he would have to take some sort of lead. 'So it was you who arranged the show in New York?'

Jerry laughed, proffering Harry a yellow-banded cohiba from his inside pocket. Harry liked him then and took it.

'Yeah,' Jerry said, taking a thoughtful suck, 'at the time we were really pissed, weren't we, Bev?, because we put a lot of faith and publicity behind that kid, not to mention a fair bit of money, and it was sloppy that he messed up those canvases so badly.'

Beverley twinkled at Harry. 'Jerry's right. It was all Gilver's fault, even though he was such a beautiful boy I could have forgiven him anything.' She squeezed Harry's arm and leered tightly at him, as if he would understand. '*Anything*. So we ended up with a dead space for two weeks. It wouldn't bother us *now*,' she stroked her row of valuable bangles, 'but we minded then.'

Jerry laughed warmly. 'The most annoying thing, though, was that he was really talented. There aren't that many people I want to show like I wanted to show him.'

'Jerry really likes painting,' Beverley interrupted, with another squeeze. Her husband ignored her.

'*You* know,' Jerry went on, 'all those nineties bottled specimens, bits of broken china, frozen wads of blood, ampoules of semen and piss, lumps of shit – pardon my French – they're all gimcrack. There's nothing wrong with it, it's all in an honourable tradition, but I'm a brush-and-canvas man myself. And Gilver could really do the trick. If I got the chance I wouldn't hesitate to offer him another go.'

Juliette had been remarkably quiet through this interchange. Harry hoped she had nodded off or even died, but she snapped upright like a pointer's ears and took a slurp of brandy. With something verging on disgust he saw that she was very tipsy. He didn't feel comfortable around women who drank.

She looked triumphantly at the three of them. 'Well even if Hal doesn't know where he is – and I'm not sure I believe him – I do.'

Horrified, Harry grasped at the faint idea she was bluffing. 'You serious?' Jerry was all business. He powdered the end of his cigar in the ashtray with a caressing motion that held them spellbound.

Beverley leaned so hard across Harry that her bangles dug into his arm and he restrained a yelp. 'Honey, how fabulous. Where is he?'

'He's in West London,' Juliette crowed, 'and I'm going to go and see him. Why don't you come? Even you, Hal,' she added, as a distinct afterthought.

Harry made a noncommittal reply and rose to excuse himself. Jerry looked genuinely disappointed, and gave him a card with their London number. They were in town for a week or so. Jerry hoped they would meet up. He asked Harry to call him. Harry did not know if he replied or not. He nodded, at any rate.

A band struck up a bossanova and dancing started. Harry left the ballroom as quickly as he could, but not before he heard the conversation pick up where it had left off.

It was just past midnight. Outside, in the sweep of the great entrance, he waited impatiently for a cab. Across the wide river of Park Lane, Hyde Park offered a velvet backdrop, dark and quiet.

He took lungfuls of cold black air and wished he could plunge in among the trees and grass to walk and think. He wished Jamie was there with him to advise him, and felt upset that Jamie had stayed behind at the last moment, not wanting to meet Juliette. Harry needed him now.

He tipped the doorman and gave Gilver's address to the cab driver, slamming the door in his impatience to be off.

XXVII

The cab dawdled along Gilver's street. As they approached the address Harry craned out of the window. Freezing air whipped his skin. The building was dark. It was a Thursday night, Gilver could be anywhere. To save face, Harry paid the cab. He looked up again then stepped back into the middle of the road. Right at the top, just visible, faint light. The bell rang for a long time. Harry pushed the buzzer again. It was half past midnight.

Standing on the frozen step he turned out to a dismal street, its pavements faintly sparkling with frost. Parked cars glittered under the street-lamps, their windscreens iced. A cardboard box full of empty wine-bottles stood against the nearest lamp-post, more bottles upended into it. Flaring its eyes at him a grey cat crouched, slipping under the protection of a car. A flash of blind-looking yellow peered from behind a wheel.

His good evening coat and silk scarf were as warm as paper. Harry shivered and buzzed again, wondering if the intercom worked. Gilver's bell was unmarked. The others carried illegible names in faded ballpoint in various European handwritings. As he was about to turn away, footsteps came slowly down the stairs. They sounded uneven; someone stumbled and cursed. The peeling door lurched open.

Gilver looked wildly at him, not yet seeing who it was. His hair was in disorder and in the faint light he looked puffy, unshaved.

'Harry? Is that you?' Gilver's voice was thick.

'I'm sorry to disturb you. Were you asleep? I need to talk to you.'

'Sleep!' Gilver arched an eyebrow and smiled a remnant of the smile Harry used to dream about. 'Far too early for sleep, old boy. C'min and have a drink. I'm working.'

Gilver turned abruptly and Harry had to follow him up the stairs. He was accustomed to his old friend's rudeness; dulled, he persuaded himself, to its smart.

Mingled with the smell of the hallway, uncleaned carpet and neglect, a strong smell of turpentine mixed with alcohol came off Gilver, moving unsteadily in front of him.

Once inside the flat Gilver did not offer to take his coat but led the way straight up the second staircase. Harry was relieved. The flat was like a tomb, he could see his breath. Closing the outer door softly behind them he glanced into the sitting room. Light filtered from the street through bare windows at the front. The otherwise unlit room was littered with packing cases, a bolt of canvas, lengths of wood. Perched on top of a box a bottle gave off a faint chemical glow that bounced on to a wall as an elliptic green smear. The room was a timber yard. It reminded him of a stage set when everyone had gone home.

He followed behind, remembering the single lightbulb hanging in the stairway from more than two years before. It hung there still.

Harry wondered what he would see in the studio. His immediate concern was that Gilver, humming some old fifties number under his breath and visibly unsteady, would stumble and fall back on him.

Reaching the top Gilver flung himself into a beaten leather armchair Harry didn't recognise, long legs stuck out, and waved airily round the room in the general direction of the chaise longue. Ignoring what he took to be an offer to sit, Harry stood.

'Oh, yes, do have a look round,' Gilver invited genially, rather loud. 'Drink?' He poured whisky from a half-empty bottle by his chair into a dirty glass. Harry took it and moved slowly round the room. The walls were covered with charcoal drawings that he had difficulty making out in the poor light; abstracts of an intense, angry quality. Propped against the end wall several large canvases were stacked, their faces turned away. The fabric stapled to them was clumsily cut. Paint came right to edges that seemed to have been hacked off, as if they had been restretched in great haste.

Two drawings arrested his slow examination: a woman with long curling hair, and a half-naked olive-skinned figure clasping a shirt round her, standing in water. He looked at both of them for some time. The woman with long hair was picked out uncertainly, as if in a dream. She had a sweet face, a little quizzical, and held a coffee cup on a table, both hands gently round the saucer. There were lots of searching sketch marks around her eyes, her shoulders, her hands. It was a study, not complete.

The other figure was not so readily pleasing. He had seen something like that image somewhere, but so different he couldn't place it. It was a very strong drawing, every line was sure: a masterful drawing. Something caught in his throat and he drank some whisky. Harry stood there for a long time. The artist he had known so long ago had only painted abstracts. They were fashionable then, although Harry never really understood why. They had not been beautiful to him as he felt paintings should be but he would never have admitted it. When Harry wandered round the National Gallery in his youth, on snatched trips to London, it was the richly coloured Italian paintings that held him spellbound. St Sebastian, shot with arrows, was his favourite. There was an astonishing colour that filled him with a sensation of ravishment peculiarly close to shame. Something of that feeling stirred him now, unsettling.

He sipped whisky from the filthy glass and came back into the centre of the room. Reflected in the vast gilded mirror, fogged with dust, Gilver sat framed. Under the overhanging lightbulb he was turning his drink, ignoring Harry and smoking. The searing light picked up grey in his thinning gold hair, heightened the rumples of his shirt and paint-stained jeans, caught at the jowls of his resting chin. Harry could not believe how he had aged. He looked unwell, blurred at the edges. The examination seemed like a betrayal. Harry turned away.

A towering studio easel holding a canvas about a metre wide and a metre and a half high dominated the room. To one side a cheap laminate table with metal legs and rubber foot buttons, the sort Harry remembered in his mother's kitchen, was clumsily covered in newspaper held at the lapped edges with scraps of bitten-off masking tape and heaped with tubes of paint, bottles, brushes, an enamel jug. Paint spattered the floor round the easel. The sickening smell of turpentine penetrated everything.

The canvas held Harry spellbound.

The figure with the white shirt was here, massive, stumbling away from the viewer. The shirt had become a sort of shift she grasped about her waist and Gilver had painted her moving through shallow water; perhaps a stream. Her skin had a sheen like a plum. Around her bare feet the water, where it caught the light, seemed to be tinged pink. Harry peered at the delicacy of her elbows jutting out, at the agonised expression seen in three-quarters. It looked as if she had been in some sort of violent struggle: there were scratch-marks on her flanks. Despite his feeling of unease there was a tremendous sensuality about the picture; the beauty of the woman's figure, the glow of her skin. He had had no idea Gilver could paint so well. He wanted to touch it but could see from its shine and rich smell that it was still very wet.

'Like it?' Gilver's voice, levelly indifferent, was startling.

Harry had been lost. He went and sat down. 'It's . . . magnificent . . . I don't know yet whether I like it or not, it's—'

'Yeah, sure.' Gilver dismissed him. 'It's all right. An experiment. I'm done with it.'

'Who is she?'

'Susanna, by way of some tart I picked up.'

Harry didn't know whether to take him seriously or not. His knowledge of the Bible was shaky, but his mother would know who Susanna was. Gilver's even tone dissuaded him from further questions.

Gilver appraised him curiously. 'You look smart. Been somewhere special?'

Harry blushed. The difference in their appearance was striking. Once it would have been the other way round. But Gilver didn't seem to want an answer and poured himself more whisky. 'You said you wanted to talk to me?'

Harry, wishing to shine in Gilver's eyes – even this new, vanquished-looking Gilver – had had his hand in his pocket, on the point of bringing out the little trophy he'd been given that night. In his folly he wanted the other man to see that he, too, had become someone. There was no point. He took his hand out again. The silver had been warm against his fingers. 'I wanted to tell you . . .'

'Come on.' Gilver refreshed their glasses. The bottle was empty. 'You were always crap at spitting it out. What is it?'

Harry sighed, his own news could wait. 'There's this woman I know.' For the first time that evening Gilver gave him a look that was almost interested.

'No, not like that. She's the editor of a magazine. She heard about you somewhere and has got this thing about you.'

'What thing? Fancies me? Do I know her?'

'Not a thing like that. Not as far as I know. She's fascinated by you, by your career, by what happened to you . . .' Harry struggled with a sense of overburdened delicacy.

'Oh, you mean by my abject failure. My . . .' Gilver cast an arm round the studio and his mouth twisted, '. . . my palatial circumstances? I'm quite a catch these days, you know.'

'All I mean is, she's determined to find you. She wants to buy your paintings – at least, that's what she says – and she wants to write about you.'

'Really?' Gilver laughed without humour. 'No one's written about me for ages. I'm sure if I bought a paper there would be an obituary. Although they more or less buried me when the house burned down. D'you remember?'

How could Harry forget?

'So what's wrong with that? Sounds very sensible to me. Not that there are many paintings to buy. All there is is in this room and those over there.' He pointed to the canvases against the wall. 'I nearly destroyed those before I moved. Don't know why I brought them with me, really, but while

I've been doing elementary woodwork these past few days I thought I might as well give them an airing. Anyway, Harry, why shouldn't she get in touch?'

'I don't trust her.' Harry blurted it. 'She doesn't care about anybody and I'm not sure she's telling the truth about you. She's asked me questions about you ever since I met her.'

'Ah, but I'm such a fascinating study.'

'Please!' Harry knew he sounded pathetic but didn't care. 'I just have this feeling that she's bent on doing something nasty. Her magazine is full of that sort of thing, she feeds off it.'

'So you think she wants to project me as a picture of rotten-ness, the defunct artist in all his grandeur, the golden boy tarnished? It's been done before, you know.'

It was horrible so starkly put. Harry shuddered. 'Something like that. I don't really know.' He felt exhausted, but couldn't give up. 'And there's more.'

'More? You amaze me, Hal, with your ingenuity. I had no idea you had been so busy discussing me with half London.'

It was so mean and Gilver's tone so acid that Harry was deeply stung. 'Ogilvy, that's unfair. I haven't discussed you with anyone. Quite the reverse. If only you knew, I—'

Gilver's voice took on a gentler note and the fierce light went out of his eyes. 'I know you wouldn't, Hal. I was joking. I'm sorry. What was the other thing?'

Harry told him briefly about the award ceremony and his meeting with the Grishers, their wish to find Gilver, and Juliette's claim that she was coming to see him.

Gilver listened abstractedly. He seemed startled when Harry mentioned the Grishers and made little comment, except that Jerry Grisher had been a decent sort of bloke and his wife a witch. But he finally reacted about Juliette. 'Ah, yes. That must be the woman who called yesterday.'

'Called?'

'Telephone.'

'But how did she get your number? I swear, Gilver, I haven't told anyone where you live or anything. Honestly, I swear.'

'Oh, I don't know. She didn't say.'

'What did she say?'

'More or less what you've just said. I told her I'd think it over. I took her number.' Gilver reached fumblingly in his pocket and brought out a crumple of foiled paper from inside a cigarette packet.

So, thought Harry, Juliette had been lying: she still didn't know exactly where Gilver was. What a bitch. And lying to the Grishers, too, to make herself seem important. At that moment Harry detested Juliette and wished he had ruined her flat.

He was feeling sleepy with the whisky, but Gilver had perked up. He hoisted himself out of his chair and produced another bottle from behind it. 'Come on, drink up, slowpoke. This is almost interesting. I had no idea anybody knew I still existed.'

'But will you see her ... them? Do you mind if—' Again Harry came up against a great stumbling-block of embarrassment. He was still taking in the tremendous changes in Gilver: the awful way he looked, the terrible place. 'Is this,' Harry gestured at the easel, 'the only painting you've done?' There, he had said it. What on earth had his friend been up to all this time?

XXVIII

'You know, you're a funny one, Hal.'

Gilver settled in his chair, one arm curled round the back of his head, the paint-ingrained hand hanging negligently by his ear. He twisted a strand of greasy hair with it. 'I haven't seen you for – how long is it?'

'More than two years.' Harry didn't like the line of questioning but still answered, trying to stay calmer than he felt.

'Two years. More than two years,' Gilver mused, and took a long drink of whisky.

With alarm, Harry saw that the second bottle was almost a quarter empty.

'And it's really nice to see you, although it's a curious time to call. It would be good to – you know – catch up on gossip, that sort of thing. But no, instead you come in here and want to know if this is all I've painted.'

Without warning Gilver leaned forward, slopping his drink, and clasped Harry's immaculate knee with his dirty hand. The nails were black. 'What have you done, Harry? What have you painted? I haven't come busting round to your flat and asked you that, have I?'

'Ogilvy, that's not fair—' The grip on his knee repelled him.

'Ooooh, Ogilvy, that's not fair,' Gilver mimicked, suddenly relinquishing Harry's kneecap and resuming his pose, a caricature of elegance. 'And for God's sake stop calling me Ogilvy. It bores me.'

He lit a cigarette dismissively and blew a rude plume of smoke up, glinting at Harry through the haze. Harry met his eyes with horror.

'No, Hal,' Gilver went on, as if he had not already struck a death-blow. 'It isn't fair. Life is bloody unfair.'

Harry concentrated on the last words or he would burst into tears. How many times had his father said the same thing when he was a boy? He had hated him for it, the smugness. His father, too, used to watch him from narrowed eyes. Sometimes Harry had gone to his room and cried.

'I only meant . . . how have you been?' In a film, Harry thought miserably, I would walk out now. Get up with dignity, stride out. I would never see him again. He couldn't adjust so fast to the monster in front of him. Through his mind, Jamie's words from their happy weekend in the cottage flashed: 'He's a bastard. What has he ever done for you?'

Harry tried to put the thought aside. Gilver was having some sort of breakdown, he was sure of it. In all the years Harry had known him, however careless he had been of other people's feelings he had never been aimlessly vicious like this: his shafts had always been tempered with humour, devilish but not evil.

Harry could see that Gilver's mind was wandering: he had already forgotten the blow, was even unaware how hard he had struck. He knew that in this state Gilver would strike out at anyone; was perhaps striking at himself under cover of his friend. It made Harry's heart fill with pity.

Gilver carried on smoking, examining his hand. He peeled a crescent of paint carefully from under a nail and squashed it as if it was a louse.

'I've been OK.' His mood changed abruptly. The horrible blackness was gone. 'Could have been better. Spent a year abroad. Muddled along. This and that.'

Hearing the too-glib tone more than the words, Harry wondered what Gilver wasn't saying.

'Anyway. In answer to your question, I just didn't feel like painting. I wasn't even sure if I could, any more.'

'So what made you start?' Cautious. Harry couldn't bear another explosion. He hated scenes, to see this wreck of a man he once loved sitting in front of him like this, riven by drink, flailing. Exhibiting a cruelty that debased him as lightly as he might try out a sordid joke.

'Her.' Gilver jerked a thumb over his shoulder. His attention diverted from Harry, Gilver's expression suddenly brightened.

Harry followed the indistinct direction as well as he could. 'The woman with the cup?'

'Yes, maybe.' Gilver poured yet another drink and gulped it down. A little whisky ran down his lip. He smeared at it with the back of his hand. 'Maybe not. Who can say?'

'Who is she?'

'Oh, I don't know. Some girl I met. Drink up, Harry. It's early.'

Harry took a small mouthful of his own whisky. It tasted foul and was murky.

There was a long pause. Gilver sat motionless, staring off towards his reflection in the mirror. Harry thought perhaps he should go when Gilver started again, his voice coming from a distance. 'She's nice. I'd like to see her again. You'd like her. Good girl.'

'What's she called?'

'Alice. That's it. Alice. I've been meaning to call her . . .' He faltered again. The cigarette had burned down to the filter and he didn't notice, taking another puff before crushing it out on the floor. He was slow pulling himself straight. 'I think I'd better go to bed, Harry,' he said, suddenly looking rather puzzled, as if he wasn't sure who Harry was. 'I don't feel very good. It's late, don't you think?' Gilver looked round the room wildly, as though uncertain where he was.

Harry didn't know what to say. His throat ached. 'Those people – will you . . .'

'Oh, them. Yeah, I'll see them. Let them come.' Gilver flashed back into focus and grinned a dazzling, disturbing smile. 'Let them come and get what they want. I don't give a fuck.'

Harry got up. Gilver didn't move. He had lost interest and resumed staring, frowning, at the mirror. He looked so old.

Harry hesitated then went to the stairs. As he reached the top and started to go down, Gilver's voice floated over the back of the armchair where Harry could see him, sitting motionless. He didn't turn his head. 'You're a good friend, Hal.'

On the stoop outside Harry leaned against the front door. His watch said three o'clock. Across the black sky, deep-purple clouds were lit by sickly green stripes hinting at rain, or snow. It was even colder than before and the street was deserted.

The fast-moving streaks blurred and gangrened. Thrusting his hands in his pockets Harry went half blind down the steps and walked away.

XXIX

Alice slept soundly. She always had. Her bedroom glimmered faintly, turned by light from the hall into an underwater cave. Hair fanning on the pillow she lay tranquil.

An abrupt shrilling from her sitting room woke her and she bolted upright. Was it a fire? Was that a fire alarm? Her head cleared, the phone was ringing.

To her waking eyes the room was black. No hint of light penetrated the heavy closed curtains. Confused by darkness and noise she leaped out of bed and ran for the phone, reaching it just as it stopped. By the handset her clock said four in the morning. She dialled recall; perhaps there had been an emergency at home. Anticipation of fear made her heart beat harder.

A local number that seemed almost familiar came up. Alice swept sleep-coagulated hair from her face and sat down. After a moment she was sure it was Gilver's.

In this room the curtains were open – she liked to walk in to natural light. Alice looked out at the tiny garden, faint and grey in a freezing pre-dawn. Straining her eyes to adjust, everything was petrified, soulless. As if the sun, when it finally struggled up beyond the dully gleaming wall, suffused her tiny external world with life. The tree at the end of the garden and her rickety iron bench came into clearer focus. She was almost persuaded that they were not shades of grey but gentle browns and dying greens.

She thought about Gilver. It was almost two weeks since he had kissed her. He had not rung, nothing. Now he was phoning at four in the morning. Alice had suffered, waiting for him to call. As days passed she gave up waiting; but the longing and incomprehension did not go away. Had that extraordinary kiss meant nothing to him, had he felt nothing as he held her trembling in his arms and kissed her again? Had he meant nothing when he said he would phone the next day and kissed her once more? Sweat broke out on her palms. She continued to scan the garden, her face blued by thin-rafted moonlight. It gave back nothing. Cold, still-cold with the total stillness of that time between night and day, the frosted grass was glassy, each blade defined.

Cloud-strands moved fast across the sky, massing into a skein like fat over a kidney, promising snow or sleet.

The warm phone might as well have been Gilver.

Alice redialled his number and waited. She did not have to wait long, he picked up on the second ring.

'You dialled my number,' she said.

'Alice.' His voice was thick, bleared. He must be ill.

'I was thinking about you,' he said.

Her heart started thumping. 'It's the middle of the night.'

'I know. I was thinking about you. I wanted to talk to you. Where are you? Are you in bed?'

Alice pulled at the thin nightdress she wore. She felt cold. 'No. I had to get up to answer the phone.' She heard him draw hard on a cigarette and drink something. 'Are you ill?'

'No,' Gilver said, 'I just wanted to call you. I'm sorry I woke you up. I'll go.'

'No!' Alice heard herself say, cradling the phone against her cheek as if it was him. 'Don't go. I'm glad you phoned. I wish you had phoned before . . .'

'I'm sorry.'

She imagined him sitting in the dark just as she was, staring

157

into blackness, the end of the cigarette glowing suddenly as he inhaled.

'Why didn't you?' His apology had been too easily made. She had to ask.

'Oh, I don't know. I meant to.' He took a swallow of something again.

'What are you drinking?'

'Whisky.'

'A whisky would be nice.' Alice pulled her feet up in the chair, completely awake now, settling into the sound of his voice as if her whole body wrapped round and enveloped it. She no longer wanted to pursue the matter.

'Would you like some?'

Alice laughed. 'What, now? At four in the morning?'

'Sure,' Gilver said. 'Can I come over? We could drink together. It would save the phone bill.'

Alice looked at the impassive garden, which answered as if it was carved from stone.

'What, at four in the morning?' she repeated.

'Yes,' he said, his voice very deep and soft.

'Do you want to?' If she said the wrong thing she would lose him. Every sense held him on the other end of the line, these precious seconds when the heat of his breath burned against her cheek.

'Yes, I want to. Very much. I'll be there in a few minutes.'

Before she had time to stop him, to reconsider, he hung up.

XXX

Light snow covered the grass and paths of Holland Park and few braved the air's savage bite. From a sulphur-coloured sky came the promise of more, more leaden snow.

A muffled figure sat bunched in a thick coat, whose unyielding wool shaped and held her as if without it she might puddle off the bench. Alice had walked and walked, skin stung red from the cold, mitten-balled hands in her pockets. Traces of tears etched on her cheeks would not leave them, although the marks were hours old. She had watched her feet instantly melt the lace of snow on damp paths and across hard black-green grass whose filaments crackled tinselly beneath her tread. Solitary crows ricocheted across the sky, bedraggled hammers.

Heavier flakes were drifting on to her coat and she rose unwillingly. Long enough and the snow, sifting down, might bury her, transform her into a snowman for children to decorate with twigs, buttons, twists of plastic and paper.

On her face, blankness masked the wildness she felt. Drained off, remnants of her usual animation burned inwards, just a sallow tinge flickering now and then to mimic the sky's pallor.

Gilver had come the night before, roaring drunk, delirious drunk. She had let him in. He stumbled inside without comment except for a heavy embrace that knocked her against the wall and fell into her bed, jeering almost at her frightened look. As if the companionable drink was a suggestion that had never been, belonging to a conversation years ago, countries apart. He managed to take most of his clothes off and fell asleep immediately.

Alice had watched him sleeping beside her, breathing heavily. She watched all night, until his breathing eased and he slept deeply. Then she slept for perhaps an hour, while dawn fought and lost against the curtains. Snow began falling.

In the darkness and half-light she studied him. Calmed in sleep, far from her, dreaming things she could not know. His head, massive in the ashy light, lay in a hammered hollow of her pillows, the head of a fallen statue. Safe from observation she looked more closely than she had dared before. Sleep had not smoothed away the ravages of drink: his features were exhausted, almost ugly. Deathly and mask-like his face taunted her.

Fear for him filled her heart.

He woke from the leaden sleep at ten. Alice had been sitting a long time, staring at the garden through half-open curtains. At a movement beside her she turned to meet his eyes, wide open, searching the room and then her with something like puzzlement.

'Alice.' As if he tried the name for the first time, tasted it. He passed a hand over his face. Sourness, of sweat and alcohol, came strong off him. She looked at him looking at her and said nothing, waiting.

Gilver stared blankly at the window, the yellowish sky. He put out his hand to touch her arm.

'Sleep some more,' Alice offered, 'you'll feel better.'

His hand closed around her arm and pulled her to him instead.

Gilver left some time later. He put his clothes on clumsily. It cost him a great deal of effort. Even though the room was not hot, sweat stood on his forehead. 'I'll call you,' he said.

When he was gone she sat staring blankly at his cup of coffee. It was untouched. Her grandmother had given her the little gold cups. Around the rim, where lips, countless times, had tasted their beauty, the gilding was worn to an ugly yellow-grey. In some places it was gone altogether. She held the tiny shell in fingers not quite steady, marvelling at the thinness of the porcelain, and drank its cold contents.

PART TWO

JULIETTE

I

As a child, Juliette had been told she was a young Elizabeth Taylor. Even though she did not know who the person with the difficult fizzy sound was she understood, from the constipated far-off look that came across her aunt and relatives' faces as they said it, that it was important. She realised almost as quickly that it gave her power over them. So long as she pirouetted meaningfully in her stretchy pink leggings in front of the television in the sitting room and tossed handfuls of black hair about she could steal any number of her brother Hugh's chips, throw tantrums and wear her dead mother's things from the shut-up box in Aunt Sally's bedroom without reprisals.

'Headstrong,' was all she got, a tone of admiration.

Juliette knew she was special, a little princess. That her Ladybird books showed that princesses lived in castles rather than a two-up two-down off the Queenstown Road didn't bother her, but she was curious about it and asked why insistently.

As she grew older Juliette began to appreciate that her special qualities must be reasserted at every step. At school it took a great deal of viciousness and bullying to ensure that everyone in the class knew who she was. Her aunt was reduced to indignant tears on more than one occasion when she heard a trembling account of how Juliette had been treated. She flew to the headmistress after only moderate amounts of sulking. Juliette was Special – meaningful pause – and needed Delicate Handling. You only had to look at the Poor Little Mite, her huge eyes, her transparent skin, the great shining clots of hair held back with a wide pink polyester ribbon that had been on an Easter egg.

Juliette borrowed the art of capital letters from her aunt and embellished it, metaphorically extending the principle to her actions. In private the headmistress was a sucker for a gale-force pout and a winsome, apparently impromptu curtsy after ballet class. Juliette saw her coming, and not just in the glass swing door on to the stage. The almond-pink tutu her exhausted aunt sat up all night spangling paid off. Juliette got the treatment she craved. That her peers loathed her was a matter of supreme indifference mixed with something close to pride.

Born the younger sister, childless, Sally Taylor was secretly pleased to acquire the responsibility of a family once the tragedy of her sister's death had been sufficiently mourned. The habit of deferring to a spoiled elder had inculcated in her the habit of worship. Sally had tagged along and been kicked out of the way all her life. She was given to understand that being dowdy only fitted you for servitude and boring jobs, and accepted it as the natural law of Second Place. Sally's sister Genevieve, Juliette's mother – a natural beauty – had been as unpleasant and domineering as her daughter promised to be under such subconscious tutelage.

When Genevieve and her husband died on their way to another fabulous holiday in Tenerife – first class, of course – Sally was genuinely heartbroken, unanchored. Genevieve had always told her what to do, often backing it up with a slap. Genevieve's autocracy extended beyond the grave. Her will made Sally sole guardian of the two children. This gave the younger sister comfort.

Sally was in awe of her new role. Plain and unremarkable as she believed herself to be, she worshipped the little firecracker that tumbled about wrecking her home, bullying her older brother and new-minted mother equally.

By the time Juliette was five she shared Sally's weekend passion for old movies and had learned to love Errol Flynn and some mysterious person called Derring Do. She had an invisible donkey called Derring Do, whom she swashbuckled and beat most ferociously, until he was run over by a Robin Reliant on the way home from her first day at big school.

As the years passed, the immediate vicinities of Clapham, Battersea and Wandsworth posed problems that also had to be flown at head-on. Trailing about the dingy local shops and the hideous hill of Clapham Junction on shopping expeditions with the drawn-looking woman she called mother was tiresome. Princesses didn't go to supermarkets and hold grubby wire baskets full of cut-price offers, she was certain of that. The admiration of passing strangers and of little boys – and of much bigger boys, from whom her new mother inexplicably dragged her with a look of fear – gave her plenty of ammunition. She knew that, in her heart, this mother saw her superiority: her charge had undoubtedly been exchanged at birth, swapped in her cot, robbed of her rightful coronet. Reparation for such foul injustice clearly fell on Sally's shoulders. They were both aware of it.

Her aunt's limited funds from working long hours in a tax office with a processed-cheese sandwich for lunch were stretched to the limit by demands to go up to Oxford Street and find something decent to wear. Oxford Street, and the long ride on the top deck of the 137 bus that it involved (Juliette conducting from the front seat or there was trouble), were, for years, the height of desirability. Juliette's rapid growth necessitated frequent instars of wardrobe, as did the importance of being beautiful and changes in the weather. Her hair had to be specially curled and she could only wear nice things as her skin was so delicate. By the time she was fifteen it might have been grafted from a rhinoceros.

During her puberty, both her aunt and her brother Hugh shrank from Juliette's cuckoo-like presence in the house. Hugh was quiet, studious. He resembled their aunt and loved her, as much as his sister allowed. Hugh was glad to be escaping shortly to university. As a child he had accepted Juliette's domination for similar reasons to those of his aunt: he remembered his mother and had been in love with her. His baby sister reminded him of her. In his memory he nursed the way his mother smelt when she bent to kiss him at the airport. She had scooped him up, mindful of him rumpling her fitted red jacket with shiny buttons, but ignoring his father's impatience. The last words he remembered his father saying were, 'Stop faffing around or we'll miss the plane.' He hoped his mother had loved him best.

When he was twelve Hugh sidled along perfume counters trying to capture the magical scent. It seemed an impossible task, but where the memory of his mother was concerned he was stubborn. He was reading about Hercules in Greek and felt that comparisons could be made. Bored shop girls were amused to help him on these clandestine forays. Anything to pass the time until clocking off. The young boy who wandered along their domains, serious and shy, had a pale face and pale eyes. His wistful look touched them. They sprayed the mutely outstretched thin arms with a bewildering patchwork of pungent odours, some of which developed into a rash.

He had come home several days running stinking abominably and dashed straight up to the bathroom. If his aunt noticed she never commented. He loved her for that. One such expedition led to a fight after he was taunted as a pussy by a group of fourth-formers in York Road and beaten up for trying to walk away. But he continued searching, until he found what he thought was the right one. He kept a small bottle under his bed, hidden in an old gym shoe. At sixteen he presented Juliette with a gift-wrapped box that cost all his savings. She said the smell was disgusting. He watched her toss it into the kitchen bin where it cracked against an empty ketchup bottle.

If Juliette had known that she tossed Hugh's memory of their mother into the bin with it she wouldn't have cared. Too small when the accident happened, she had no mother to remember. Besides, she was descended from higher stock.

After that Hugh kept out of her way, studying as hard as possible to get a good place. Once he had left for university, where he planned to stay for the rest of his life steeped in the classics, he never spoke to his sister again. In retaliation, as an adult Juliette always called herself an only child and an orphan.

By seventeen Juliette was uncontrollable and did as she pleased, having recently taken over the best bedroom. Her aunt was relegated to Hugh's old room at the back and told herself it was understandable when she heard Juliette play music late into the night, or not come home at all.

Juliette attached herself to a very fast set, all of whom had more money. By dint of pretending that she went to the country at the weekends – a mysterious place with large grounds, a keeper and a possibility of turrets – she was able to excuse herself from costly jaunts. Instead she got a Saturday job on the local newspaper, taking round the mail, making tea, and having her bottom patted by any man who was passing. It gave her enough money to buy the things she wanted but could no longer wheedle out of her aunt. No one ever came back to the house. It was too awful, she hinted darkly, but she put up with it.

Juliette thus made herself a romantic figure whom her friends admired. She was tall and leggy, her long black hair kept shiny with an endless stream of different products. She studied magazines and sat in cafés in Sloane Square and South Molton Street whenever she could duck off school, getting ideas on how to move and dress. After school she went to bars, sometimes with her friends, sometimes not. She looked older than she was and had no fear of sitting on her own. She never had to sit for long. Long legs and short skirts, the high heels she carried in her bag, flashing glances and tossing hair got her all the attention she needed. What were men for, if not to buy drinks? On the few occasions when Sally, worried sick, asked what Juliette did when she didn't come home, she learned that Juliette stayed with her great friend Olivia. Juliette's scorn that she should dare ask was so humiliating that Sally pretended to be content. Her own difficulties at work, where the office was being restructured, made it hard to keep track of a lying adolescent.

At first it was true that Juliette stayed with Olivia. She had stayed there once. It was a highly satisfactory evening. They got drunk on neat vodka in Olivia's bedroom and went to a nightclub on the King's Road, where Juliette pretended not to be impressed when Olivia exchanged obvious familiarities with the owner. Olivia's parents were away for a month in their house in the Maldives. As a pledge of eternal friendship

Olivia gave her one of her mother's many cashmere cardigans. Juliette stole forty pounds from a kitchen drawer out of the stuffed envelope from which Olivia paid the maid.

Her friends called her Jules, a name she liked and which separated her from the tedium of home. She felt it had something exotic and fast, something of the Riviera and fat airport paperbacks about it. When she was out, she lived the life Jules lived. Jules had a rich boyfriend, with access to a private jet, called Stefan. Stefan, who was madly sexy, was often abroad, negotiating a racehorse for some important client. But he was a handy backup for getting her out of scrapes.

One particularly hot July evening they went to a bar with three of their other friends.

They changed at Jessica's house in Cadogan Square and wore little silk dresses with tiny straps. Olivia, just back from a fortnight in Rome, was gloriously tanned, her long blonde hair bleached almost white. Juliette had fake tan, but her legs were better to start with and she knew how to use the spray-on colour well. She put something on her hair that she found in Jessica's mother's vast bathroom which made it shine almost blue-black, and scented her skin with an expensive cream whose name she wrote in the notepad she had begun to carry.

At eleven the three other girls went home. They were studying hard and wanted good grades. Olivia, who couldn't care less and had a trust fund to prove it, waved them off disdainfully. 'B-List,' she said, laughing across the table at Juliette and tossing her hair back. 'Let's get up to mischief.'

Despite her arrogance, Juliette's forays into mischief were rather limited. Bottom-pinching, hand-holding and a few attempts at kisses from lecherous men who wanted something back for her glass or two of wine and a handful of greasy bar snacks were as far as she had got. She was impatient to test the extent of her power.

She invested Olivia with everything she felt had been stolen from her. Olivia, in a curious way, was her birthright, the only living thing for whom Juliette felt an approximation of love. Together they became invincible, particularly since Olivia said casually one day that Jules only had to ask if she ever wanted more cash. They hugged and Juliette prolonged it in order to get a very good look at Olivia's new pearl and diamond earrings.

It was actually rather boring sitting in the bar. They did not have many resources between them, save discussing school and the girl who had recently got into trouble and couldn't do her waistband up.

It was a smart place, most of the people were older. Olivia had her eye on a group at the bar. There were four of them, all around twenty. They shot covert, curious glances at the two pretty girls sitting together giggling, drinking vodka tonics – Olivia's mother's drink. Olivia had singled one out, with floppy dark brown hair and a leather jacket. He did not seem aware of the intense heat. She thought he looked daring, like a pilot. Juliette and Olivia giggled, inventing names for their potential Lotharios, who seemed to be having a debate that involved them.

'They're deciding whether to come over,' Olivia pronounced, worldly. 'It's difficult with four of them. That one at the end looks really boring as well. I think he's an accountant. He'll stop them.'

Juliette wasn't listening. She had turned and was staring out at the bright street through big, ornate wood and glass double doors whose curved, bevelled panes sparkled. All the romance of London was around them, its scent of hot summer air wafting in. All this, like a handful of jewels strewn across a black velvet box, and Olivia was getting excited over those dreary specimens. Juliette knew nothing was going to happen and didn't want it to. She would have liked a Big Mac. They had not eaten and the vodka was making her bilious; she preferred rum and Coke. It was half past eleven. A dark, shining car pulled up at the kerb, passing the doors so that only the back end and its bright bumper were visible. A double soft thud came of the doors closing; two men swung in from the perfumed darkness, disrupting Juliette's glittering perspective. The one in front looked straight at her as he entered, tawny eyes in a tanned face turned on her as if he had come to meet her. Blood fanned into her own face but she continued staring straight at him, an interloper interrupting her placid enjoyment of the view. His sudden smile broke her composure. She smiled back.

He walked straight towards their table, only breaking his gaze to glance at Olivia. His companion, nice-looking with short-cropped red-blond hair, followed. They fell gracefully into seats at the next table. Expensive clothes, ease and warmth beat off them. They were perhaps twenty-six or -seven.

'Hello,' said the one who had transfixed Juliette, now addressing them both, 'we desperately need lots of champagne. Will you share it?'

Olivia kicked into action in the way for which, years later on the stage, she was famous. Swinging round from her desultory appraisal of the other men, her hair a flail of wet corn, she bent the surface of an unflawed face to this new challenge. Olivia had green eyes that shone in different shades from grey to moss. They now spat emeralds. 'Yes, please,' taking them both at a glance before flashing a smile at the one with the army crop, 'we've been waiting for you.'

After a bottle and a half of the most expensive champagne on the list – Juliette knew because she'd had a furtive look earlier – Gilver and Jack suggested they all went to Annabel's, if that wasn't too ghastly an idea. Gilver was a painter and Jack was on leave. 'An officer and hopefully a gentleman,' he offered fatuously, patting Olivia's hand in a way that was not remotely polite.

It was Gilver's car outside. His driver was getting bored, he said. Olivia kicked Juliette delicately under the table with her Blahnik toes. The thin silk of Olivia's dress showed her young nipples, the whip-like flatness of hips and stomach. 'Would you like to, Jules?'

Also under the table, Gilver's tawny hand was caressing Juliette's falsely bronzed bare knee in small circles that made her even more dizzy than the champagne. His thumb flicked imperceptibly at the flimsy edge of her dress with each circulation, stroking the skin under it a little harder.

'Mmm,' she said, trying not to faint, 'why not?'

They left the champagne. Gilver tossed some notes on to the table without looking at the bill and enclosed Juliette's thin arm with his hand as they walked to the car. The hot grip was a manacle. 'Jules is a nice name.' His voice made her feel as if he had run his tongue the length of her body. Gilver slid into the front of the car and gave directions, turning to grin into the vast back seat. 'Don't let Jack misbehave.' He laughed. 'Put down the arm-rests and sit tight.'

At the club they drank more champagne and danced. Olivia was sitting in Jack's lap, kissing him, trapping his head in a golden net. Juliette's head spun. When they danced Gilver almost had to hold her upright. 'Let's go home, Jules,' he said, running the back of his finger lightly up her stomach where the silk clung in the heat. She looked towards the table and he caught her meaning.

'Jack will take care of her, I promise.'

Outside Gilver's house, Juliette drew back a pace. Gilver laughed and told her not to worry. She stumbled and he carried her upstairs and tossed her on to a big French bed draped with white. Her head still spinning, she lay quiet while he stood at the end of the bed, tall, taking off his clothes unhurriedly, watching her watch him.

She had never seen a man completely naked except in a film, not even – certainly not – her brother. Gilver's body was perfect, beautiful. His erection embarrassed and fascinated her, her eyes were drawn to it. She giggled, flushed, and said he looked like a lion. He smiled with an ease that suggested he'd heard it before.

He stood still for a moment so that she could admire him, before moving on to the bed over her. To her surprise he did not kiss or stroke her in the way she had learned from films, but calmly removed her knickers, lay on top of her and started to fuck her. Juliette tried to wince away from him, shocked by pain. He put his hand over her mouth in a gesture that was almost soothing and carried on.

The pain increased and Juliette started crying. She was crushed beneath him. He shushed her, kissing her lightly on the forehead. After struggling half-heartedly beneath his weight she passed out.

Juliette woke with a start to Gilver's hand jammed between

her legs. Her head hurt, her body hurt as if she had been torn. She started to sit up but he pushed her firmly back down. 'Lie still,' he said, kissing her. She began to relax, thinking that at least this was nice, like the movies she loved, and took his kisses. So close to hers that they engulfed her view, his eyes were pure topaz. She found herself swimming in them. His hand gentled and caressed her thighs, pushing them apart.

'Don't,' she gasped, escaping his lips. 'It really hurts.'

Gilver kissed her again, harder. 'It's all right,' he murmured abstractedly, suddenly entering her with tremendous force, so hard she was stunned. 'Good girl,' he murmured, kissing her shocked white face tenderly. 'Just lie still.'

Juliette pulled her things together while Gilver showered, his cheerful whistling grating while she stumbled round the bed looking for her other shoe.

In the shower Gilver thought about her. He would take her for a slap-up breakfast at the French place near the Oratory. She was quite a girl, Jules – a jewel, in fact. He hadn't had a fuck like that for a long time. As he soaped the few pale hairs on his hard chest, running his strong hand over his strong body and admiring its muscles, he grinned to himself. She'd seemed more experienced in the club; provocative. It was nice to find she was rather sweet after all. Perhaps he'd take her somewhere at the weekend. Then he remembered he was going to Nice for a party. It wouldn't do to take her there. He had someone else in mind. But certainly the weekend after, or maybe the opera: he had tickets for *Un Ballo in Maschera*. She'd said she had never been to the opera so she might like that. What was she – twenty, twenty-one? She'd be fun to have around for a bit.

When he came back into the bedroom, blazing white, pale lemon and blue in the strong sunlight, full of perfumed white roses from Moyses Stevens, he expected to find her still in bed, waiting. The thought aroused him.

The room was empty. He called her name in case she was snooping around downstairs and went to look, but she was gone. So was the linen jacket that had been on the back of a chair, which dumbfounded him, as it was one he was particularly fond of. There was no note.

Strange girl, he thought, towelling himself off, disappointed. Must just like one-nighters. He hoped he'd run into her again.

Had Gilver looked out of the window at the sun-strewn mews he would have caught sight of Juliette at the far end, limping across the cobbles, his jacket crumpled round her, hugged to her chest.

II

For quite a while afterwards Juliette tried not to think about him at all. If she did, if she let her guard slip, she suffered attacks of panic. When she missed her period, things became easier to contemplate. At least there was something real to think about, plans to be made. She left home the day after her discovery, with no warning.

When her aunt got home from work she saw a folded sheet of paper torn out of a lined block on the sideboard, wedged under a bowl of mixed nuts. She cried with something shame-fully mixed with relief. The child was only a fortnight shy of her eighteenth birthday. Sally drank two wine glasses of Bristol Cream and decided to let it go.

Juliette borrowed money from Olivia to rent a tiny room, a smelly cubby-hole on the King's Road over a shop that sold curious items of clothing run up in the basement, records, and bric-à-brac. Drugs were dealt too: when Juliette found out, she used it as leverage to get a job there in the evenings. At weekends she went back to the newspaper and having her bottom pinched. Only through ceaseless activity, she thought, would she not go mad.

She registered with a doctor and lied about her birthday. You girls, he restrained a sigh, telling her to pick up a paper bag full of mixed condoms from the dispensary on the way out.

It was very early on and she got an abortion fairly easily. It wasn't easy when she went back months later with severe pains and the doctor said there was a chance she might be infertile. She should arrange an appointment for some tests at the desk. He was a nice man with wavy hair, not more than thirty. He was sorry. If she had come sooner.

Juliette didn't cry when he told her. The doctor put that in her notes and that the patient was traumatised. He suggested counselling, which she declined. What more could he do? She seemed tough enough to cope and she was an adult.

'I'll be all right,' she had said to him, smiling, he thought with brief concern, too rigidly. She was very attractive. Often it was the good-looking ones, but not always. He wondered if she would really be all right. She said she was an orphan. She had a place at university. It wasn't any of his business.

Juliette closed the door of the consulting room and walked straight out of the surgery on to the sunny street.

As if she swam through deep water, Juliette moved through university passing exams with high marks. She was popular, good to look at. She took lovers absentmindedly and they sometimes wondered at her disengagement. Some sort of sex goddess, some sort of ice-queen. No one got close to her, except in that way for a night or two.

Her determination not to think about Gilver crystallised into hatred when she saw him in a gossip column in a magazine, flirting, cavorting, successful. Her intention to put behind her what had happened between them changed: she read everything she came across. Somewhere there would be a crack in his armour but she couldn't discover it at this remove. Everything he did glittered. Even when he had a flop in New York it somehow wasn't his fault. As years passed she did not forget her loathing but time distanced her from it. She found she could deal with it by putting herself into a kind of coma.

After getting a degree she took a job as production assistant on a magazine about babies, motherhood and layettes. Her best friend Alice had spotted the small boxed ad in the *Guardian* and cut it out, wondering if it might be a good start. Juliette pretended disinterest but rang up the moment Alice had left. She thought that, at bottom, Alice had suggested it on purpose, some sort of evil sixth-sense masquerading as sweetness. You couldn't trust anyone; certainly

179

not your closest friend. Although the irony of her new job rankled, it *was* a place to start and she learned the business.

Paul met Juliette at a product launch at the Ritz. He offered her an intricately stuffed olive. The tailored suit from Jaeger was too old for her but made her look unusually vulnerable. Paul was the only man she had met who didn't try to go to bed straight away. For that reason alone she agreed to his rapid suggestion of marriage and let Alice catch the bouquet. Paul proved hard-working and solid, earning loads of money. He accepted anything she did and encouraged her. Probably he loved her. How did you tell?

She had brief flings behind his back when she calculated they might further her career, without the slightest feeling. Her calculations were rarely wrong. So what if it made men crazy about her? It served them right and helped her along. She deserved success.

Eventually she was powerful enough to put aside her feelings until she could use them properly. In this way she got on with her life. Divorcing Paul was as uninteresting as marrying him, except that he was generous and gave her a lot of money. When she got the cheque she wondered if she did love him after all.

Like some strange mockery it was Alice who brought Gilver back into her orbit. Juliette had always imagined that if he was thrust upon her – and she could see that it might never happen – it would be at a party, a dinner, a grand event. Not through Alice, whose social life Juliette had never considered in the same light as her own. It was unexpected, frankly annoying.

Not that Juliette couldn't have arranged something to

happen on her own, but even thinking about Gilver sometimes paralysed her and sapped her normal vigour. The notion of forcing a meeting was horrifying. So she convinced herself that if fate threw him towards her she would act, but only then. She told herself it would be better that way. Even so, Juliette was surprised to find something like rage boiling up when Alice told her over the phone about meeting Gilver Memmer. It was clear that Alice liked him, despite a feeble attempt at dissimulation that wouldn't fool anyone. She had never heard Alice sound like that. Alice was stupid enough to believe she could be attractive to a man like Gilver. Her friend's happy voice increased the depth of Juliette's irritation. The suddenness of what she had so long anticipated took her completely by surprise. A great heavy pair of locked iron doors that gave into another universe, so massive, so stubborn that they must be prised apart, flew open without warning. She stood before the future naked, speechless and shaking.

Collecting herself in a heartbeat, she stepped forward. It felt much harder than she imagined, but it was possible. With the split-second knowledge of possibility, pent years of certitude flowed back. She warmed to the task.

She would turn it into another assignment, no more, no less.

III

A bitter draught, Juliette thought, a bitter pill. It was an inconsequential thought but it pleased her all the same. She liked the sound of the words, their shape on her tongue, taste in her mouth.

Her bag and a bundle of *Rogue* proofs were scattered in the hall where she had dropped them: she was running late. Too bad. Gilver Memmer would have to wait until she was good and ready.

Standing by her bedroom window, its sills and sides curving seamlessly to meet slabs of dough-coloured linen and concrete walls to either side, she rolled a stocking up her leg. The sheer black slipped up her skin, tight at the thigh like a noose. Its soft constriction was pleasant. She started to roll the next, dreamily watching snow fall perpendicular on to the dark moonscape of the street below.

Gilver waited. It was a large place, expensive. The woman, Juliette, had suggested it. He was curious and had agreed. Her voice intrigued him on the phone. Its depth and suggestion of more depth were compelling. He felt something like nerves, to which he was unaccustomed. Once he had been so sure of everything. Now he seemed to know less and less, and the grim realities he dealt with made him daily more uncertain, which was puzzling. He drank some more whisky. He could overcome it, it was momentary.

She was half an hour late. He signalled to one of the waiters idling at the end of the bar, laughing with each other, sporting with a glass-cloth. A handsome young man with bleached hair tweaked into spikes flicked the end of the damp cloth on to the collarbone of a waitress, a hard flick. Gilver thought he could see her skin start to darken.

He shifted and made a more overt sign. The waiter took Gilver's empty tumbler gingerly. I do not wait tables in the other world, his gesture implied. Gilver ignored him and consulted the list. He ordered a serious bottle and poured a glass when it arrived. A woman was approaching the table, twisting through the crowd jammed along the endless bar. The longest in London, they said. He had watched a lot of women and wondered if it was her but this time he knew. She was seeking something. The defiance of her chin, her self-assured look.

She was extremely attractive. Tall and slim with high breasts shown off in a low black top. Shining dark hair falling around her shoulders, a short, shiny skirt, fine black legs, ankle boots. Moving as if she was oiled. Holding his glass steady against the table he watched her come towards him. She saw him and smiled slightly, triumphant, with dark red lips. 'You're Gilver Memmer.' It wasn't a question.

He rose. She noticed his steadying hand holding the edge of the table.

'God!' She laughed, sweeping back her hair and smiling widely. 'I've had a hell of a day. I need lots of champagne.'

She paused for a split second, staring at him, almost as if she expected him to say something.

'My thought entirely,' he answered.

Juliette sat down. She'd come straight from the office, she continued, taking the glass he poured. Easily she began telling him about the magazine. But of course he must have heard of it. It was an interesting life. That was how she had heard of him, come across him in some articles, seen his face, admired his work. She'd always wanted to run into him. She was his biggest fan.

The first bottle of champagne was nearly empty and he ordered another. She was leaning conspiratorially across the table, breasts plunging into darkness, cheeks pink. She pushed strands of hair out of her eyes, smiling all the time. She longed to see his work, wanted to buy something – if he'd let her.

There was more than that – Juliette put her hand on his arm. She told him about meeting the Grishers, apparently not noticing Gilver's slight start at her touch, what a wonderful coincidence that was, and about how they would like to show his work again. Of course he must allow her to choose something first, before they snapped it all up.

Under the table her knee brushed against his leg. He could feel how finely boned it was, imagined the faint hiss of nylon. He moved his leg slightly and her knee pressed back while she discoursed merrily about the Grishers, how she had promised to bring them to him – if he would let her.

Her knee was between his legs.

Suddenly she said she had to go, she had an early start, she always went running before the office. It had been fantastic to meet him. Her body withdrew itself and she gathered her things, sparkling.

Gilver followed her carefully out of the bar. It was his impression that he had drunk most of the wine. She skimmed between people who moved aside for her while his shoulders brushed clumsily against them. He helped her on with an expensive, soft black coat and sweeping wrap of fine red stuff from which scent came. As he sat her coat around her shoulders she nestled into him and swung round, laughing into his face. Her hair brushed his cheek with the same warm scent.

Juliette danced from foot to foot on the iced pavement, hooing out white clouds of breath, amused by them, while he called a cab. 'I'd drop you somewhere, except I think it's the opposite direction.' She beamed, her lips just catching at his cheek. They had arranged for her to come to his flat the next day, Saturday, at teatime. She turned her head the other way as the cab drove off.

Gilver stood unsteadily with one foot in the gutter and watched her go. He walked all the way home, trampling the crisp pavement.

IV

Juliette had not known how she would react when she met Gilver again. Going into the wine bar had been the hardest thing she had ever done. Seeing him brought everything back in a confused rush. But the state he was in, the way he drank, how his hand trembled when he poured, shocked her further. She needed to think about that.

Walking the length of the bar to find him, crossing so many years, was dealt with by imagining she was in a film. Perhaps a double-agent in a James Bond movie. The dangerous one with a stiletto in her stocking top. This thought engulfed her in the dazzling smile that sliced through the crowd, and that Gilver saw.

Juliette was certain she would know him instantly. He had

carved his name on her, after all. She thought it unlikely –
prayed it was so – that he would recognise her in return. She
knew she was a beauty now; it was said often enough, but it
was a hard beauty. Youth was long gone. Softness and sweetness, had she ever possessed them, were nowhere. And, practically, she had changed the colour of her hair a shade or two,
her skin was now naturally pale and she went by her full
name. There was nothing to connect her with the cannon
fodder in the silk slip wearing too much perfume and a pair
of fake pearl earrings from Arding and Hobbs.

V

Gilver took more care than he ever had getting the flat and
the studio ready for Juliette's visit.

He rose early. After a shot of Scotch and some coffee he
began tidying up and shutting things in cupboards. There
was a clean sheet for the bed, although the pillows were
creased, grey. That didn't matter. He threw the cover over
them, straightened the piles of books on the floor and chest
of drawers and tried to make the curtains hang evenly, a hope-
less task. A long vertical gash of about fifteen inches gaped
in one of them. He had stumbled, still drunk, one morning
and caught his foot, ripping the weak silk with a horrid
screeching. At the top the curtain was lopsided. The room
was dingy.

Walking into the sitting room was no better: it looked back

bleakly, not helped by silent, death-like light faltering in. It was freezing. Cold beat unceasing into the flat, against which the bar fire made little headway, glowing its pathetic patchy orange. Gilver put the oven on. Perhaps things would improve by teatime. Hastily he dressed as warmly as possible and went out. The snow was deep. Cars had become cartoon cars, round-edged. Roads and pavements were gritted to mucus-grey, but fresh white flakes were falling.

The unloveliness of urban snow, clinging haphazardly to piles of rubbish and scabbing on doorsteps was everywhere visible. So different from the glittering fields and mountains he used to love. Those aching, sharp blue skies you dared not look at, blinding; blinding too, the snow and doubly lovely; the lacerating air and clean scent, the sense of health and vigour. A sharp sleet flurry came and stung into him. He put his head down. There were relatively few people about, although it was market day. Gilver crunched and slithered to Portobello, breathing out stertorous clouds like a hippopotamus spraying water, clapping his hands in loose old leather gloves, silk-lined. His nose was running, the warmth of the whisky long since evaporated.

Something had to be done before Juliette came. She couldn't see the flat like that. Not a woman like her. Alice, he was certain, wouldn't have minded. She would pretend it was all fine, say something encouraging. Alice, it came to him, was kind. When had he seen her? Was it a few weeks? Seemed like ages ago. He ought to call. Had he said he would? It didn't matter just now. Alice would wait, would have to wait; he put her out of his mind. She was the patient sort, she wouldn't hold it against him. He hadn't exactly slept with her anyway, had he? Just for comfort in the morning, it hadn't meant anything, he was drunk. She would understand that. She was grown-up. She'd asked him over after all, she knew it would happen. And she could always call him.

Thinking about Alice was uncomfortable, he'd come back to that later. But Juliette! That was a different matter. It made his pulse quicken. God, what a girl. Breeding in every line, but style with it, not wishy-washy. She reminded him a bit of Eugenia. They'd probably get on. Or hate each other like cats. The thought made him grin. Arched back, fur up, spitting, Goya's *Gatos Riñendo*. That was more likely.

The smell of her perfume, the thick soft feel of her coat, the sensation of her slim leg between his, teasing him, her eyes sparking at him. It ran through him with heat and aroused his desire for her. He'd never known anyone like that.

What on earth had Harry been on about, jealous little queen? That was the point. Harry was a sad, embittered failure, always tagging along. How dare he try to make up that ridiculous story about Juliette, warn Gilver off? For God's sake, don't say Harry fancied her too. But then a woman like that could probably turn anyone. How could you resist her? He wanted her and there was no reason why he couldn't have her – except that he had to do something about the flat. She was used to the best of everything, you could see it, she knew how to judge. He knew she would judge him.

What she had said about being a big fan of his painting suddenly came back to him. He had that, of course. He had almost forgotten it was the reason she wanted to meet him. She knew who he was, who he had been. The thought was pleasing, making a sort of connection between them, something to build on. He would show her what he was doing and she would see that he still had it, that he was still someone. Showing them paintings always worked, got them going. Strange thing but true. And he could talk up the fire. A bit of sympathy might not go amiss.

Her meeting the Grishers was strange as well. He had put all that behind him; now it was as if it had all been planned.

Gilver had never given a tinker's cuss for destiny but it struck him abruptly that perhaps there was something in it, after all. If he could get the Grishers to promise him another show he would be made again. Visions of his old life rose before him, warm, brightly lit: the fun, the parties, sex. Hanging about at the Groucho; judging the Turner Prize. Fêted.

Across the almost empty streets the solitary figure bundled heavily into a fraying coat, too-long hair stranded with snow, lurched and slid red-faced towards the flower stall.

VI

Juliette was lunching with the Grishers in the Metropolitan. They liked to move with the times. Privately, Juliette thought their movements rather jerky.

They all ate out of bento boxes, Beverley stabbing at little bits of fried flour and marinaded tuna like a raddled crow. She was wearing a cardigan that looked crocheted from gold string with a wide binding at the edges. Indefinable Chanel, might be original. And a polished snakeskin skirt of whity gold with beige bits. Juliette priced the lot and flipped out her cash register drawer before they had even sat down. The amount of gold, down to a chain round Beverley's scrawny ankle and Jimmy Choo foot, wouldn't have gone amiss on a Christmas tree in a shopping arcade.

'You look breathtaking.' Juliette kissed Beverley's ear, checking how recent the scars above it were.

From the admiring glances of other diners she knew she looked lovely. She had seen *The Age of Innocence* on video and was particularly taken with a saucy pelisse the Countess wore, which seduced poor circumscribed Archer. Juliette had had her tailor make a tight-fitting crimson velvet dress, cut low and trimmed with sable. The fur nested happily against her skin. She had had a sable wrap with a sharper shot-red silk lining made to go with it, and liked the way you could toss it about seductively, or drop it at the right moment.

'Wow,' Jerry gasped, his arms held wide to scoop her into an embrace. She caught the look on Beverley's face. So did Jerry. He looked at Juliette sheepishly, reluctantly letting her go, holding her chair with a defiant flourish. 'You know I can't resist beauty,' he addressed his wife, 'so how could I ever resist you?'

Juliette liked Jerry and his vaudeville banter more on the second meeting. He seemed to have no front. The need for social graces – beyond common good manners – had evidently passed him by. He drank his wine with voluminous relish and ate with gusto, finding the immaculately presented food fiddly, confiding that he preferred meat to look like meat and vegetables on someone else's plate.

Beverley had recovered from her acid attack and asked after

Harry. Juliette couldn't help. She suggested vaguely that he must have gone away for the weekend to celebrate his award. Her tone conveyed Bognor. 'Nice young man,' Jerry approved. 'Is he married?'

Beverley gave her husband a look. 'Don't pretend to be winsome,' she said, tapping him on the sleeve with a claw. On her hand the veins stood up.

The conversation turned to art. The Grishers had been busy and were pleased with what they'd seen. They said they had been to some studios and to the Royal College. It was important to spot trends. Jerry had made a very satisfactory purchase that morning in Cork Street. 'Overpriced but I know someone who will kill for it.' He was pleasantly flushed, drinking brandy. Beverley hinted he might like some soda. He drank the brandy off and waved for another. 'That watanabe stuff, or whatever it's called, gives you a thirst,' he said.

Juliette leaped into the breach. 'I'm going to Gilver Memmer's studio later on today,' she announced. 'Very short notice I'm afraid. But I thought I'd mention it in case you want to join me there.'

'Sure we want to.' Jerry spoke without consulting his wife, who had a hair appointment.

'Now there's a handsome young man.' Beverley livened up. 'Has he married, do you know, dear? All the girls were crazy for him back then.'

'Gosh.' Juliette pretended to try to remember. She was actually thinking how much nicer she looked than anyone else in the restaurant. 'I don't think so. Funny, isn't it, how the most handsome ones sometimes stay single?'

Jerry was lumbering along. 'You're surely not suggesting that he—'

'Oh, shut up, Jerry.' Unexpected fondness softened Beverley's tone. Once they must have been Beauty and the Beast. Now it was a hard choice. Smoothly Juliette told them she had arranged to go to the studio at six. She admitted it was a bit late, but the light was so awful anyway, and it was the earliest Gilver could manage. Perhaps they would like to join her there at six thirty?

Beverley calculated that she could get her hair done, after all. She turned a more amenable countenance to her husband. It depended on him.

He wiped his lips. They were going to a dinner later. Political. You know. Couldn't be avoided. Finance, that sort of thing. Tiny portions on big plates. The sort of nonsense Beverley liked. He gave her a grin and a nudge that would have tipped her off her chair, had she not been so ballasted with metal. So there was no reason at all why they couldn't come along first. Beverley fiddled around with a personal organiser, presumably juggling this new interruption into their schedule.

Juliette thought her pathetic, but even so, not to be toyed with. 'Quite,' Juliette said, 'so this might work out rather well? Of course, if . . .'

Jerry put his large hand over hers, an upturned soup-plate with hairs. He had nice warm hands. She wondered precisely how rich he was, and how old. 'We'll be there with pleasure,' he said, firmly squashing a ring into her finger without meaning more than a pat.

She gave them the address and flurried off in a cloud of musk.

Park Lane sparked and glittered beneath a sudden blue sky. Over the road, trees poking out of a white blanket glimmered.

Pillow-sized lumps of snow plopped from them. Birds careened in the bright air, looping and planing on cleaving wings, hoping for thawing insects to fly into their beaks.

Juliette shot out of the Metropolitan a furred jewel. It was just before three. Her imperturbable lie to the Grishers gave her a little time to be alone with Gilver, not much. She did not have a plan, trusting that the incubus of jealousy and hatred that had grown into the space where her heart had once sat would surely rise and strike him dead – or at least something along those lines – when they met.

She snatched the cab from the doorman with ill-concealed impatience and neglected to tip, tossing instead a fragment of a smile, which he took happily, heated by the velvet-upholstered ball of her left buttock as she climbed grace-lessly inside.

While the cab bowled along she remembered her recent impression of Gilver, how awful he looked, overblown. His face sagged. He was alcoholic, it sang from him, a cracked tune she had heard before. Lust came off him too. He wanted her and he was a wreck. Satisfaction curved her mouth. She saw the driver looking at her through a spark of light in the mirror, questioning, wanted some of it for himself. She laughed, threw a teasing crumb of conversation and made him wait at a wine merchant near Moscow Road.

Gilver had bought armfuls of flowers, lilies, roses, freesias, every scented thing he could find that wasn't frostbitten, and put them about as well as he could. He lit a few candles and blew them out again, depressed by the effect. The flat had the air of a church.

By keeping all the windows shut the temperature was

satisfactorily snug. Thick scent from unfurling flowers was almost sickly but he was getting used to it. How different they looked from the flowers at the mews! Every room filled with them, changed long before they drooped. He put the thought aside. These would have to do.

He had bought wine and brandy. Little cakes and pastries from Maison Blanc, chocolates, plump dates. Some wonderful cheese, pâté, salmon and bread from the best delicatessen in the neighbourhood sat hopefully in the fridge. He spruced himself, searching vainly in the mirror in the studio for something. The effect didn't seem too bad. He sucked in his stomach and smoothed his hair. At least he hadn't lost that. Not much, anyway.

He took away dirty tumblers and a couple of empty bottles and straightened the cloth on the chaise.

There were flowers here too. A bottle of brandy and the last of his best Bohemian glasses stood ready on a card table; there were only two left. The rest were broken. A round seventeenth-century majolica dish filled with flame-coloured grapes, another with marzipan lozenges that were out of season but tasted all right.

It was two thirty by the time Gilver's preparations were complete. He was over-excited and hadn't eaten all day except a *calisson* and some grapes. There wasn't time to eat now. He opened some red wine and drank thoughtfully, standing smoking by an open window. Sun broke through and lit the street with flaming, blinding white and blue. It was a Christmas card, lovely to look at.

Joy and hope surged in his breast. The despair that had crushed him all year lifted by the second. Something was going to come right, things were going to change. He could feel it and wanted to hurtle towards it. He drank the rest of the wine and tossed the bottle, for no reason, out of the window. It made no sound.

The bell rang just before four, as darkness began to fall.

Climbing the narrow stairs to Gilver's flat Juliette took in neglect and dirt with approval. Junk-mail and leaflets littered the squalid hall. Under the twisting handrail many balusters were broken off. He had sunk further than she could have hoped. Any last trace of the nervousness she felt as her cab approached evaporated and at every step exhilaration replaced it. Juliette felt almost drunk, although she had been careful to take only water at lunch.

Gilver opened the door to the flat and she saw that he looked rather wild.

'Hello, how well you look.' She beamed, peeling off her gloves with care but refusing his invitation to take her wrap. He was dignified, but his eyes glowed with the amber light she remembered, momentarily unsettling. I shall have to be careful, she told herself, turned from him, trying not to shake, before returning with a bright smile. 'It is dreadfully kind of you to find time to see me. You must be so busy.'

Gilver demurred. He asked if he could offer her something to drink.

'Oh, how nice!' She contrived to look startled. 'I almost forgot, I brought you a present.'

Thanking her for the bottle of champagne he carried it into the kitchen.

She followed, taking a good look round. The smell of lilies was so overpowering it made her feel sick. While Gilver opened the wine she wandered delicately, aware of herself, touching things. She didn't find much to admire but made the best of it, exclaiming over a writing table on spindly legs loaded with hastily squared piles of books and papers. There was a lot of dust. It was not remotely to her taste.

'I mustn't have too much,' she said, taking the glass. His finger touched hers. She pretended not to notice. 'I drank loads at lunchtime with the Grishers.'

'Are they coming?'

'They're going to drop in on their way to a dinner, they couldn't make it earlier. I expect I'll be gone by then. I hope that suits you. May I see what you're doing?'

He was watching her, stalking her. She had to get away from his eyes. All the time they stood close like this they bore down on her; she was giddy under them. Like no other eyes she had ever seen, eyes that trapped you. Even though she was sure she hated him his presence was terrifying. It was worse than she had imagined.

Gilver drained his glass and turned to lead the way upstairs to the studio.

The spell broke. She breathed, pulled her wrap around her and poured her drink into a bowl of cream roses, pink blushing their edges. He was too far ahead to hear the water in the vase spit.

The flat was very warm, too warm, but Juliette felt cold. She picked up the bottle and followed.

She approached the big easel painting that dominated the room. It was compelling, its size demanding attention even before the surface held it. Juliette forced herself to look closely. The portrayed woman, who appeared to be escaping something, or someone, brought her to a standstill. Juliette noticed the blood-tinged water round her feet. Though the subject repelled her she could see it was well painted, more than well painted. But still it unsettled her.

Gilver stood silent, a pace behind, she felt him. If she lost strength now—

'May I have some more champagne?' He filled her glass, raising his eyebrow at her, a gesture that stabbed from her memory. He filled his own.

'Down in one?' She was desperate.

He joined her, watching. 'You remind me of someone.'

'Me? I expect you've seen my picture somewhere. I've certainly seen plenty of you.'

Was he convinced? She didn't want him to think. Desperate measures. She grasped his hand, which was hot. 'Tell me about the drawings,' she suggested, pulling him lightly towards them. 'Let's have some more to drink.'

Gilver held her arm as he showed her what he had done. At least his attention was deflected. Perhaps he would not feel her heart exploding. Perhaps he would not see – as she could when she glanced down – the fur around her breast trembling with each rapid beat of her heart. To be given away by the pelt of a damn ferret! The ridiculous idea calmed her slightly.

She had had no idea it would be so difficult. Sweat was starting. She did not know if she could continue standing, nodding monosyllables, smiling.

Juliette looked at the charcoal drawings in a haze, with no idea what they were or what Gilver was saying about them. Then Alice's face came into focus out of a smaller one and she tensed. What in God's name was Alice doing here?

'What's the matter?'

'Oh, nothing.' She collected herself at once. 'What a nice drawing. Who is she?'

'A girl I met. It isn't finished.'

'Did she sit for you?'

'No. I drew it from memory. I don't think it looks much like her.'

Juliette wanted to differ. She bit her tongue. The thought of Alice in the room, watching them, was intolerable; yet the unexpected jolt steadied her a little. 'Is she a friend of yours?' She felt rather than saw his sideways glance. She should not have expressed so much interest.

'I suppose you could say that,' he said, using an insinuating tone.

Its vulgarity infuriated her. How dare he try to make her jealous? To think that she might be jealous! But his arrogance served to calm her further. The pounding of her heart became manageable.

She moved away, to the stack of paintings facing the wall. 'And these?'

'Old things.' Obviously he wasn't interested in them. 'I'll show you if you want.'

Juliette fought to gain control. Smiled at him. Arched her back and smiled as brightly as she could. She took a couple of steps towards him then sat on the chaise longue, bending to look at the card table set with titbits. 'Could we look at them later? How lovely all this is. Did you do it for me?' A glance at him showed that her archness was working.

Gilver moved the armchair close to her, pulling the table within reach. 'Yes, of course. Will you?'

'Yes, please.' As much warmth and gaiety as she could muster. She had to remember that she was in a film and this wasn't real; she was a *femme fatale* and could do anything she wanted with him, anything at all, just as he had done with her.

He busied himself pouring two large brandies. The champagne was finished. She had managed to leave the third glass on a ledge.

What did she want from him, this man who had hurt her so long ago? Was it even the same man, the one before her, lost, desiring, not knowing her? Could you still seek revenge after so many years, feel hatred? Was it her he had wronged so long ago, or someone else? They had both, surely, changed so much. She did not recognise herself any more. So why should she recognise him? Sometimes when she looked in the mirror she wondered who she was.

What did they have in common now except an experience, an injustice, of which only she was aware?

Should she, like some some Greek harpy, some Roman plotter, seek him out in the darkness of night and harm him, from behind, unknowing? Or confront him with the past, tell him what he had done, present herself before him and in so doing show him what a monster he had been then? Had he been a monster? . . . It was so long ago. The brandy made her sleepy, she didn't want to think. Danger she could not afford. She roused herself.

Yes, he had been monstrous. That was certain . . . but was he now? What was he now? Where, too, was charity, where forgiveness? The Bible told you to forgive. Could this be the greatest test of her life, the one that would shape her for ever? If she forgave him—

'You're miles away,' Gilver said, watching her staring into the clouded mirror, her brandy tilting in her hand, an amber disc with a blood-red meniscus. 'What are you thinking?'

VII

Time was frozen, hung. The smell of lilies.

What in God's name had she been thinking all these years? Vague ideas of making him seduce her, running from him, accusing him of rape, denouncing him in the eyes of the world. Things she had been thinking two days ago, things she had been thinking for what seemed like all her life. It had driven her. How to punish him for what he had done to her, how to bring him down.

Gilver lit two candles on the little table.

Looking at him across the soft light, as he leaned forward earnestly, clasping a drink on his knee like a lifeline, she saw that her work was almost done without her. He had been brought down, he was down. Had time, which had tormented her, been her ally all along? Those words at the end of *The Count of Monte Cristo* that she had read at school, 'Wait and hope': what, if anything, had she been hoping for? Revenge, yes; but not in this way. It had always been liberally splashed with violence and glory. But this—

Her thoughts of revenge were hard to grip. It was not too late to grasp after them. Yet it seemed that if she wanted revenge she would have to find a fresh reason, for the man before her was wretched, a lock of hair greasy across his fore- head. However angry she had felt all those years, whatever nebulous plans of retribution she'd made, this felt wrong. To strike someone who was down – what joy could there be in that? Pleasure had always been mixed, bitterly, in her concept of revenge. What pleasure with him like this? To strike at him now would have no more refinement than kicking a dog.

Not that, at this moment, he seemed completely wretched. There was still fire for her in his eyes and a smile on his beautifully shaped lips. He was without doubt the same man she had once met; but as if a coarse caricature had been swapped for his face, as if drink had laid a rough cloth over his features that you might strain cheese through, holes cut for the nose and mouth. It wasn't that he was ugly, he was not. He was still the shadow of a good-looking man. She could see that this was the case, even with hatred momentarily damped to disinterest. But if one knew how handsome he had once been—

With terror Juliette thought, Does this happen to all of us? Has it happened to me? She wanted to look behind her in the mirror, to comfort herself with her own beauty. She sat still; nothing happened. She moistened her lips with brandy.

'That painting – it's nothing like anything you've done before, is it?'

Gilver leaned back. The edges of a puzzled look had been forming on his bloated face. He relaxed. 'No, it isn't. It's interesting that when you haven't done something for a long time, something that you do, I mean – the thing you do – that when you come back to it you have to find it again. It's as if . . .' he chose his words carefully '. . . as if it has grown on its own, in parallel with you . . . Does that make sense?'

'I'm not sure.' Against her will she was interested in what he was saying. It was the echo of her own thoughts. Yet, Christ, she couldn't afford to be interested in anything about this bastard. She had feigned interest in him to get what she wanted. It was too exhausting to experience what it really felt like. She must leave. He was speaking again, gently, and she did not move.

'And you're afraid of what you're doing, too. You know it has grown and changed independently, but what will it be? Will it be any good, will you be able to do it?'

Juliette pursued both trains of thought. 'You seem to be saying that you can't control it, that the painting is something different from you, apart, not done by you. It's . . .'

'I know it sounds mad,' he interpreted, slowly, 'but I promise you it isn't. It's terrifying, yes, but not mad. And you either find you can live with it and build it back into yourself, or you can't.'

There was a strange fur in Juliette's mouth.

'And can you, this?' She gestured towards the easel. She hated it.

'I don't know.' Gilver smiled suddenly. 'I know it's a good painting. I hope that doesn't sound too conceited. That doesn't mean I know why I did it or if I like it. Or if I'll do anything like it ever again. I was compelled to do it.'

'Compelled?' Her heart started pounding; she needed to buy time again. Compelled! Juliette drank her brandy in a gulp, anger flickering again, but not very strongly. Had he been *compelled* that time with her? Had that been mere compulsion that you could slip on and off at will? Something that he might or might not do again? Was that how he dealt with moral responsibility, attributing it elsewhere, parcelling it off?

Gilver refilled their glasses evenly. He hadn't picked up her agitation. Perhaps it didn't show, or he wasn't seeing. She noticed he was flushed. She had meant to get him drunk, at first, and now it looked as though he was. It had blinded him.

She tried again. 'That woman, those marks . . .'

'You mean, were they real?' Straightforward.

'No, I—'

Gilver leaned over and touched her hand. The touch was shocking. She withdrew her hand hastily, fiddled with the front of her dress.

'You do wonder, don't you?' He appeared not to notice the slight; nor was she sure if this was an advance. Talking of painting seemed to have cooled his ardour for the moment. You might even think that if he had a passion, it was this and not that. He continued to lean forward; his hand, where he had stretched it out to touch her, still hung bizarrely in a sort of mute appeal. An undressed glove-puppet. And his repeating the question – he was not leering at her, he was interested. 'Hasn't it struck you that paintings aren't real? Not even the most realistic ones? That's what painters do, surely you know that.'

'I hadn't really thought about it.' She knew she sounded vague. She didn't need a lecture on art. What the hell was she doing here? Her sense of purpose was slipping from her with each second that passed.

'You don't like paintings, do you?' His voice was different. He was drunk all right, but his voice had changed dramatically and it wasn't the drink.

The smell of lilies, released again, was horrid.

Gilver stood up and looked down at her for a second, then walked off to the easel and stood in front of it, arms crossed. His footfalls on the wooden floor brought back reality.

She watched him, feeling absurd, glued to the seat, clutching her brandy so tight the glass was damp. This wasn't the scene she had imagined. It was clear that he was thinking and she was afraid of what he might say. If he had not been drunk he would have come at the question – *why was she there?* – straight away, she sensed that; but he was feeling his way slowly and he was confused. If there had been nothing else, the knowledge that she wasn't really interested in his work would have spurred him at once to ask it, or to rudeness, or to a reaction of some sort.

It wasn't just drink that had slowed his thinking. He was muddled too, she sensed, by the attraction he had felt for her in the bar, which she had now seen ebbing away as she failed to respond at every turn. Why was she so different, when she had flirted like crazy with him the night before? He must surely be trying to work that one out: *why was she there?* He would come at it, find it, the question. She could almost hear his bleared brain ticking. It was the only question to ask, after all. She knew that if she so much as moved, he would ask it. She sat, hoping for a miracle.

The phone rang.

'The Grishers!' Juliette almost screamed, too loud, glad of an interruption. Abruptly Gilver went downstairs. He did not look at her.

Exhausted she checked her watch. It was a quarter to six. Perhaps they were cancelling. It didn't seem to matter, she had messed everything up anyway, with her ridiculous half-formed idea.

The hatred she had counted on to direct her was confounded now that she was there, once he had talked, proved himself normal, articulate, even. Different from the endoskeleton of loathing she had shaped herself with for so long: Gilver was a real person. Above all, that was what laid waste the scheme she had harboured all those years: he was different and she could not do anything about it.

Had she, even now, expected them both to react to each other in the same way as they had that night? Leap into each other's arms, drunk? She had been seventeen. What was he? She had never asked. It didn't matter. He wasn't young any more.

Even as she thought this Juliette saw, with a sort of guilty astonishment, that she had never allowed herself to consider, not even for a split second, that she had wanted to go to bed with him the night they met, from the moment she clapped eyes on him walking towards her with his friend. What he did, how he behaved, had been unforgivable. That she had wanted to, she had never admitted.

It seemed as if it had happened to someone else. She felt exhausted and started to pull her wrap closely round her, ready to leave. The encounter had been a failure. She had lost her nerve.

Perhaps he would find some way out of the desperate life he was living. For it was desperate. These things put out for her, the flowers, the food, the wine. You could smell a sort of taint coming off them. Like an old gentlewoman in reduced circumstances grasping at gentility: laying out a fine embroidered cloth with the folds too rigid to iron away; the best china, its gold a little worn, roses painted on the side; frail biscuits on a plate, a doily.

Juliette picked at the beautiful grapes, translucent red sacs in the candle flame, wondering where Gilver had got to. He seemed to have been gone ages but it wasn't the case. Ten minutes. It couldn't be the Grishers. Jerry would be a barker on the phone. It must be someone else.

While Gilver was downstairs she went to the drawing of Alice on the other side of the room, in case it spoke to her, or she could steal strength from it. The face, fixed in a calm smile, a Mona Lisa smile almost, gave nothing, yet it served to remind Juliette that time had passed and was still passing. She had to get out.

Without warning Gilver reappeared at the top of the stairs, fidgety, smoothing his hands on his back trouser pockets. A lot of men did that when they were nervous. Instinctively, Juliette darted away from the picture of Alice. He didn't notice.

'Wrong number,' he said, clearing his throat and sitting down again. 'Do you have time for another drink?'

'I should be going,' she said lamely.

Why had he lied? It caught her interest. Dimly she saw the drawing of Alice out of the corner of her eye. Surely it couldn't have been—

Gilver poured one for himself. His hand trembled, but it might have been a trick of the light. 'So, why did you come?' he asked at last, the liquid still flowing from the bottle and both their eyes bent on it as if it was gold.

This was it.

Head still bent he spoke again. 'In the bar the other day I thought you—'

'No.' It was all she could manage. One more word and she did not know what she might say. She rose abruptly.

Gilver got up too. He looked into her eyes, searched her face. She saw that one pupil had a dark fleck in it and looked away.

Gilver caught her hands in his, holding them too firmly for her to escape, and she did not try. 'I'm sorry,' he said.

VIII

Juliette looked at Gilver's hands encasing hers. Like driving gloves, she thought incoherently. He held them loosely now and his own were very warm. She slipped hers away and turned from him where he stood motionless.

Incredible. What was it, fourteen, fifteen years ago? She was back there, seventeen, the room full of beautiful morning sunlight, the magnificent bed, priceless things, silks at the window catching and playing with the sun. Trying to find a shoe under the bed. The pain came back.

'Come and sit down.' Interrupting her thoughts, Gilver's voice was kind. He just touched her shoulder, hesitant, but it was enough to make her sit suddenly. Gilver took his place in the armchair, close, and handed her her drink. 'You're as white as a sheet. Drink this.'

She took it from his hot hand and downed its contents. The brandy was warming.

The woman he had met, so self-assured, flashing sensuality and control, sparks coming off her as she sailed, memorably, into the bar to meet him, might have been someone else. Juliette looked smaller, bunched into her fur while she drank, the short glistening hairs moving softly around her. She did not look at him but somewhere else, far off, and he waited.

'So, why did you come?' he repeated, after a while.

She looked at him, searching for the man he must have been, the one she had spent so much inventive anger on all these years. Not this man, real concern on his face, unsure of himself. Not this man, certainly.

'Don't you know?' She still had to gain a little more time

in order to find her way. But if he suspected at all, if he remembered anything, she must go back there, whether she wanted to or not.

'No,' he answered slowly, 'no, I don't. I have no idea. I would have liked to think—' He leaned a little closer towards her, her straightened back.

Without understanding it he saw something like terror in her eyes. An incomprehensible look. She must be very highly strung.

Juliette, unaware, scarcely seeing him through a blackness that threatened to spew out and engulf her, felt her heart pulsing in her throat, as if she might choke. She was so close to saying it. The relief it would be, just to speak and not care for the consequences. She straightened even more.

Gilver saw pride flow into the face opposite; colour; a sort of magnificence as she pulled herself up. He leaned away again, feeling helpless.

Juliette's blood beat relentlessly in her head. She saw the helplessness and uncertainty on him. Christ, how she could make him suffer. She was giving him – what? – grace? Or just an easier way out for both of them? Or cowardice: was that it? Was that all it was? She could scarcely breathe.

When she finally spoke again her voice was different. 'The Grishers will be here any minute, won't they?'

Gilver blinked. 'Yes. Oh, yes. Will you stay? I'd like it if you could.'

Juliette looked into his eyes and remembered them again. She was too exhausted to stoke her hatred. He looked tired, worn. He didn't know her and could not touch her. 'No, I don't think so. They should concentrate just on you, the work.'

'Which you don't like.'

'It's not for me, I think.' She sought refuge in the subject as a dying man might drink from a stream, choosing her words one by one. 'What you said about coming back to something after a long time ... and finding it changed?' He nodded imperceptibly, fixed on her face, poured a little brandy into her empty glass.

She cleared her throat and went on, 'Perhaps it's the same for me too.'

'I'm not sure I—'

'I remember you from long ago . . .' As if she was walking through fire, forming the words from gouts of her own flesh. She gave up the incipient struggle almost as soon as it was begun. 'And ... it's changed for me too.' She felt weak and drank a stinging mouthful.

Suddenly Gilver seemed relieved. His hand, gripped hard round his glass, relaxed. 'Ah,' he said, ambushed intelligence and something like admiration lighting his eyes. 'I never thought of that. So you liked what I painted once, but now ...' He turned her words over. 'I really never thought of that.'

Juliette thanked a god she had never worshipped. Gilver had not found her. She was safe for the moment. This must end.

'To be honest, I don't like that painting. But I can see that it's good. I hope ...' Juliette stood up, properly this time: she was going. She looked down on him and gritted a sort of smile. 'I hope they like it, I hope it works out.'

Gilver walked her downstairs and opened the door on to the street. 'Will you be all right?'

She turned. A flash of fury that he almost mistook for the one from the bar came. 'Oh, good Lord, yes! I'm fine.' She rejected him. She had done with him, for now.

'Thank you for coming,' he said, 'thank you for—'

Juliette went down the steps fast without listening and he watched her go.

A cab appeared by magic. They probably always did.

Unusual girl. He felt as tired as if he had had a fight with someone and climbed the stairs slowly to wait for the Grishers.

IX

They arrived five minutes after Juliette left. Gilver was relieved they hadn't all met. He was still running the afternoon over and over, trying to work out what had gone wrong, but forced his attention to Jerry.

'My,' the visitor said, moving round the studio slowly, 'you've changed your tune.'

Gilver was unable to tell if Jerry was being cautious, dismissive. Good or bad, he couldn't tell. Juliette still bothered him. He shook himself and followed a pace behind.

Even more antique and monstrous than Gilver remembered, Beverley perched on the edge of the chaise. She dusted the blue brocade smooth with her hand before lowering her snake-skinned rump on to it. Her eyes followed them round the room while she ate half a marzipan sweet when no one was looking. Through the mirror, Gilver watched her snap the other half into her handbag.

Jerry went round one by one. He turned back the canvases in the corner, with Gilver's help. 'Oh, these look more familiar.

What, in God's name, did you do? Stretch them with your teeth?'

This was his only comment, but he looked a long time all the same. They turned the unwieldy squares outwards. Of the easel painting, Jerry said nothing, except to peer closely. He came back and sat down hard in Gilver's chair, spilling out of it. Gilver sat next to Jerry's wife on the chaise, thinking that if it was a seesaw she would pitch up and out of the skylight. He noticed how she moved over, glinting at him from stretched eyelids while they talked. He didn't remember her so quiet.

Jerry took the wine he was handed, and crammed a couple of sweets into his mouth. He unpeeled a cigar and offered it, trimming another for himself. 'Well. How long have we got, Bev, before we go and set the British government to rights?'

'It's fine, Jerry. Ten minutes is fine. The cab's waiting.'

Jerry relaxed and lit Gilver's cigar, appraising him frankly. 'You've changed your style a lot.' He turned and waved at the five paintings. 'Those need stretching properly. They're useless like that. You cut them out with a penknife or what?'

Gilver nodded.

'Well, you can sort that out. It's kind of funky. Bev and I like to move with the times, but we haven't moved quite that far yet. This one,' he jerked his thumb at the easel, 'this one's pretty strange, but I'm getting used to it. No idea what it's about.'

Gilver started to speak.

'Don't have time, m'boy. I daresay there's some sort of symbolism in it.'

Again Gilver opened his mouth but Jerry stopped him with a second wave of the hand. 'As long as you know what it's about that will do for me. I'm sure you'll make it clear. Can't show it on its own, though.'

Completely focused on him, Gilver forgot to exhale. He coughed. A thread-like hand patted him on the back. He asked Jerry what he meant.

'Drink less, Gilver, and wash your ears out, or you might miss the way the wind's blowing. Paint me another nine and you've got a show.'

Gilver was so astonished he couldn't speak. The older man grinned. 'Keep them clean. The people who buy from us might just about manage a bit of spanking in their spare time but that's far enough.'

Gilver made one last attempt at speech but Jerry was bent on his own train of thought. He looked quizzically at his cigar. 'On the other hand . . .'

'Jerry!'

Jerry buffeted his wife fondly. 'Joking. We're a country of puritans now.' He turned back to the main subject. 'And make sure they don't all fall to pieces. Send them ready-crated. I'll cover it.'

'Do you mean . . . ?'

'Godawlmighty, Gilver, are you getting Alzheimer's? Sure I mean. Here. I'll show you.'

He drew a cheque book out of his pocket and wrote on it with a flourish. 'This should get you started. It looks as if you need it. We'll work out the details in the morning. Bev and I go back tomorrow night.'

X

Going into work, for Alice, had become agonising. Ever since Gilver had come to her weeks before, it had been impossible to think straight, to concentrate. Words she was supposed to correct on the screen melted in front of her eyes and she had to read everything twice, panicking in case she overlooked mistakes. In the middle of long passages about architecture or the Middle East she found herself thinking about him instead of what she was supposed to be doing.

Something he said, or the feeling of him kissing or touching her, as if it was happening right then, seized her stomach so hard that she was oblivious to the huge, spinning office, the clatter of her colleagues. She had read a story once about a sub-editor famous for never making a mistake, a bottle of champagne growing dusty for the one who caught him in error. A triumph of paradox, it told how the sub-editor went blind. Alice often mused over this simple parable. She was blind now, with a mixture of love and longing that ate her. It was as if the bottle had been smashed over her head.

She looked repeatedly at the phone on the desk, wondering if she dared call him, fighting the temptation.

If he did not call, how on earth could she? What would be the point?

He had come to her that night, insisting on it. Alice replayed the evening a thousand times. Desperate, drunk, burning with a force that scared her. When she opened the door he seemed larger than life. When he made love to her in the morning she was obliterated.

'Where's the copy on the Potsdamer Platz?' A shout from the news desk.

Alice pulled herself together. 'Coming in five,' she called back, frantically scanning the column once more before sending it.

He had held her down and made love to her like someone possessed. She clung close, holding him as hard as she could, trying to wrest some of his strength from him. He was too strong; his strength broke her apart and Alice, who felt almost as though she fought for her life, had never felt so glorious. She washed up somewhere she didn't know, and basked. If he walked up to her desk now she would beg him to take her on the floor.

Charles was just visible on the far side of the room, narrow shoulder-blades sticking through his jacket. He came into the office every few days and made sure, as she did, that their paths didn't cross. Alice found herself slinking along walls and taking unusual routes to her desk, head down, to avoid any chance of accidentally meeting his look. Probably he did the same.

She had never felt so alone and couldn't understand why Gilver had deserted her again. Was he really so ignoble?

She couldn't go on like this. It would destroy her. She had to talk to someone.

Looking up she saw the news editor hoving to, brandishing a proof. He did not look particularly pleased. 'Nice job.' He lounged satirically over the back of her computer. 'Might be a good idea to use spell-check. Are you feeling all right?'

'Yes,' Alice stated, with determination. 'I'm fine. Why?' She liked the news editor. He had a bleak sense of humour and once took her out for a cripplingly cheap lunch when he found out it was her birthday. All you could eat for six pounds. 'Alice, you're one of my best subs. But these past few days...' He looked uncomfortable. 'You've seemed a bit distracted, and there have been some strange things you wouldn't normally do.'

'Oh,' Alice observed weakly, 'I'm sorry.'

He scrutinised her again while she tried not to evade his searching examination, without success. 'You look pale. Maybe it's this flu. Why don't you take a few days off? You haven't had any holiday for months.'

'But it's almost Christmas. I've got some time booked then.'

'It doesn't matter. I don't like to see you unhappy.'

Alice looked at him in astonishment. 'But I—'

'Alice. Take a few days off. Come back after Christmas. We'll cope.'

Eyes finally crinkled into a nice blue smile, he tapped her computer cheerily with the rolled-up proof. 'That's settled, then. Push off when you've done that. Before I change my mind.'

He went back to the news desk, the calm stroll of the almighty.

Alice got home before dark, and started cleaning her flat, which was already clean. The trouble with being – however kindly – sent home was that it threw her even more on her own resources. Washing the kitchen floor for the second time, she knew she would explode if she didn't talk to someone. If she couldn't call Gilver, the only person left was Juliette. Past caring whether it was sensible, and with no idea what to say, Alice dialled.

Juliette was alone in her office. She had sent her assistant Daisy downstairs to check in an enormous delivery of cashmere burnouses, which she imagined on a flock of girls with nothing underneath, rollicking among the sheep-strewn hillside of Bodiam Castle for an Easter special, the Luxury of Lambswool. It didn't bother her remotely that cashmere came from goats as Daisy, reckless, pointed out. They would cross that bridge when they came to it, Juliette replied tartly, and if Daisy had had enough of being a goat she could be a lamb and go and iron the entire consignment.

Juliette had been in a tricky temper for the past few days and everyone in the building was keeping a low profile. Crying in the basement, Daisy was glad to get out of the direct line of fire. Even if it meant two hours' ironing, which was surely not in her contract.

Alone with her thoughts, Juliette debated calling Alice. A week had passed since the meeting with Gilver. The memory of the drawing tacked up in the studio was still unsettling, unfinished business. It was as if Alice had somehow been an observer – distinctly unbidden, as far as Juliette was concerned – of a matter no one could ever know about. What Alice knew, if anything, was almost secondary to the sense that she had ventured where she had no right to be, into Juliette's domain. This problem must be tackled: it was a mark of how drained Juliette was by the encounter that she had not yet called.

Her natural inclination to dominate everyone within her sphere had been undermined, as if one had got away. After what she felt was almost superhuman clemency towards Gilver, for which she deserved the Iron Cross or whatever it was, she was in no mood to be gentle with anyone else. Particularly Alice, who had blundered in without an invitation. Alice had to be assessed and Juliette was angry enough with the entire world, now, to do it.

She'd tried Alice's number earlier but was damned if she was going to leave a message.

Juliette's private line rang. She snatched up the receiver with customary impatience to meet a hesitant greeting, She did not let Alice get any further. 'Guess what,' she announced, without preliminaries, 'I saw *your friend* Gilver Memmer the other day.'

Alice did not miss the sarcasm, though for a reason she could not put her finger on, it seemed misplaced. Juliette's attacks were usually unerring. Not knowing what to say, anyway, Alice relinquished control of the call. It was inconceivable to imagine telling Juliette what had actually happened with Gilver: she'd had the vague idea of talking about him under cover of pretending to talk about someone else. But she had not expected to hear the name that filled her thoughts; it threw her off balance.

'Really?' She was almost speechless.

'Yes. Quite a coincidence, isn't it?'

Paralysed, Alice said nothing, wondering what on earth Juliette meant by coincidence. Juliette couldn't possibly know! Alice pulled herself together, recalling the other's obsession with him two years before, her delight after the fire. Given all that, she wondered just how much of a coincidence Juliette's bumping into Gilver had been. Of all the possible replies she tried to pick an inoffensive one, to make her tone bright. 'Where?'

'Oh,' Juliette lied breezily, almost as if Alice had not spoken, 'some big arts dinner, frightfully grand, *everyone* was there. He was sitting right opposite. Can You Imagine That?'

A strange sensation came over Alice, yearning and loathing rolled into one, but she managed to keep her voice steady. It was all too easy to imagine Juliette sparkling at Gilver over a table, drinking expensive wine, flirting in a low-cut dress. She took a deep breath. 'That must have been nice.'

'I don't know about *nice*.' Juliette wasn't giving an inch. 'They're all much the same. You've been to one, you've been to them all and believe me I have. But it was interesting to see him after so long.' She paused meaningfully, giving Alice the opportunity to say something, bare her soul, reveal her secrets.

There was silence at the other end and Juliette, with a slight edge in her voice, tried a further prod. 'I can't believe you once thought he was handsome, Alice. Have you gone mad?'

This was unexpected. Alice couldn't work out where Juliette was coming from. 'I—'

Juliette interrupted: 'Yes, he looked absolutely dreadful. A complete wreck, horrible. You gave me the idea that you rather liked him?'

Alice had the sensation that Juliette was determined to make her say something particular, at all costs. But why, and what, Alice wondered, when it was she who had made the call?

'I did think he seemed quite nice . . .'

Juliette almost guffawed. 'Really, Alice, you have the most appalling taste. No wonder you're still single. I've never seen anyone go downhill so fast! He's disgusting. And have you seen his *flat*?'

Alice began to understand, albeit dimly. If she said yes, Juliette would know that more than she had ever admitted had happened between them. Even though Alice wanted to talk about him with almost mad desperation, it must be on her own terms, not goaded by someone else. She should have

218

known it would be like this if she rang Juliette. It always was. Time had worn the grooves between them too deep to jump. She had been a fool to call.

Alice had already lied – by neglecting to tell the truth – about visiting Gilver two years before. Now, after so much more had happened, didn't seem the moment to start.

But why had Juliette seen the flat, and when? In one of those horrific leaps jealousy masters, she saw the scene. How stupid could she be? They must have rolled back to Gilver's flat after the dinner, drunk and exhilarated, and—

'Alice?'

'Sorry,' Alice murmured, sick at heart, 'no, I haven't.' She grasped at courage and strengthened her voice. 'Why? What's it like? Did you go after the dinner?'

It was Juliette's turn to be discomfited. Accustomed to lying, she had run away with the story before refining its details. How, indeed, had she seen the flat if not after the supposed dinner? Naturally she could have made an appointment to go another day. But to seem so interested in Gilver, after just saying how dreadful he was, didn't serve her purpose. 'Yes, exactly.' She snatched Alice's towline. 'He wanted to show me his work.'

'And what was it like?' Alice ground out the words, compelled into fresh falsehood.

Was Juliette having an affair with him or not? It came to Alice, with sickening clarity, that this was the only thing that mattered. Whatever she had rung for was subsumed by the need to know. If Juliette and Gilver were having an affair, unbelievably painful though the thought was, it would explain everything. She had to keep on with these ghastly questions.

'The work or the flat?'

Juliette's voice was jumpy and took Alice by surprise. It wasn't the tone of a lover on the defensive, either. There was terrific rage in it. Against me, Alice wondered, or against him? 'Both . . . What were they like?'

All the time they talked, Juliette played close attention to Alice too. She was so rattled herself that her friend sounded plausible. Alice had never been there, Gilver must have been telling the truth, extraordinary though it seemed. He must have drawn Alice – when was it? – when they met, years before. Why on earth would anyone want to draw Alice? But there it was. Juliette had not thought to ask how old the sketch was. Yes, that must certainly be it. It must be an old drawing. Why hadn't this occurred to her before? She had been so shaken when she saw it. Suddenly she felt at ease, ready to take back control.

'Disgusting, completely disgusting.' Her anger flowered. 'He lives in this completely vile place and does these pathetic things that – well, frankly, they're disgusting as well. And, you know, I'd even wondered about doing a piece on him, a sort of comeback.'

'Will you?' Alice intended sounding obtuse. She had never heard Juliette so cranked up. Had Juliette made a pass at Gilver and been rejected? It didn't sound like the other way round.

'You're joking, surely. He's finished. I wouldn't touch him with a bargepole. A comeback! He deserves a send-off.'

There was a terrible silence.

'Anyway,' Juliette continued, as though that matter was now closed, 'why did you call?' She was looking at the clock.

'Oh.' Alice, flooded with hideous ideas that made no sense,

was scarcely able to get words out. 'Just to say hello, and wish you a happy Christmas. We haven't seen each other for so long.'

'Well, that's terribly sweet.' Juliette had no further use for conversation. Her secret was safe and she had decided to deal Gilver a blow from which even Lazarus would throw in the towel. 'But I've got to go now.' Flicking through the new *Tatler* while they spoke, Juliette had just seen that a handsome banker and a woman who made jewellery for Asprey's were divorcing. There had to be a story in it at the very least. 'I have to interview a banker in five minutes,' she announced.

'Well, happy Christmas—' As Alice started to speak Juliette put the phone down.

Alice stared at the bookcase on the far side of the room. The flat was eerily quiet. Someone cranked past on a bicycle. They rode over a stone. There were three books with orange spines next to a turquoise one sticking out slightly crooked. One of the orange-backs, yellow with age, was *Pride and Prejudice*. Alice knew it by its width and wondered what the other two were. She almost got up to put the crooked book straight but it seemed too much trouble.

The table next to the sofa was speckled with dust. That would need wiping off. She would do it tomorrow.

What did Juliette mean? The threat in her words was unmistakable.

Alice racked her brains. Juliette had always been interested in Gilver. Her exuberant reaction to the fire at his house had seemed, even at the time, too strong, almost gloating. There must have been something between them once

221

that had made Juliette dislike him, which she had never told Alice. Alice had always known Juliette was vengeful, never tolerated slights, and felt a sudden rush of concern for Gilver. But surely he could look after himself. Whatever it was must have been long ago. The thought of some sort of relationship between Gilver and Juliette was so unpleasant it reinforced her decision not to call him. If he wanted her he would have to seek her out. If he couldn't tell the difference between them, couldn't choose, she would force herself to forget him.

To her astonishment, for the first time in her life, Alice compared herself with Juliette and came out on top. She looked out of the window in guilty disbelief, half expecting to see someone pointing in, rebuking her. Yet why was it that wherever she turned, she came up against him? Whichever path she took, as in a maze, instead of finding the exit, she turned a hedged corner next to a cracked statue and came out at a clearing with Gilver sitting in it. She longed to go and sit next to him, but if she took one step forward he vanished through a gap she hadn't even seen and went off laughing with someone else.

In the rapidly darkening room Alice, alone with her thoughts, preoccupied almost past endurance, could have been a painting by Rossetti. Hands clasped in front of her, a mauve tinge cast by the fading light on the paleness of her skin, her eyes metallic in the grey air. Gilver lived only fifteen minutes' walk away. It might as well have been a hundred miles. Maybe he was there now, staring out of the window at the dusk. She tortured herself with wondering who filled his thoughts.

The telephone rang. Alice watched it in case it would relieve her, be him, and tried to stifle disappointment in greeting her mother.

Her mother didn't like the way Alice sounded. That Charles, she scolded. He had never made Alice happy, no wonder she was upset. She needed a change of air. Alice should come home. Too miserable to argue, Alice agreed, if only to get away.

A few minutes later she was packing a leather grip with worn, looped handles. She had bought it in Florence on a sunny day years before while a boy with long brown fingers waited outside the shop. She loved that bag, even though the zip was broken.

Her parents picked her up at the station in time for supper.

XI

Cecil Court, one of those narrow old streets you could miss if you didn't know how to look for it, was swept clear of snow. It was just before ten on Monday morning. Few American tourists had ventured out of their hotels to search for coloured prints that they would be assured used original pigments and had definitely not been cut from books.

Gilver's shoes crunched the scattered gravel, shining wet, salty. A faint smell of whelks, he imagined, bad drains. Cutpurses must once have huddled here.

The air was freezing and he rang the bell of one of the little shops impatiently. It didn't open for another half-hour, according to the faded card in the window, red ink along a ruler, neatly underscored twice in black that was now grey-green, a colour belonging to another time. There was a movement at the back of the shop and the door-catch released with a sharp buzz.

Many years ago, when he was rich, he'd struck up an acquaintance with Corot, the print dealer. He had been there even earlier, as a student, looking without intending to buy, sifting through mounted prints with Cellophane folded carefully over them, prices handwritten on sticky labels on the back. Once when he had money in his pocket, he had taken a fancy to something. Corot, who didn't have a lot to do, showed him why he shouldn't buy that, but something much better. As they shook hands all those years ago the elderly Italian had announced that everyone said his first name was unpronounceable; he'd got so used to being called Corot he had almost forgotten how to say it himself.

Over the following years he showed Gilver how to look, what to look for, how to look for what should be there but wasn't, how to look for what was there and should not be, how to judge the weight of a line, to assess the quality of an engraving stone and engraving tools; how to judge the paper and funny little marks that seemed to have no place, but did. Gilver knew a lot about colour, but Corot showed him things about pigments he had not dreamed of.

Corot was almost sixty then, standing five foot six in an old black suit that might have been cut in the fifties and a black polo-neck sweater. Gilver never saw him in anything else; except once, for a funeral, he added a red carnation. 'We can't be sad all the time,' he said, winking, 'not everything rhymes with sorrow.' Which was disconcerting.

The dealer was much older now and even shorter. His hair had faded completely to wispy tar and he came to the door slowly using a stick. It wasn't just for show, he leaned heavily on it. Gilver saw that one foot was bandaged and stuck into a carpet slipper. Not any old slipper though: monogrammed leather, GC.

Corot recognised him immediately. His eyesight was as good as always, he said proudly, offering the left hand, which wasn't arthritic. He asked Gilver to shut the door and pull down the leather blind. 'Come in,' he said, 'come and sit. Long time, Gilver, you don't look so good.' He offered a cup of tea, gunpowder, and a little curled biscuit.

Gilver had a portfolio with him, which he held out to the old man without comment, first loosening its ribbon ties.

Carefully, Corot opened it. 'Ah,' he said, looking unhurriedly through a loupe at each of the four Dürer engravings inside. 'I sold you these for a great deal of money. Do you want them valued?'

'What are they worth?'

'A greater deal of money.'

'Can you price them, Corot?' Gilver took a sip of tea, which was completely cold, the way Corot preferred to drink it. He had forgotten how ghastly it tasted.

'To keep or to sell?' Corot looked at him kindly, the engravings carefully nested in his lap. 'The two things aren't always the same, you know.'

Gilver said nothing. He finished the tea.

Corot was studying him. He shut the folder as if it was a butterfly and put it to one side, taking up his own cup and stirring it slowly. 'I read about the fire.'

'Yes.' Gilver was noncommittal.

'I read that these were destroyed.' Corot rested a hand delicately against the folder, fingers flat, the fingers of a resting effigy, his gaze not shifting from Gilver's face. He paused before going on. 'And that they were insured.'

'Yes. That's what the papers said.'

'So why?'

Gilver looked round the small room, the racks of prints, the dried air. Such a long time ago he had been happy here, almost as if it was home. He couldn't place how he felt coming back, how to fit in. 'You were kind to me in the past, Corot, more than once. You taught me things, helped me . . .' He dried up, getting no encouragement, and started again. It was no use. Scarcely looking at Gilver now, past him, Corot sat as if no breath entered his body. A fine print in silver-point, the faint taste of scorn coming off him. Gilver pulled himself together. 'I need the money. I'm getting ready for a show, I need it to tide me over. There's almost nothing left.'

Corot moved his head slightly to look at him, a flat look, and let out something that might have been a cough. He got up with obvious discomfort. 'In the circumstances I can give you a third of their true value – their true value, mind – but not more. Do you want to think about it?'

'You're very kind.' Gilver patted the dealer's other hand, curved round the ivory bulldog topping his stick.

He waited while Corot went slowly into the back. Gilver knew he had difficulty opening the safe but wouldn't admit it. He came back after some time with a half-glued fat manila envelope and gave it, smiling, to Gilver, resting his hand on the younger man's arm as he seated himself. 'I know how much you loved them,' he said. 'Newspapers make mistakes sometimes. Will you tell me?'

Gilver looked square at him. 'I went back for them.'

'Into the fire?'

'Yes. I rolled them in my jacket. It was all I could save.'

'It was a stupid thing to do, maybe?'

'It was terribly hot.' Gilver smiled. 'If there had been six I might not be here.'

Corot said nothing. Despite age, his eyes were sharp. After looking for a while, calmly studying Gilver's features as he might estimate the provenance of a drawing, he spoke, not relinquishing his hold. 'This is one of the strangest things you learn: what seems to be wrong can sometimes be right. You could have let these burn. I'm glad you didn't. The law – and art – have often been uneasy bedfellows. Art – this – this is the most important thing. I was once afraid that—' He looked intensely at Gilver, his face up close.

'I know,' Gilver returned simply. 'I lost my way. But I really am working again now.'

'And you're certain this will help?' Corot gestured to the envelope Gilver had not yet put away, out of politeness.

Gilver nodded.

'Then I'm glad for what you did.'

They shook hands. Corot asked him to flip the card to 'closed' on the way out.

After pulling the stiff door to behind him, Gilver put his collar together against the cold, the packet snug against his chest. At the end of the court he hesitated, whether to turn right into St Martin's Lane and cut directly down to the Strand, or left into New Row and Covent Garden. A shortish man grazed against him while he paused, passing him on the left side and taking the direction of Leicester Square, lost at once in a crowd flowing towards Nelson's Column. People were always in such a dreadful hurry, Gilver thought, turning the other way and starting to whistle.

Two hours later, he was on Eurostar.

XII

It was the week before Christmas. Everyone in Paris scurried against a biting wind, rushing to work, to buy presents, to do anything that would get them out of the blast.

Gilver sat in a café on the corner of Place St Sulpice, amazed at the number of small dogs jerked along on leads, skidding in the wet. Why did the French like dachshunds so much? That was surely one of the great mysteries.

It was mid-morning. He had a cup of good coffee, a square of chocolate to the side, a small whisky. He never tired of the way the waiters pronounced whisky, almost as if they were sneezing, a little bit of contempt thrown in. '*Vous êtes américain?*' – you must be if you drink that muck.

They had stopped asking now.

The sky was leaden, but over the big *place* it was light lead, not oppressive. Fast-moving clouds kept the colours changing through a lacing of hawthorn branches round the square. This was one of his favourite places. For the past two weeks he had come every day, usually at mid-morning, like now, sometimes the afternoon. It was a good way to start the day. He liked to see how things were the same, and different. In the second week he spotted someone pass who had passed before, a man with a hairy dachshund. This made him feel as if he belonged. In the café one or two people, like him, came a few days running – tourists, he supposed. Then they were gone. He liked it that one day the square seemed swept clear and gleamed, silvery, the fountain with its clumsy lions carved as if from aluminium lit by streaks of wintry sun. On others, leaves from who-knew-where would be bowling and blowing about on the breeze, children running after them, like hoops.

He'd walked around a lot, been to the Picasso museum, the Louvre, the Musée d'Orsay, into a lot of galleries. For miles one thin yellow morning to see the Rodins where the mangled legs and arms of a near-botched torso in the garden pitted her splayed legs against his gaze. Gilver stood, his nose almost pressed to the slash flying between her thighs, until a guard told him to move on.

Renewing an acquaintanceship, reminding himself who he was. He felt good here. Apart from waiters and museum staff, shop girls and men in *tabacs* and wine stores, he spoke to hardly anyone, deliberately avoiding conversations, difficulties; taking some meals in his indifferent room in the Marais, reading a book. There had been plenty of opportunities, plenty of glances and half-smiles. Had he wanted to make a new friend it would have been an easy matter. He ignored the inviting glances and read his novel, his newspaper, or just turned the other way. It was strange to feel more contented keeping to himself; he couldn't remember when he had ever felt like that. He had no wish to be rude, he just wanted to think, to see, to think again.

He pulled a postcard out of a paper bag with dentate edges and started writing to Harry. Another whisky, single shots.

He was drinking less, with care. It was easier here. No one gave you that look.

Gilver knew how cruel, how unfair he'd been to Harry. But he hadn't thought about it much until now. He was doing a lot of thinking all round. Not only a damn good sort, Harry was shrewder than Gilver had ever given him credit for. He had felt there was something odd behind Juliette's interest in Gilver from the start. How had Harry known that? Almost as if Harry understood him better than he did himself.

Gilver had spent a lot of time, too, wondering about Juliette, their extraordinary meetings. He had known such exhilaration, confusion, felt so excited and so let down. It was as if she had had a thing about him for years and then it just wasn't there any more. Yet she seemed so keen the night they met! You couldn't mistake that, the way her leg found his, the way she looked and looked away. That stuff about not liking his paintings any more was weird too. However he turned things over they didn't make sense. It was exasperating. Like the opening to a great ballet, the thrill before the curtain went up, the building chords, the rippling melodies that sing in your heart. Then when the curtain finally goes it reveals Punch and Judy, batting each other over the head and squeaking. Yes, Harry was shrewd. Sensing something was wrong, Harry had tried to protect his friend, without knowing what he was protecting him from – nothing, as it turned out. Trying to look after him was Harry's crime and Gilver had punished him for it. 'Dear Hal,' he wrote, 'I'll be home when you get this. If you're still in town please let's have a drink. Sorry I was stupid. Forgive me? Love, Gilver.' He had chosen a painting from the Musée Salé, two boys reading, one over the other's shoulder, their hands massive, sculpted. Even though he was going back the next day, Harry would appreciate a French stamp; it was more romantic.

A patch of sharp blue appeared between the scudding sheets of cloud, like a kite, strings of bright blue bleeding off it. It started to skew and smear, cirrus riding the fast-closing gap like rows of quills.

He watched, fascinated. If you could capture a sky like that, the fine veils, the masses, the ever-changing colours . . . Turner had done it pretty well, but with a strange palette. Gilver didn't like his colours. But maybe there was a way, if you worked hard enough, layered the paint thin enough, used your arm and brush as if they, too, were sky, free, floating.

With the second whisky his spirit lifted further. Despite the penetrating cold it was a beautiful day. He took a notepad from his pocket and sketched. Definitely a good background for a painting. Maybe a painting in its own right. And the trees, crossing and crossing, the fingers of old women or the skeletons of birds.

Having spent half an hour wandering along rue Buci, Gilver lunched in a narrow Sephardic restaurant. Its dark inelegance was appealing, and he waited at the counter to be seated. At last, a matter of indifference, they gave him a shiny pile of salmon and taramasalata with pallid, vicious peppers on the side. His appetite hadn't been so good for ages.

After eating with relish he went shopping, wandering along the boutiques looking in all the windows. They were decorated with restraint, but stuffed with lovely things: some cufflinks with a pair of twined sailors, azure enamelled on silver, made him laugh; a beautiful shawl, rich green cashmere with fine black and gold embroideries hand-worked at the ends. Holding the shawl's softness against his face for a moment, smelling the warm wool, he decided it would be perfect with red hair.

He strolled in the Luxembourg gardens and sat on a bench with pigeons bickering round his feet. In the evening, after supper in a restaurant near the hotel, he went to a movie. The story was straightforward, romantic, with a wonderful Schubert score. The heroine looked a bit like Alice. During a particularly enthusiastic grapple from the hero, a stolid-looking baggage handler, Gilver remembered the night he spent with her and knew he wanted to see her. A quick nightcap later he went back to the hotel and packed his suitcase.

XIII

'Don't you think he was a wonderful Darcy?'

Alice and her mother were watching the old black-and-white *Pride and Prejudice*. Greer Garson had just sent Darcy's aunt packing from the sweep of lawn that was patently an indoor set with stuck-on leaves. Everyone held their head very high, their back very straight. From the bowels of the sofa Alice, who felt anxious and regretted coming, conscientiously pulled herself upright to take a glass of sherry.

Her mother had a point. As she put it, the contumely on

Laurence Olivier's lip had a genuine ring about it. 'Well, they'd been through the war, you see.'

Alice's mother had come at her with surprising darts and rushes for the past few days to get her to talk. Straight-on questions failed, so now, as over a trench, breaking into Alice's solitude, her mother popped up, chatting about something that seemed to have nothing to do with anything, manoeuvring with curious side-windings round to men, relationships, and the single status of her only daughter. Like a rattlesnake playing chess.

Alice sipped her sherry and wondered how many passes this foray would take.

People who had been through the war had different values: one. They valued the importance of life, honour, working as a team: two. These days young people don't care about anything except themselves: three. Your father slaved two years to put the deposit on the cottage in Shillingford before he proposed, although we were walking out, of course (a proud glance spanning decades off into the shrubbery beyond the french windows, from where ominous thuds came): four, check, half-nelson. Alice's mother waited for her daughter to speak, so full of this big question that Alice had to look away. They both peered out of the window. Her father came suddenly into view from behind the faded shed with a pair of shears and an axe.

'Gordon attacks that rhododendron every year.' Smoothly her mother diffused the unproductive situation as she had once thrust spoonfuls of linctus. 'I've asked him not to take it back so far.'

He strode silently up to the almost black bush and struck a large branch clean off with a single blow. She winced. 'I don't know how it survives. But, then, they're very resilient. Unlike us.'

During the pause in which she knew she was supposed to speak, Alice rebelled. She had let herself be bullied into coming; taken advantage of, in her weakness, by the person who understood it most. She was not going to be harried into betraying her heart if she could help it. Merely by coming she had already exposed herself too much. She said nothing.

Her mother regrouped. 'How is your little garden?'

The moment safely past, they faced each other across an uncrossable gap of gardening techniques. Alice went into some detail over the blight patches on her tree's leaves.

With a slam of the back door, her father was stamping for attention on the mat. Her mother got up to help him off with his jacket, patting Alice's head with her dry hand over the back of the sofa.

Alice had said she would come for a week. She couldn't take it back now. Her mother asked, knowing the answer, if she would stay on for Christmas. Her cousin Jake, his wife and the two children were coming down from Edinburgh. It would be nice, no one was going to sleep in her bedroom. Jake was bringing a goose and some Scottish salmon. There was plenty to go round. Aunt Emily had sent a massive hamper from Australia – well, not from Australia, of course, Fortnum's – and it had some of that ginger marmalade Alice always liked. Alice yawned discreetly. There was a cupboardful of ancient jars at home.

On the last morning they went for a walk. Gordon didn't want to come. He ascertained, after a brief interview over supper, that Alice still had some sort of a job and seemed to be in reasonable health; bowels in order, that sort of thing; although it was perplexing that she hadn't settled down. But as long as she was happy – this last was a criticism – he could turn back to the history of the SOE with a clear conscience and Radio 4.

'What about getting a little dog for company?'

Here we go, thought Alice, resigned to it, hardening, ambling along next to her mother. They both had thick coats. Sevenoaks was frozen solid. Through several layers of botany wool the other woman's arm felt thin. Alice explained that it didn't seem fair leaving a puppy in the flat all day. She'd thought about another kitten, though, or a cat from Battersea Dogs' Home. If her mother asked her about Baxter she knew she would burst into tears, and looked the other way.

Keen to salvage a horn button from the pavement her mother missed the moment, speaking on the way up as an afterthought. 'You're not happy, Alice.'

They trudged further in silence, not exchanging a glance.

'Is it Charles?'

'I left Charles, Mummy.'

'Did you? Probably a good thing. He wasn't right for you. You need someone to encourage you, dear. It sounded as if he only cared about himself.'

Taken aback by the forthright remark, Alice didn't even feel defensive. Her mother had never met Charles. Nevertheless she voiced the truth. 'No, I know.' She kept an even pressure on her mother's arm as they walked in step past a row of festering cottages with a picket fence. 'It's someone else.' A sop of some sort.

'Is this one interested in what you do?'

Alice did not know how to begin to answer. He had been, when they first met. She wasn't even sure if it mattered. All that mattered – she thought of Juliette and grimaced the other way again.

'And you're in love with him.'

The bluntness took Alice by surprise. Was it that obvious? She panicked and deferred. 'I suppose so. I don't really know.'

Her mother stopped and stood in front of her, holding her by the wrists while Alice picked at a lump of frozen sod with her toecap. 'That's the most important thing, if he's worth it. Is he?'

'I don't know,' Alice repeated, uncomfortable. Despite thinking about nothing else she was too tired to know anything. Was she in love with him? There was no name for how she felt. She wished she could hate him. She didn't want to discuss it.

'What does he do?' Tireless, her mother tried a different tack.

'He's a painter.' Every word seemed like betrayal, as if she had been enjoined to secrecy, or as if the other's scrutiny might throw too strong a light. The pain of being forced to look closely was too much; she moved, stubbornly.

They started walking again. A woman came the other way, led by a fat black Labrador that snuffled noisily at their groins. Alice shoved it off pretending to pat its ear. The beginnings of a growl came.

'Untrained animals should be muzzled,' her mother suggested, not yet out of hearing, before resuming. 'Gordon always thought you should go out with someone like that.'

Doubting that her father had ever thought about it at all, let alone the niceties of the matter, Alice kept quiet. Her mother carried Gordon before her like everything else.

'Is he any good?'

'Yes, very.' As terse as she dared. It didn't work.

'Does he love you?'

Her daughter stared hopefully at an oncoming bus. One quick push and— 'I don't know.'

'They don't always tell you. I think they think it makes them less manly. Why don't you ring up and ask him?'

This time Alice stopped short, in amazement very close to rage.

The older woman smiled briefly. 'We didn't do it in my time. But then the phone was only for really important things – you know, business. No one rang up just for a chat. But love seems to be all anyone thinks about these days. It's all they talk about on television. If I was young today . . .'

Hands in pockets, Alice stood, horrified by the whole conversation, determined not to be shown Gilver through her mother's eyes.

'That's what girls do now, isn't it? That's what I'd do if I was you. No point making yourself miserable when you could just find out, one way or the other.'

She gave Alice a smart kiss on the cheek and turned her by the coat-sleeve to march back. Alice let herself be turned.

'Give him a call when you get home. I would.'

Alice's mother never called London 'home'.

XIV

Gilver had been back from Paris for almost a week. The flat needed airing, although the air that came in was shrill.

In the bedroom the empty frames that had hidden his Dürer engravings were stacked against the wall, the cheap ripped-out prints scattered on the carpet. He threw them away. He fixed a lampshade over the lightbulb dangling above the studio stairs and vacuumed for the first time since moving in, with a new purple and yellow toy from Selfridges.

The exhilaration he felt at starting work was astonishing. Most of the week was spent stretching a set of large canvases on linen, the best he could get, its surface more beautiful to him than silk. He strained the cloth over the stretchers with one smooth flex of arm and hand repeated endlessly, late into the night, and primed each one with care. The hot rising stench of boiling rabbit skin, which he had always found foul, pleased him where it clung to his clothes; his largest brushes smoothed its anaemic toffee to a flawless sheen, working out spittle-slicks of bubbles. Clearing away the timber at the end was a bore but he did it, and bought some heaters.

In between he lugged a lopsided Christmas tree from Portobello Road that was going cheap because it had lost its top six inches. 'There's one fairy won't be getting any fun this year,' the man said.

Three crates of mineral water arrived from the local off-licence. Gilver hadn't drunk water for years but he had never felt so thirsty.

*　*　*

It was Christmas Eve and Harry was going to drop in on the way down to the country, just to say hello. Jamie was already there, stuffing the goose. They spoke on the phone. Would Gilver come too, wouldn't he be lonely over Christmas? They could play games.

That was what he was afraid of, laughed Gilver, who had broken off what he was doing to take the call. Why should Christmas be lonely? he added. He was working. But he wanted to see Harry before he left London. Gilver started to apologise again.

'Don't,' said Harry simply. 'That was then.'

Harry bowled in with a fine bottle of 1978 port. His hair was cut and curled all over his head, what there was to curl. It suited him. He was swathed in a big yellow scarf. 'It's my new look.' He beamed, pleased with himself. 'Jamie chose it.'

'He has good taste,' Gilver lied.

Harry failed to conceal his pleasure. Gilver hadn't acknowledged Jamie before.

Harry undid the cufflinks, fussily wrapped with woven ribbon and put them on at once, although they looked horrible with his sweater. Over the port he talked about his new commission, very hush-hush, a family job. He said he was looking forward to starting in the New Year. Beaming, taking Gilver in. 'You look much better. What's happened?'

Gilver decided to take it as a compliment. It was true, he did. He told his news.

Harry expressed pleasure at Jerry's offer of an exhibition. He could tolerate any amount of success in his friends; a rare commodity, but he didn't know any other way. He was pleased too, although he thought better than to remark on it, at the effect it had had on Gilver.

After exchanging news they went upstairs to the studio. Harry glanced up, where the brand new lampshade flourished, and said nothing. The set of great blank canvases was neatly stacked. One was already mounted on the easel, the table set up with clean paper. Nearby, the floor had been scrubbed, although most of the splotches were still there. The three-foot-square canvas Gilver was working on was full of light, as if it pierced through scuddy clouds. Chalk-marks showed the outline of a woman sitting at a table outdoors with a coffee cup and a book. The loose underpainting seemed to move and shimmer. Harry couldn't imagine how it would come out.

Gilver sipped the delicious port slowly and looked at what Harry had given him, a second-hand copy of *Tess of the D'Urbervilles* with marbled endpapers. 'Nice story,' Harry observed, 'rotten ending. No one would do what Tess did, not in real life. See what you think.' Gilver wasn't sure what he was talking about but said he looked forward to reading it. While they talked, Harry went round the studio again. He stood for a while in front of the picture of Alice before coming back to Gilver. 'I'm glad this is still here,' he remarked, genuinely pleased. 'I like this one. What's happened to her?'

'Who?' Gilver, watching him closely while apparently absorbed by the flyleaf of his present, pretended not to understand.

'You told me she got you started again, ages ago. *You* remember.' Gilver looked deliberately vague.

For the first time in his life Harry felt exasperated with his friend and showed it. 'You know perfectly well who I mean.'

To make matters crystal clear he pointed. 'Alice, the girl with the cup. How is she?'

'Oh, I don't know.' To Harry's surprise, Gilver lunged out of his chair and went and hung out of the row of windows. The sky was sharp, bright, the air bitter. Gilver took great breaths of it. Stripped plane branches across the street caught his attention, he could use them in the painting, the way they scratched at the light.

'Gilver!' Harry was insisting behind him.

Gilver brought his head in so sharply he banged it on the frame. 'Did you know, Harry, that if you lean as far as you can out of this window you can see All Saints? Come and look.'

Harry stared at Gilver as if he had lost his wits, ignoring the doubtful blandishment of a distant view of the ugly tower he knew well. He astonished himself by not feeling cowed and stuck to his ground. 'What do you mean you don't know? Hardly the Christmas spirit, is it? You say she got you going again and you haven't even sent her a card? I call that jolly mean.' He looked reproving.

'How do you know I haven't sent her a card?'

Once Harry would have let it go. He was enjoying himself. 'Well, have you or haven't you?'

Gilver shifted uneasily and tried to crack a walnut on the floor with his staple-gun. It mashed to pieces under the too-heavy blow.

Harry was still staring accusingly at him. 'You see. Mean. Bloody mean. Surely it's the least you could do. Anyway. I've got to go. Thanks for the cufflinks, I love them.'

After he had gone, Gilver lined up a row of walnuts and cracked them perfectly, one after the other.

He went downstairs and stuck his head in the fridge. Bacon,

cheese, ham: not exactly festive but it suited him. He wandered about and put on Schubert's 'Ave Maria'.

What did Harry know? Of course he'd thought about Alice, especially – if he was honest – now Juliette wasn't in the running; but still he hadn't been in touch. He had thought, many times, of the way he had left her, barely saying good-bye. He'd been in such a dreadful state. Gilver shrank from thinking about that night. He'd been drunk as a skunk and did not want to recall the way he'd behaved. You didn't want people to remember you like that, another strong reason not to call. How on earth could she forgive him?

As each day passed it became harder to make contact, impossible to explain his behaviour. He had always considered himself a gentleman: how did this look? It must be at least a month. Still, Christmas Eve was as good a time as any for getting humiliated and Alice had every right to tell him to leave her alone.

The possibility was troubling. He didn't want her to. As long as he didn't call, he reasoned, it couldn't happen.

Yet Harry was right, even though – luckily – Harry didn't know the half of it, would be horrified to know the truth. It *was* bloody mean.

Gilver picked up his favourite brush, a fat Whistler with bristles worn down from grinding against the canvas and 'Il Famoso Pennello', like a second-rate tenor, branded on its tubby handle.

The distraction didn't work.

He wondered where she'd gone for the holiday. Tucked up round a roaring fire with friends, somewhere remote. Or Venice, breathtaking at this time of year. That would suit her. He would have liked to know what she was doing.

Gilver didn't feel like painting and went down to the bedroom with Harry's book, humming to the miraculous music. Wrapped in flame-coloured tissue paper in a white box, the cashmere shawl lay on the bed. He shook it loose across the bedcovers. He hadn't definitely decided to give it to her anyway, he assured himself, he could easily find a use for it. It would look well on the back of the chaise, its rich colours enhancing the blue of the silk.

The port was good. He put the bottle in the kitchen and made some coffee.

After wandering around a while longer, he picked up the phone. Perhaps it wouldn't hurt to leave a message, seasonal greetings, that sort of thing. It was only polite.

Alice was looking at the backflap of a turkey when the phone rang from the sitting room. She had told herself repeatedly that she liked spending Christmas on her own. When Charles had rung earlier that morning Alice lied without a second thought and told him she was going away. As for Gilver. She shoved a handful of sausagemeat up the cold bird.

Her mother's advice two days before was insane. Nevertheless she had thought of nothing else. Her mother! Absurd. That her own mother had suggested it determined her in the other direction. There was no way she was going to call. She wasn't even sure if she would see him if he called her. He had hurt her at every turn. Even the consuming attraction she felt could not alter the fact of his being a drunken boor, that he had bruised her. For the first time since she met him, Alice found herself wondering if it might be best to call it quits.

The phone was still insisting. She decided to let the machine

243

answer. It was probably Charles again, anyway, checking. He was enough of a sneak for that.

Her hands covered with pimples of sausage, she couldn't see the dishcloth and went to the answerphone covered in it, ready to listen to Charles grovelling out a second helping of Christmas cheer.

The moment Gilver began she knew him. That voice. If she was honest, she had never really expected to hear it again, and sat down, heart hammering.

The message filling the room was brief. He wished her a happy Christmas. He'd been away. He'd got her a present. Would she call him when she got back after the holiday?

Abruptly the machine snapped off.

While his quiet voice crashed round the room, Alice absent-mindedly smeared sausage on the back of the sofa, ready to grab the phone. At the last moment she stayed her hand; the machine clicked. She examined her sausage-trowelled sofa with interest. Why should she make it easy for him? Anguished that she hadn't answered, she felt a strange contentment at the same time. He would have to try harder than that if he wanted her. It was not as if she had been sitting waiting for his call.

XV

Shut up in his cold studio in the middle of January, Gilver worked on the paintings Jerry had asked for as if his life depended on it. The first, the seated woman, was finished except for the face, which eluded him. He was trying to paint Alice's, using the drawing and his memory; but was scalded by the fact that the last time he had seen her he was so drunk he could only just focus. He couldn't remember exactly the colour or shape of her eyes, the tone of her skin; his attempts to render them were like fumbling in the dark. The only thing he was sure of was her hair. If he sat, as he often did late at night, too exhausted to move, looking with curiosity at what he had done during the day, he fell into thinking about her. By shutting his eyes he could see her hair change in the sunshine from red-brown to flame. He did not feel able to capture that yet but felt it was not beyond his grasp.

In the passion of working he was unaware of seeing or thinking, his hand and eye moving ahead of and beyond him. But afterwards, in this quiet time, elusive shapes came from the canvas as the light struck it in minutely different ways. Sometimes he imagined he could see her and started up, eager to capture it in paint, only to find that as he shifted his position she was gone. Despite these various proofs of failure, he clung to the stubborn belief that by the time he finished the others he would remaster his skill enough to do it, to find her. There was no time to contend with the thought that he would not.

When he had drawn her before, thwarted by her repulsing him, she sprang formed to the paper without conscious thought. He barely knew her then, not as he had known her since; yet the drawing seemed truthful in every line, had almost come to be Alice for him.

This was part of the problem: his drawing had become as real to him as she was herself – which was comfortable, it contained no reproach. In order to paint her as she really was now, after the passage of time, after the night he had spent with her, he must go back to her. And he was afraid: not that he couldn't master the drawing once he saw her, but that she might reject him. So he continued insisting to himself that it was possible to paint her – a matter of technique – knowing it for a lie. Later, he told himself, if he still didn't hear, he could get in touch. After all, it would be much easier if she sat for him. That was all he was prepared to admit.

Even though his skill had rusted through long disuse, with every stroke of the brush, every well-drawn line, power came back, increasing confidence with it. Gilver put the portrait of Alice to one side and concentrated on the first of the other paintings, part of a series that was building in his mind's eye as he worked, Biblical figures from far back in his memory that seemed to grow of their own accord.

Revelling in his work with a sensual thrill that, wryly, he occasionally found indecent, it struck him that he had never enjoyed painting so much, or even grasped the true point of it. Once he had painted for the things it brought, too complacent in facile skill and ubiquitous popularity to do more than walk his talent on a slack rein. Much as wealthy women, he thought soberly, had walked him.

Now he painted because he must. There were no pretty women hanging on him, marvelling at the meaningless abstracts he used to churn out. No one to sweep off with him to a club, a dinner, an opening. No one to come back afterwards, stirred by the aura of success he wore. Just him, a cold room, a canvas.

He met the challenge Jerry had thrown down with mounting excitement, going to bed aching and rising early, bounding upstairs to see what he had done, how it had settled overnight. Since he had something to do there was no time for anything that held him back. He drank less. Hunger and thirst were forgotten for hours on end.

Sureness increasing by the day, he experienced what he had almost given up for ever. Laying down colours as gently as he might stroke the bloom on a woman's cheek, or thrashing out a ground in a welter of something close to fury, he lost all sense of the passage of time and worked until he could hardly see. A slab of light hauled slowly across the long room from dawn to sundown, which gave him the peculiar sense of being a tiny figure on a mechanical German clock, a sixteenth-century *nef* in the form of a gilded ship; or he might be a nielloed *Landsknecht* jerking round a jewelled castle, ruby-specked doors opening and closing as the sun rose and fell. The stabbing strut of his easel marked the hours.

Captive on its stand in the middle of the room, the new painting took on various aspects with the changing light. Gilver's pace sped or slowed with it. He noted the different qualities the colours wore, how they changed at dusk when the spectrum shifted into ultra-violet, until his blues sometimes sang out, until he felt a sensation so piercing it was almost pain.

'Whan that Aprille with his shoures soote.' The words he remembered from somewhere rolled softly round as he worked.

One morning a week later the bell rang. Unwilling to break off, Gilver ignored it, but whoever it was persisted until he had to go down.

The FedEx courier wore a surly expression and glanced pointedly at her watch. He took the packet back up to his flat and made some tea while he read the short letter it contained.

Jerry didn't bother with chat. There was an unexpected slot for a show at the beginning of April and he needed to know immediately if Gilver wanted it. Otherwise the gallery couldn't guarantee anything until the end of the year, perhaps next. As if courting no answer but yes there was also a contract, setting out terms, and a cheque. At the end of the typed letter, Jerry had scrawled, 'Keep them clean.' Gilver smiled at this. He reread the letter, signed the contract, threw on a jacket and went to the post office.

XVI

The sensation of strength Alice got from not answering Gilver's message lasted a couple of days. Christmas passed in a mountain of turkey. By Boxing Day she began to doubt her wisdom: it was unlikely he would phone again after such a clear signal to call back. This depressed her, but it was of her own making.

After surviving a New Year's Eve party in Battersea with friends from the newspaper asking if she was all right, she made a conscious effort to pull herself together. You couldn't spend your life sighing after someone. Life was not a romantic novel, however attractive a prospect that might be. It was probably best if they didn't see each other. So Alice persuaded herself, feeling hurt that Gilver hadn't called again.

She decided to try to write as a distraction, even though her heart was not really in it, and hunted out a draft of a play from two years before that she had intended reworking into a film script. To her surprise the writing did not fit; sat uneasily, pinched. There was a large crocodile clip snapped on to it, nipping it in. Bits, Alice was quite sure, were so po-faced they could not have been written by her own hand at all. It was as if Charles had dictated them.

After struggling to overcome this perturbing sensation, and the sense that she was trying too hard, she tore it up and started afresh. What began as an idea based on Gilver began to absorb her. Characters started getting ideas of their own; the Gilver character hurled himself out off a balcony for no reason at the end of scene three. Alice started enjoying herself. She pushed her writing table up against the window. From outside, where she glanced up from time to time to watch the changing colours of the sky, came the sound of migrant birds returning with fresh, higher notes. Pinpricks of milky green sparked her blighted tree and the forsythia thrust out a handful of perfect yellow stars. Sometimes, when Alice opened the window, leaning against the sill to stretch her arms and back, the sharp hint of sap drifted in as days then weeks went by.

XVII

In the last week of February Juliette waved Eugenia off at the airport following a twenty-four-hour visit. In her eagerness to get away she worked hard at a parting smile. Eugenia exclaimed that she couldn't bear to go on her own, they'd had such fun together, hadn't they, she wanted to squeeze every drop. Juliette hugged her goodbye, unconsciously making a tourniquet out of Eugenia's scarf.

The day before had been one long shopping trip. If they walked past a plate-glass window without going in, Eugenia's face acquired a look of stubborn disappointment as if the riches of the Indies might be captive inside. Unaccustomed as Juliette was to give in to anyone, she persuaded herself that foreign nobility might have allowances made for it, a sort of unmerited *droit de seigneurina*. Nevertheless the two women's progress, down streets and in intimacy, was slow.

A month before, she had sent Eugenia the promised invitation for the end of London Fashion Week, with seats to the coveted final show. Eugenia rang back with her flight almost at once. She loved those little golden chairs and couldn't wait to meet. They had so much to talk about. You bet they did, Juliette thought.

To pass the time till Eugenia arrived she called Marcus, the American banker. At their first meeting she had interviewed him over lunch in the Ritz and they went straight up to bed afterwards, as Juliette had planned. It would have been a waste of an expensive room otherwise, although fortunately that bargaining chip didn't have to be played. Having made such an impetuous investment – day rates at the Ritz weren't as attractive as she had been led to believe – it made sense to continue, and Marcus proved accommodating. He seemed, moreover, to be under the impression that they were going out, and there was no reason to deprive him of such a pleasant thought. As rich as she'd hoped, he made Paul's finances look like tiddlywinks.

Juliette told his secretary to go and get him, she hadn't got all day. There was an unnecessary amount of paper-rustling before Marcus came on the line. He expressed pleasure at hearing from her, conceded that, yes, the meeting she had hauled him out of could wait a minute and hoped they were still going to the concert later.

Juliette sawed off a hangnail. It was grim, darling, she was tied up for the evening – a rich backer who knew absolutely nobody in town – they'd have to postpone their date, she knew he wouldn't mind. After all, she hadn't arranged it on purpose.

Marcus temporarily back-burnered, she bent her attention on Eugenia. Of all the people Juliette could use to get at Gilver she was clearly the most useful: after all, they had gone out for years. Gilver's presence at Carolina's christening, Juliette reasoned, could only mean that the pair of them had never lost touch.

Once Eugenia had been fed and quartered, Juliette worked hard in pursuit of her prey, asking endless questions about life in America and Vienna, Caro's orthodontics, painstakingly uncovering people in common. The short trip was almost over. Eugenia's suite in the very big hotel was full of shopping bags. Having helped carry them in with ill-concealed temper, Juliette proceeded with caution. Over a large jug of martini after the final show's party she progressed from the sofa to the bed, until they were both sprawling on its great expanse at two o'clock, like naughty teenagers.

Eugenia was going home the next morning. Until now, Juliette had found out nothing interesting, except to disabuse herself of the notion that stereotypes didn't exist. Eugenia was even more superficial than she'd dreamed. Yet, however foolish Eugenia seemed, she wasn't actively stupid. Her oft-vaunted friendship held a wariness Juliette was quick to discover, patient in disarming. Although their conversation turned early to Gilver, Juliette's touch stayed light. Whenever his name was mentioned she couldn't help drifting off to the apparently far more fascinating topic of handbags and belts. Sensing from the first that Eugenia was on guard she kept her foil buttoned. In consequence, throughout the day their exchanges had been dull and profitless. Juliette noticed with satisfaction that each time she danced out of Eugenia's reach, the Countess became increasingly frustrated by the fobbing off. It was clear she wanted to reminisce. She was practically making hand-signals.

At last, lolling on a pale mohair throw, Eugenia's defences started to come down. Maybe, Juliette decided, because she was leaving shortly and felt safe; or because Juliette's disinterest had piqued her one too many times.

She wanted to know how Juliette knew Gilver. Juliette heard the question Eugenia really asked over the drumming in her head and ignored it, pressing the small of her back against the lime *toile de jouy* bedhead to steady herself. Her reply was oblique, though she crossed Eugenia's sharp glance with an odd one of her own. She scarcely knew him, but thought he was wonderful, and his work marvellous. Didn't Eugenia think so? Eugenia knew him so well.

Eugenia reminded Juliette that she hadn't seen Gilver for a very long time. Her face looked peculiar as she said this; round her smiling mouth the skin seemed to vibrate. Juliette mustered a sweet returning smile, flipped open a copy of her own magazine and bent to read it.

Thwarted, Eugenia began again. She so hoped Juliette had managed to get in touch with Gilver using the number she had given her? Juliette put aside the copy of *Rogue*, looking rueful. 'The most *stupid* girl in my office . . .' Eugenia nodded, commiserating on the woeful inadequacy of staff. Juliette ignored her complicity, '. . . *lost* it before I had a chance to call. Can You Believe That?'

Eugenia, astonishingly, appeared to. 'So you sacked her?' She nodded encouragingly as she spoke.

Juliette hid her annoyance at the interjection. After that, she said, she felt simply *too* silly to call and ask for the number again. Seeing Eugenia's complete acceptance of this, Juliette made a mental note that she couldn't have spoken to Gilver for quite some time. She didn't know whether that was useful or not: she was still feeling her way. But it was important to know precisely where she stood. If Eugenia had been in contact with Gilver recently, everything was blown apart. Juliette never played card games where you had to guess another's hand, disliked risks. It was the main reason her career was so successful, and why she had left Gilver in peace for so long.

After yet another martini, the moment had surely come.

Juliette was absorbed in examining the stitching on a chiffon top, humming under her breath. 'Look at this,' she exclaimed happily, tugging the delicate stitching this way and that like a jackal nipping at the tender underbelly of a newborn fawn, until it gave way. 'Tat!' The triumph with which she tossed the sundered garment aside, the repeated withdrawals, appeared to be too much for Eugenia who had never been able to stand losing someone's attention. Under its even tan her skin paled to an interesting violet.

As Juliette cast around on the heaped bed towards a valuable pink scarf, Eugenia spoke at last. Her revelation went beyond the other's hopes.

Juliette was such a good friend that she had to tell her now – it had sat heavily in her heart, *schatz*, to fib – that Gilver kept her company when she was expecting her child.

'How very sweet of him.' Juliette was smooth, waiting, streaming the scarf between her nails. 'What a nice thing to do, to stand by you like that.'

They both agreed that Gilver was a terribly nice man. But then Juliette had always thought he must be. And that proved it. Did Eugenia have a picture of Caro with her?

Hanging over the side of the bed to get her handbag, Eugenia showed muscular upper legs. She came up for air with her wallet and took out a snapshot. After admiring the black-and-white photo at length, Juliette relaxed against the bedhead, trying to look bland. 'She's adorable. Does she take after her father?'

'*Ach*, not at *all*,' Eugenia confided, leaning forward from her end of the bed as if Juliette was partially deaf. '*She* has *very* dark hair, *very* black eyes. No one would ever think—' Eugenia caught herself up abruptly and shot a look at Juliette.

Juliette wasn't paying attention again, twisting round to the bedside table to put down the photo and top up their glasses. Eugenia's colour faded back to normal. Juliette balanced a shoe thoughtfully on her palm. They both made shadow-birds out of their fingers and thrust the shoes on their hands.

Juliette had photographs of all Eugenia's husbands in a file at the office. Each one had dark hair, dark eyes. Suddenly, Juliette wanted to look at all the other things they'd bought, in all the other boxes. She said her legs had gone to sleep. This renewed interest in flim-flam pleased Eugenia, who had sometimes, during the day, felt short-changed. By the time they finished, the vast room looked like a church bazaar. Bed, carpet, even the bedside table, were buried under mounds of tissue paper and ribbons.

Juliette left the hotel with an armful of impetuous gifts, which impediment she dropped among the pile of rubbish bags outside her flat.

On the drive to take Eugenia to the airport next morning it was obvious Juliette had an appalling hangover. Hunched in her corner the entire journey, judiciously moaning, quite unable to speak a single word, her fond leavetaking of the Countess was conducted in throaty monosyllables.

A tall, slack-bodied traveller, straight off the red-eye, had been slumped at a coffee stand for almost an hour. His second cardboard espresso was cold in front of him on a circular red table and he watched the travellers rushing past with jaundiced indifference. The bounce of a striking brunette speeding towards the exit acted on him like a tonic: she radiated sex and vitality. Even if he hadn't seen her half an hour earlier, drooping in, arm-in-arm with his ex-wife, he would have noticed her straight away.

Leaving the coffee without paying – it was rubbish – Anders grabbed his overnight bag and ran after Juliette, exhaustion forgotten, catching up as her driver opened the car door. She knew him at once from his photograph. Waving away his introduction she motioned him inside.

XVIII

Daisy had put a heap of mail on the editor's desk. There was a lot in March from all the design shows. As usual, as soon as she got in, Juliette divided it rapidly into two smaller piles: action and bin. Half-way through there was a thick envelope with a New York stamp marked personal, which Daisy, well trained, hadn't touched.

The writing was unfamiliar. Juliette ripped it apart and pulled out a very smart invitation to the opening of an exhibition of paintings by Gilver Memmer in the Grisher Gallery, New York, on 1 April. A note from Jerry hoped she could come. Holding the card in her lap she read it again, then checked the envelope for anything else. She told Daisy to go and buy some coffee, then put the invitation in her top drawer.

The date was less than a fortnight away. During the morning, Juliette opened the drawer at least ten times and read the card, glancing around to make sure everyone in the office was about their own business. It was almost unbelievable that anyone could prepare a show so quickly. When they met, there had been only that one repellent painting. It was all he'd done. He'd told her so. She had wondered since if the Grishers turned up after she left. Evidently they had. But she hadn't calculated he could come back this fast. When she had seen him he was a wreck, drowning in his hovel.

She went over how she had felt in the days following their meeting. Robbed, cheated of revenge by his pitiful state. She had tried to tell herself it was generous-spirited to leave him alone, but the truth was, she had no choice. And in a curious way, as time passed, rather than accepting this and forgetting it, writing him off, she started instead to consider his degeneration a personal insult.

How dare he escape her like that? How dare someone she had ever been associated with become so wretched? It almost reflected on her! If anyone found out they might even laugh at her behind her back for knowing such a failure. Strictly illogical though this was, Juliette didn't give a toss for reason unless it suited her own situation. It seemed to her that, by being so pathetic and vanquished, Gilver had snatched any justification for retribution away from her, leaving her with an unsettled score. Further, to her way of thinking he had exposed her to the possibility of mockery. This was irritating at the time and, as weeks passed, the sense of dissatisfaction grew until she could think of little else. To come so close to something after so long only to have to run away at the last minute was intolerable. It had eaten into her, hour by slow hour.

In childhood she'd learned enough from Hugh's teatime dirges on Greek heroes – Hercules in particular – to know that the last bloody thing you wanted was a Pyrrhic victory. So Juliette, convincing herself that her clemency had been stupid, began her campaign afresh. Yet despite toiling for months to get at everything she could about Gilver, so far it had been as productive as sweeping out her brother's beloved Augean stables with a twig. Nevertheless, now obsessed with her own failure as much as her contempt for Gilver, she searched for the way to destroy him, to manufacture an instrument that would not fail.

She remembered that afternoon in his flat, thinking that you couldn't strike someone who was down. It had seemed likely that everything she had pieced together about him these past agonising months would be useless. This thought, too, had added to her burden of daily anguish. But, not prepared to acknowledge defeat, she had carried on, bleak in her feeling of pointlessness.

Until this morning.

Juliette pulled the drawer open yet again and took up the card, running her fingertips over the writing on it. If this expensive, engraved invitation was to be believed, the fucker was up again, more spectacularly than she could have imagined. Any qualms about striking at him were no longer valid.

For the first time since she had torn open the envelope, Juliette felt calm. A smile crept on to her face, which she subdued at once. No one had seen it. She scraped her chair round to the schedule taped on the wall. An issue of the magazine was due out the day before Gilver's show. All the pieces were written, photography taken. They were going to start laying it out. The day he'd picked for the opening – April Fool's Day – was sublime.

Juliette marvelled at this for a while, before ringing Production and telling them to clear that crap about the new band off pages five and six. Yes, so what if it was an exclusive? She'd give them a bloody exclusive! She waited until everyone had gone home. No day had ever seemed so long. Finally alone, she took a file from her locked bottom drawer and tipped the collection of loose papers and photographs it contained on to her desk.

XIX

'Gilver Memmer is a parable for our times,' she wrote. 'He enjoyed unparalleled early success in his youth, during which he was the toast of the town, taking London by storm. Surrounded by fashionable people, Memmer had a string of gorgeous, high-profile girlfriends.'

She laid photographs of them in a row, some torn from back copies of magazines, others printed out from the photo-library. Seen together like this they bore a passing resemblance to Henry VIII's wives. 'But going out with Memmer didn't do them much good,' she went on. 'One died in a mysterious drowning in Lake Lugano; the case is still open. Another – the top model at *QT* – fell out of favour with her agency after they split up. She hasn't worked since.'

Juliette scribbled numbers on the photographs with a Chinagraph and typed out captions, left to right. She put the pictures in a plastic wallet, and continued.

You might almost think that Memmer's huge (she erased this and put 'preternatural') success was sucked from those closest to him, as if he preyed on them like a vampire, drawing strength from their wealth, glamour and beauty before tossing them aside.

Nothing stopped his meteoric rise – even what would have been, for most people, disaster: after a New York gallery offered him a major show at only twenty-eight, when he was already wealthy, the show was cancelled. His paintings, it was rumoured, fell apart before they reached their destination. This abject failure was laughed at in the press on both sides of the Atlantic.

Nevertheless, the artist [pictured inset right/left/above/ below aged twenty-eight, at a dinner at the French Embassy] continued to trade on his reputation and his social connections, using the goodwill of his many friends to maintain his position in society.

Juliette reread what she had written. Not a bad start. It was ten o'clock.

After this catastrophe he disappeared completely from the artistic scene, although he became even more prominent socially. New artists, more in touch with the taste of the time, sprang up to replace him.

At the end of almost a decade of spiralling dissipation and – coincidentally – at the exact point when Memmer's money ran out, he hit the headlines once more. His house in Knightsbridge went up in flames during a party. The police report hinted strongly at the suspicion of foul play. There was a second, unanswered question of an insurance scam. (She had a handsome young police sergeant to thank for that tip.)

At this point Juliette paused. How was she going to play it? She got up to stretch her legs, wandered over to one of the large factory windows and tilted a small section open for some air. An area of Covent Garden Piazza was visible below, brightly lit; young tourists sat cross-legged in one corner, a few tramps wandered about with cans of beer. Faint shouts of laughter and some drum beats came through the opening. She shut it.

The man she had paid to follow Gilver hadn't had any luck

until the morning in Cecil Court. Until then he had been a costly waste of time, but something made her hang on. Later that day, after an excited phone call, she went down and met him at the back entrance of her building. He was huddled into the rubbish-strewn doorway next to a downpipe, lit up with his offering. She despised him. A life spent following people about had left unpleasantness, which was hardly surprising. She stood pressed against the wall, as far from him as she could manage.

It had been hard, he told her, to get a clear look through the window of the print gallery without being seen. He emphasised the lengths he had gone to, the skill. Juliette cut him short: embellishment didn't pay better rates; she wanted to know precisely what he had seen. He told her how Gilver went in with a sort of folder and came out putting a thick envelope into his coat. The man showed how thick with his fingers, made the gesture of putting away. There was no doubt of what was in it. Through the window grille he saw the man in the shop looking for a very long time at the contents of the folder and tried to describe them to Juliette. There had been a few of them, the old man took them out one at a time.

'How many exactly?' Juliette was losing patience. The number mattered, everything mattered. She had told him that from the start. A child could have given a more accurate report.

He gathered himself at her tone, considering for a while: there were only four, yes, he was sure. Juliette made no comment and he repeated the number, less certain, as if four might be a bad thing. He tried to describe them to her; drawings, he thought, it was hard to see.

Juliette wasn't impressed. A wild-goose chase from start to finish, she announced dismissively, none of it was important.

261

Memmer was obviously showing the dealer some of his own sketches, selling them. She had paid the man off.

She stared, unseeing, out of the window and pondered what to do. Fraud: such an ugly word but, even so, could she prove it if she had to? Those engravings could be on the other side of the world by now or shut up in a vault. And the dealer might prove difficult – you never knew where you were with murky little crooks like that. Even if she did prove it, would it even matter to the sort of people Gilver knew? Mightn't they consider it rather a wizard wheeze? *Serve those insurance bastards right, good old Gilver.* Moreover, rushing back into a fire and risking his life to save some mouldy engravings, when there were so many sensible things to choose instead, either made him look like a hero ('Painter Puts Art Before Life!') or a complete idiot.

It was possible she would get him into trouble with the law, but that was far too small a prize. His name, his honour, was the goal. This wouldn't do it at all. It was better to hint at it, to leave a whiff of something. Maybe she could use the truth in a better way another time, keep something in reserve. In the unimaginable situation that her article didn't have the anticipated effect she could keep this as a *coup de grâce*: if he managed to haul himself off the ropes, it would knock him out cold. Juliette went back to the computer and began typing again:

No charges were brought against Memmer. There was insufficient evidence to prove wrongdoing.

(There was no formal evidence at all, according to the young sergeant, merely suspicion; but Memmer was hardly in a position to argue and she didn't think the police were going to pick a fight with her. If they did, surely *Rogue's* lawyers could get round it. What did she pay them for?)

After the fire, and the question-mark of *possible fraud* surrounding it, Memmer simply disappeared. Perhaps the humiliation was too much for him. You might have thought he was dead.

That last sentence was a nice touch. But it could be better. She changed it:

He might as well have been dead. In fact, *Rogue* has traced him to the dismal place he holed up in after the fire. There, faced with complete failure, he started drinking heavily, losing both his looks and his artistic judgement. He resorted to painting pathetic, sadistic images, whose only merit was to reflect his own downfall, his own depravity.

If only she'd taken a picture of that painting! It would have been so easy when Gilver went to answer the phone. What a missed opportunity, in retrospect. But where could she have put a camera? In her bra? She hadn't had a bag.

After a cup of machine coffee she sat down again. It was late. Her production team needed the copy first thing in the morning. She typed 'cross-head: WHAT'S IN A NAME' and underlined it.

His first name – Gilver – a strange word that reminds you of gold tarnished to a baser metal, like silver – grew to fit him. And his even stranger surname . . .

With a stroke of brilliance that astonished her, Juliette hit

her stride. She looked with admiration at the words string-
ing across the screen, her bad typing scarcely keeping up with
her thoughts.

'Memmer' . . . where does it come from? It reminds you
of the German hypnotist Mesmer, a charlatan who
mesmerised his patients into believing he could cure them
of any ailment with a ludicrous invention, a monstrous
piece of quackery, called 'animal magnetism'.

Juliette added another photo to the growing collection, a
picture of Gilver with his eyes caught in a hideous flash of
the camera so they glowed eerie and flat like fog-lamps.

Yes, in the early days Gilver Memmer mesmerised everyone
he met with his own animal magnetism, his seductive charm,
until they believed that his indifferent works were somehow sublime, that he was godlike. They worshipped him.
  Like the emperor's new clothes.

Juliette took this out, she was going off-course. She cracked
her finger joints thoughtfully.

Crosshead: DISGRACE.
Why did Memmer run away from the world and become
an alcoholic wreck, a sad, depraved shadow of the man and
the artist he had once been, so that even his old friends
couldn't find him; so that if they did they scarcely recognised him? Was it because he had a Dark Secret? Was it
because if the world he moved in found out it would

ostracise him? Is this why, too cowardly to face the music (*Rogue* readers liked melodrama) he ostracised himself?

That secret was an illegitimate child, the product of an adulterous relationship with a scion of one of the noblest families of Europe, a cheap scandal whose discovery would exclude him from Society and destroy the honourable reputation he traded on.

As if she put out cards in a game of patience, Juliette gently set down the last photographs from the file. Gilver. Eugenia. Anders. Carolina. Knave, Queen, King, Ace.

Surely this would get her promotion to the board.

XX

Gilver was busy writing the gallery a list of names, trying to put down people who might actually come to his opening night, or whom he wanted to be there. It was curious but he couldn't think of many and sat for a long time with an almost empty piece of paper.

His old life seemed so far away. Though he still thought of it fondly, it might have belonged to someone else, someone he'd read about in a supplement or seen on the news. Even Alice was mixed up in there too. Gilver did not send Alice an invitation. He wrote her name on one of the few kept to be personally dispatched and held it in his hand for a long time before realising he didn't have the courage to post it. He had been such a bastard, not calling. There had been a hundred opportunities to phone, or put a note through her door, she lived so close by. To ask her now, in this way, to hide his confusion behind a piece of pasteboard, was a sort of cowardice he had always despised. And then, too, he knew she did not have much money. Asking her to fly all the way to New York just to see him was an impertinence that had been in his hands to avoid. Why had he let her go like that, just drift away until she was beyond his grasp?

Gilver put the invitation in a drawer in his writing desk, with the vague idea that when he came back he could make it up to her.

He toyed next with the idea of inviting Juliette only to dismiss it almost at once. Surely she wouldn't come. She had made it very clear that she hated what he was doing the day she came to his studio. Watching her disgust then, through a protective cloud of champagne and brandy, had been more perplexing than painful. That afternoon he had been so intent on her that he would have gone as far as destroying the painting of Susanna, if only Juliette had agreed to go to bed with him, if she had made it a condition. He wouldn't have cared less.

In recollection this was an appalling thought. If he had done so – if they had done so – it would have destroyed him, broken him; he knew with horrid certainty that he would never have painted again. A devil's bargain, from which Juliette's indifference had saved him. He owed her that, although she could not know it. Nevertheless, there was surely no point in asking. What he had done since they met mattered to him more than anything.

Burning to meet Jerry's impossible deadline Gilver had worked ceaselessly. Exhilarated by mortal combat with impossibility, his past life fell from him at a speed that had nothing to do with the real passage of time, almost as if it husked, broken away. Staring at the practically blank page brought this home. He had penned only a few names where once there would have been columns. Not long ago his only reason to do the show was to recover a glorious past, to get back to how things were before. That was his ambition, so he began. But things had changed: the work was an end in itself, and a beginning too. The genuine labour he poured into these silent presences, familiar as any lover and perhaps more so, was quite different from how he had once worked. Looking back, Gilver saw that it had not been work as he now understood it at all.

He had been a charlatan, a trickster. They were painful words to apply to yourself. He had something the world wanted that seemed at the time to cost nothing. So he gave it, unable to resist the reward.

Struggling on with the list he looked up at the paintings lining the walls, nearly dry enough to crate. Almost finished, touches needed here and there. Varnish could be added in New York if the paint was stable enough. They pleased him.

The only outstanding problem was the picture that didn't fit with the rest, the most important one to him: the portrait of Alice. As soon as he got up that morning he put it on the easel. He had drawn her sitting reading, light splashing the table and catching at her book. Her face was still unidentifiable. A sculpted blur, tones and shades marking out the mouth and downturned eyes. He had worked the surface over and over again, only to scrape it back, polishing it away with turpentine.

It was terribly frustrating: it might almost be Alice, yet

it wasn't. This uncertainty, his inability to paint something that looked the way he remembered her, mirrored how he felt.

There had been plenty of time to call and ask her to sit for him, as he had first intended. Then everything would have been so simple. But he always put it off, inventing one reason or another. The easiest subterfuge was to work on a different canvas, defer the problem. His guilt at not calling for so long spurred him. Intoxicated by what he was doing Gilver felt entitled to leave everything else – Alice – in abeyance. Now there were no other canvases left to hide behind.

They hadn't seen each other for months, during which he had travelled further than in his entire life. Two months ago she was still real to him, he still wanted her. Neglecting her under cover of his obsession with work, she too had moved away, as blurred as the painted woman's face. Inside him a voice argued, Why not leave the painting as it is, unfinished? It was so easily done. He tried to shut his ears. If he did, it would be the most damning testament of all.

Sighing, Gilver drew a line under his brief list and folded it. He put the envelope by the top of the stairs and went back to mixing colours, looking hard at the elusive face on the easel, still hoping stubbornly that the answer would come.

XXI

It was one of those transparently lovely mornings that press on your heart only to fade without warning, as if they had never been. Admiring the cloudless sky and first blossom, Harry walked with a spring towards his office. There were a few things to tie up, some stone samples to check, before he took a flight to New York for Gilver's opening the following evening.

They had not met since Christmas. When the invitation came Harry had felt a surge of pleasure almost as strong as when he won his own award. He understood the importance of this show, how success or failure on the opening night would determine Gilver's career. His bag was packed, he longed to be there. Jamie was meeting him at the airport and was very excited: they were going first-class, a hotel was booked off Washington Square. Jamie wanted to get a good look at that sad bastard Harry cared for so much, to try to work it out. There was just no way – even though of course he wasn't jealous – that his lover was going on his own.

Strolling along, Harry admired the bright colours of people's clothes, their sunny hair, and drew in the particular scent of early spring with short happy breaths. Life felt good. A letter had just arrived saying how delighted his client was with progress, how well Hal was doing.

His client! If only he could tell his mother she would burst with joy. As he walked, avoiding cracks in the pavement, he tried out different ways of phrasing thanks, ready for when he got back: 'Sir, the honour is entirely mine.' What a fantastic thing to say! Did it sound too obsequious? He'd test it on

Jamie later. If Jamie's lip curled, they would find something else.

A crocodile of children was coming the other way, blue coats and berets with pompoms. Mittened hands clutched a pink and yellow cord along the length of the line. A tiny tug-of-war team. It made Harry grin. One little girl shot him with her green see-through gun, squealing with laughter. There was time for a quick coffee before the office. It was too gorgeous a day to miss out on, and his favourite café was just up ahead. This decision made, Harry dropped in at the newsagent to see if there was an advance mention of Gilver's show in the *New York Times*.

All the foreign papers were on a rack by the door, sugared-almond colours ruffled by a slight breeze. The typefaces intrigued him, held the key, he suspected, to the histories of entire continents or political movements. They were not so different from the symbols cyphering matter and the cosmos that used to entrance him in physics. Building equations he had often been struck by the fact that one symbol, shunted casually in or out of a parenthesis, could blow worlds apart or save lives. Or like Chinese brush-strokes: delicate movements of the wrist had the power to declare love or war. Those finely judged strokes. How much finer, surely, was painting, where so many brush-marks came together, were judged, in one moment. Harry began to be nervous for his friend. The exhibition mustn't fail.

Inside, behind the newsagent's counter, the girl beamed back at his greeting. Everyone looked so nice today. She blushed.

Next to the till were the gossip magazines with their salacious headlines. Under the giant word 'Unmasked!' in a slab-like sans-serif, Gilver's face took up the entire cover of *Rogue*. Harry knew he blanched, scattering the counter with coins in his haste to buy a copy. If only he could have bought them all. The shop girl started to ask after him, but Harry was half-way out of the door.

XXII

Alice rose late. She did not start work until noon. Despite a sharp wind she took breakfast at a wobbling iron table outside her french window, scanning the paper in case there was a funny April Fool's Day story. The wind scuffled with the pages, forcing her back in.

Two hours later as she strolled into the office lobby, she noticed that the receptionist was reading a copy of *Rogue* at the desk on the far side. Even at that distance she knew the face on the cover. It must be a prank; in a lurching moment she knew this was impossible. Running, Alice snatched the magazine from the startled young man's hand without comment and went straight back out of the revolving doors so fast she knocked Charles's cappuccino down the front of his trousers without even seeing.

XXIII

The great glass front of the Grisher Gallery flooded the wet sidewalk with light, making its concrete bright silver. No one in New York could remember an evening like it. It was filthy weather. Scourging winds blew horizontal sheets of water straight along the streets, spewing out at intersections like jammed faucets, mowing down pedestrians doubled against the blast. Vehicles were forced to crawl, their windscreens impenetrable waterfalls. Hail pellets mixed with thick ropes of twisting rain lashed and spat walkers into sheltering porticoes. All planes were grounded at JFK. Incoming aircraft were cancelled or monstrously delayed, circling in treacherous crosswinds over Manhattan, trying for a toehold. A light aeroplane had already crashed in a field in Brooklyn, beheading a big dog. They couldn't find the owner's tag until the pilot was found crouching under a tree unharmed, clasping something metal.

People said it was an evil wind.

Given the weather, it was astonishing that five minutes after Gilver's show opened the gallery was packed, the best turnout Jerry could remember in twenty years. Beyond the windows a determined clump of photographers crouched under tarpaulins. Jerry tried to think who the snappers could be waiting for: they had huddled outside for almost half an hour. He sent one of the staff out with some wine in plastic cups for the poor sods trying to hold up flapping oil-cloths with freezing hands. Probably there was nothing much else on that night, which was a piece of luck for him and Gilver.

How did the boy do it? Jerry mused on this for a while before going to find the woman from the Guggenheim, whom he had left motionless in front of Gilver's Susanna, talking briskly at someone down a mobile phone.

Gilver was still in his hotel a few blocks from the gallery, too nervous to hang around before the start in case no one showed up. Once, such a thought would not have entered his head.

When he had got back from the hang, at five, there had been an anxious-sounding message from Harry. Strained, brief. He and Jamie would be there on the dot. He must have rung when Gilver was at the gallery checking everything was hung right, the catalogue in order. Trust Harry to sound worried. Anyone would think it was him having the show. Gilver listened with a tolerant smile and went straight out again for a haircut. They'd see each other in a couple of hours, they could talk then. Harry had probably forgotten his cufflinks.

From inside the barber's Gilver heard the wind pick up. The sky changed in seconds from overcast to black. A tree directly outside started rocking; its branch-tips tapped the glass. Across the street a poodle tied to a fire escape started a pitiful yelping as rain came from nowhere and fell on it like a mudslide, sopping its curls to a dark mass.

Gilver fought his way back to the hotel, hunched against mounting wind. At the end of Horatio Street steel hulls of spray seemed to be rising up off the river, but it was probably his imagination. The gallery was only a quarter-hour walk away; traffic always seized up when it was like this. It was extraordinary weather but he enjoyed a good storm. For luck he had laid out his old dress suit, immaculately pressed. He placed the fiddly quartz studs carefully in a new shirt, the best he had been able to find that morning in a lightning detour down Fifth Avenue – a shortcut, he fibbed to himself with guilty pleasure, to the gallery. Somehow, in the rush to get ready, he'd forgotten to pack his own.

The hotel room was sparse but practical and in its full-length mirror Gilver looked himself over. The suit fitted as well as ever. Working on the paintings he'd lost weight. Three months of unremitting labour had taken away the slack look, brought colour to his face. He grinned at himself, tried out an imaginary handshake, met someone else with a raised eyebrow and, satisfied with the result, slapped on a little Vetiver. He turned his head this way and that in the narrow glass. The barber had done a good job. After a frank but dignified conversation on the subject of Men Today, Gilver had finally agreed to judicious highlighting, glad to be cajoled into something he'd already decided on. The effect was better than expected: it took years off.

He checked the room, finished his spiked orange juice and battened on a thick overcoat and huge umbrella for the howling walk to the gallery.

Juliette's car was booked to pick her up at seven sharp, the time on the card. Her hotel was uptown and she reckoned on a twenty-minute drive. To pass the time she rang Marcus, who said he would try to join her as soon as he could get away from a meeting. He sounded peculiar and said he had to run.

She wasn't in any hurry to arrive, having no intention of getting stuck with the Grishers, just in case they'd seen the piece in *Rogue* the day before. Even though it carried no byline they would still blame her, probably guess she wrote it. Stuff them, they were rolling in it. If they couldn't tell Gilver was a bad bet by now, that was their lookout. They knew what sordid crap he did. They should give up the business. And tonight, she thought cheerfully, they would find themselves moving much faster with the times than ever before.

Juliette subdued a slight regret for Jerry. But he knew what she did for a living. What could you expect? It was her job to tell the world the truth. Gilver was a monstrous sham and by now everyone must know it. Even so, best to give the Grishers a wide berth: Beverley had horrid-looking finger-nails.

It should be easy enough to keep out of their way. By the time she planned to get there, Juliette had every reason to believe the gallery would be packed. She had certainly made enough phone calls and Daisy had told her the London phone hadn't stopped ringing. Yes, the gallery would be full. The more people who turned out to get a good look at Gilver, to see his hateful paintings, laugh at his embarrassment over her article, the better. She tried to imagine the state he would be in when she arrived. If he hadn't already slunk out through the back.

Her zip was tricky to do up, it must be all that water she had drunk on the plane. But the final effect was magnificent, the ratio of skin to frock satisfactorily high. Juliette smirked at her reflection as she screwed diamonds into her ears and clamped a bracelet made from four coal-size lumps of quartz cobbled with thick gold foil on her wrist. She was expecting Marcus to propose over dinner after the show. Nervousness probably explained why he had sounded odd. If this didn't do it, nothing would.

Sipping a second glass of champagne she stared out at the lashing rain, which excited her even more, and waited for her car.

XXIV

From the instant Alice opened the snatched copy of *Rogue* on the pavement outside the office and read the piece she had only one thought: she had to find a way to reach Gilver. Back at her flat she managed to book a flight that would get her there just in time, the last seat. Hunting for her passport she didn't stop to think why she was going. She didn't want to think. If she did, she knew she might change her mind. This was the only thing to do, she told herself, there was no choice.

She knew Juliette's appalling writing style at once – but the horrible rantings against Gilver took her breath away. For whatever reason, Juliette was out to destroy him; this was the send-off Juliette had threatened. If only, Alice thought, she had followed her instinct at the time, tried to warn him; but she had been angry and did nothing – and now this. Full of guilt, convinced something terrible was going to happen, Alice was sure he would need her.

At Heathrow she ran to pick up her ticket. The desk clerk started to say something but Alice rushed off without listening to look for the flight. A crowd was shoving and milling round the nearest bank of overhead monitors. She pushed through, blinkering bad-tempered glances. Even as she found the right slot her plane time crumbled to nothing on the screen. 'Delayed' came up in its place.

Alice tore back to the desk, cursing the slippery floor, and barged the queue, pushing aside a man trying to ask the same question without a second glance. There was no point doing that, he said, finally attracting her attention with a touch that made her jump, amusement somewhere under his voice. It wouldn't get her there any faster. The flight was delayed, hadn't she heard? They all were until further notice, they couldn't land. What did she want to do about it? Parachute?

Alice stared at him in rage, ignoring his gentle humour. Her eyes were on the point of filling with tears. He smiled. It surely wasn't as bad as all that, was it? There'd be a flight soon, they could go together. This last was said without tawdry inflection and through her slough of consternation she noted it.

His name was James, he said; he was an antique dealer with a shop in Pimlico. He held out his hand.

Alice had been grasping the magazine so hard that her own hand was sweaty, the palm stained with ink. She faltered.

'It doesn't matter.' James laughed pleasantly at her concern. 'I'm pleased to meet you.'

He offered to buy her a consolation cup of coffee and bent to pick up the magazine she'd dropped. Alice looked at him properly for the first time. Ordinary, with rather kind grey eyes. He peered at her more closely. 'You're really upset, aren't you?'

His concern was too much: Alice turned her head the other way.

'Come on. Let's get you a stiff drink.' James swung her bag over his shoulder and she moved with him away from the thrumming crowd.

XXV

Bundled into his coat, his umbrella a tilting shield, Gilver wrestled towards the gallery, all enjoyment gone. He forced grimly forward, every step a fight, so rarely able to peer from under his impervious armour that he walked past the door. The brightness of the crowded window made him realise where he was and at the last moment he ducked back.

Closely watching everyone who went into the gallery the photographers paid scant attention to what was clearly a canny passer-by escaping the wet. They sympathised and wondered where the fuck the artist's car had got to. Their scout had double-checked that he wasn't inside, only a few minutes ago.

Gilver took the crush in dimly as an immediate obstacle to be overcome. He was freezing, his outer clothes soaked. Keeping his head well down he shouldered straight through to the back to leave his things, looking neither right nor left. His passage went unnoticed, except by Harry, who had been scanning and rescanning the room to Jamie's increasing exasperation ever since they arrived.

Harry glimpsed Gilver from the other side of the gallery:

a black shoulder, a swatch of darkened hair. He knew that head. 'He's here,' he whispered, nudging Jamie in the right direction. Jamie tried to crane over the packed mass, following Harry's gesture, but Gilver was gone from view.

'I won't be long.' Harry spoke quietly, urgent. 'I have to get to him before anyone else does.' Jamie touched his lover's arm; a resigned gesture that might have been restraint. Harry looked at the hand in a way that made Jamie, biting his lip, immediately let go. Harry disappeared.

Sodden outdoor things quickly put aside, Gilver only took in the crowd properly on reopening the connecting door between the service room and the gallery. In the shadow of the doorway, still unremarked, he looked the room over in astonishment. Half New York seemed to be out there and quite a few from London. The place was actually humming, a note that sounded higher than he remembered, almost hysterical. The thought was ridiculous and he shook it off, trying to see if there was anyone he knew. There were journalists from major papers and glossies. That was to be expected: his name must still have some currency. But also scattered among the strangers were many faces from his past, people he knew he hadn't put on the list. How on earth had they heard about the show?

Over there were Lucy and Max Cavender, Lucy fatter than ever while Max – Gilver saw it clearly – eyed a stunning girl in a yellow halter-neck across the top of Lucy's head.

He could see his ex, the painter Deborah, with short hair that suited her, chatting up someone he knew from the *New Yorker*. And if he wasn't mistaken that was Anders, a head taller than the rest, stifling a yawn near the door – as boring and bored as ever.

Very near Anders a head tossed impetuously. Gilver caught a flurry of bronze. Surely it wasn't Eugenia? He'd sent an invitation and heard nothing. But where was her new husband and why was she standing next to the old one?

Beginning to put this question into action, Gilver started moving out from his concealment when, from two directions, Jerry and Harry broke from the crowd. Harry's forehead was furled like a Pekinese's; Jerry was beaming and sweaty as usual, half a cold cigar propping his lip.

They arrived in unison. Jerry slapped Gilver's arm but Harry hung back, with a look of despair.

Gilver made a surprised face towards the heaving room. 'What on earth—?'

'Thank God you made it.' Jerry was as pleased as punch. He misunderstood Gilver's expression. 'Yes, it's astounding, isn't it? But you shouldn't be surprised. The paintings are great – great! You have to come meet some people. I've got two senators, the Guggenheim and a multi-millionaire. They've bought four between them and are haggling over another. You've got to see it to believe it. Beverley's got them in an armlock, I don't know how long they'll hold out.'

Gilver wasn't sure if he had heard straight. He was too busy looking at Harry who, empurpling, obviously needed to say something before he fainted.

Jerry didn't expect dismissal after delivering such news, yet even he looked concerned by Harry's throttled expression.

Distracted by his friend's blotched countenance, Gilver waved Jerry away. 'Fantastic! I'll find you in a minute. Tell her to sit on them.' The senators could wait. Anxiety poured from Harry's face. 'Now, Hal, whatever is the matter? You're all puckered. It can't be good for your complexion. Have you seen Max?'

Harry ignored the question and pushed his friend into the dressing room without a word. He shut the door behind him and leaned against it. Gilver was astounded: Harry had never shoved him in his life. Success must be making him bold; it was quite impressive. 'I say,' he smiled at Harry playfully, 'I've just been in here. Don't you think it's rather late to shut the stable door?'

'You don't know, do you?' Harry blurted. He'd been going insane with worry.

'Don't know what?' Gilver appeared to be brimming with good humour. He had just taken in what Jerry said. Almost half had sold, perhaps more by now. It went beyond his wildest dreams. He tucked away the happy thought for the moment to listen to Harry, a smile still on his lips. 'I don't know lots of things. What?'

'What that – that *bitch* has done?'

'Hal, I've no idea what you're talking about. Has someone done something to upset you? Surely it can't be that bad. We're *definitely* on the wrong side of the door. We should go and get a drink. I'm going to have several. You look as if you need *lots*.'

Again Harry restrained him, palms flat against Gilver's studded chest. 'She's written a piece about you in *Rogue*.'

Suddenly Gilver knew who the bitch was, although he couldn't grasp what Harry was on about. But Harry's tone was disconcerting. It didn't sound like it was a great write-up. Taking stock of Harry his pleasure faltered. 'How bad is it?' Simply. He would come at why later.

Harry looked as miserable as a stuck pig. 'It couldn't be worse.'

'Then tell me.' Gilver sat down and folded his arms, looking up at him.

Marvelling at the other's poise, Harry remarked how good Gilver looked. He had been too flustered a few minutes ago to notice anything, but now he saw. Better than ever, in fact, much better than at Christmas. A complete transformation. Graceful, handsome, ready to hear whatever he had to say. A change that beggared belief. Harry's evening was fast becoming surreal.

He shook himself: there were more important matters at stake. They would have to go back into the gallery at some point, it was Gilver's show – and what a show, he'd overheard the word 'genius'. But that would have to wait too. He collected his thoughts, seeing Gilver watching him, a game smile still on his lips. 'She said vile things, stupid things, about your girlfriends, about the fire at the mews . . .'

Gilver could tell that Harry, red with embarrassment, didn't want to go on. 'There's more, I'll be bound,' he suggested helpfully. 'Don't be afraid to tell me, Hal. You're the best friend I've got.'

Suffering as he was, Harry heard these words and the tone they were said in quite separately from everything else. Something Gilver had never said, definitely never meant. It gave him a surge of joy and of courage. 'She said you were a con-artist, that you're sadistic, that your paintings are rubbish . . .' He was overwhelmed again.

Gilver didn't take his eyes off him. 'Go on. It's all right. No surprises so far.'

Harry's eyes went wide with amazement, but he obeyed,

all in a rush. 'And that you've got an illegitimate child by Eugenia, that you cuckolded her husband. And there were pictures. It was awful.' He gestured through the closed door. 'Half of them are out there because of it.'

'Only *half*?' Gilver had not batted an eyelid.

Harry shuffled, not sure whether he felt more wounded by what he was saying or by Gilver's remorseless equanimity. He swallowed. 'I asked the other half to come. No,' he looked at Gilver with clear eyes, 'I *told* the rest to come.'

Without warning Harry found himself swept off his feet in a hug so astonishing he was never quite sure, afterwards, if it really happened. Gilver looked into his face for what seemed an age, weighing him, as if he saw him afresh. Harry could barely breathe. Gilver's arms round him! Time measured itself in his heartbeat.

Gilver set Harry down. 'OK, Hal.' When Gilver eventually spoke he was level-voiced, calm. 'You're very brave to tell me that stuff. I wondered what she was up to. I'll read it for myself later, bedtime reading. Now, this is what we're going to do. We have to go out, put on a big smile, and show them what we're made of. I honestly don't care what the silly cow has written.'

Smoothing his hair, straightening his already straight back, Gilver threw the door wide and strode in front of a trailing Harry into the vast room.

As they slammed the door behind them something happened: the excited conversation went dead. All sound switched off with a snap and everyone turned to where Gilver stood, erect and smiling, Harry hovering behind.

Confronting the expectant mass Gilver still didn't know precisely what Juliette had written, but he trusted Harry's judgement. He scanned the faces quickly again, noting their expressions. However they dressed it up, most were there to gawp. Taking his time, taking each one in, he stepped forward. Catching a familiar face, nodding an elegant greeting, moving his eyes and constant smile smoothly on. Coming closer he analysed the distinctly strange look on every face: curiosity – what? – anticipation. Gilver returned the doubt and bated attention with disarming ease.

He continued, a one-man phalanx, sensing that Harry had fallen behind somewhere. The silent crush fell back around him, opening, like the Red Sea, towards the exit, until he stood alone in a human corridor.

Do they want me to run the gauntlet, Gilver wondered, catching Eugenia's eye round someone's head and flashing her a grin. She scintillated back and waved, sapphires glinting briefly in the air. Something in the atmosphere relaxed.

Gilver thought he had everyone's attention now and held up his own hand. A gesture he'd seen in *Ben Hur*. It worked here, too. 'Friends.' His measured voice carried right around the gallery. Each word seemed to take visible shape in the room, sculpted. 'Every one of you is here tonight as my guest. I am deeply honoured you could come.'

Far behind him – Gilver fancied it was Harry – someone clapped loudly. The noise fell into silence for a split second followed by a downpour of relieved applause.

Around him the ranks closed in. Gilver joined his party.

XXVI

Just as the applause inside was fading, Juliette's big car skidded up, later than she had intended. Fucking traffic. The wind had dropped but it was still drizzling. She peered, fuming, out of the car window at the glowing gallery, awash with people. Her anger reached a pitch at the sodden photographers, shaking free of their makeshift coverings, hanging around outside by the door.

Juliette sprang out of the still-stopping car. 'What the hell are you doing here? Why aren't you back at the lab?'

The one from *Rogue* took the brunt of her attack. 'He never showed up. We got the rest of them, though.'

She was taken by surprise. What a coward! How typical! She hadn't thought of that. About to mollify her remarks she suddenly caught sight of Gilver, his back to her, through a sort of gap in the throng. Clear as day. 'You stupid bastards. Come *on.*'

Juliette imploded through the double-height doors just as Gilver turned round. From behind her the photographers unleashed an electric storm, catching his best side framed by a crowd of evident well-wishers. Juliette, the black hole at the centre of a balled aurora or the heart of a malevolent sunflower, glowered like a fury. So bright the firestorm Gilver could only just focus. Undaunted, at ease with flashbulbs, he bounded up and locked her in a firm hug, crushing a huge lump of her bracelet into his stomach.

The photographers, cold, bored and pissed-off with the vicious slag, got the hug as well. *That* was a syndication shot.

'You and I need to have a talk,' Gilver mentioned kindly in her captive ear, mid-embrace. '*Now.*'

Without acknowledging Harry's approving nod or the open-mouthed admiration of what must be his boyfriend, Gilver took Juliette's arm hard and marched her towards the back. He flung open the door into the dressing room without letting go of her, smartly striking Anders and Eugenia who were jammed against the trestle table in an unambiguous embrace. They flew apart. Eugenia straightened her neckline and slapped Juliette in an unbroken sequence. Save the violence, she was as unruffled as a receiving line. 'You are a silly tart, not to mention *incredibly* bourgeois.' Eugenia addressed Juliette succinctly. 'Call yourself a journalist. I think you've already met Caro's father.'

Anders gazed the long way down to his feet, unable to meet Juliette's eyes. After brief hesitation and without looking up, he volunteered his hand. Juliette just stared at it. Eugenia pushed him ahead of her into the gallery without further comment, considerately slamming the door shut with her foot.

Alone in the room from which the others had so recently precipitated, Gilver invited Juliette to sit on the only chair. Her volition spun out too, she did.

In the struggle to understand how everything had gone awry, why the crowd round Gilver had been so pleased with themselves and with him when she arrived, Juliette looked very lovely. Her colour up, she glowed. She sat without knowing she moved.

Eugenia's words clanged in her ears. It couldn't be so, could it? But Anders — that pallid creep, hand held out like a slab of veal — hadn't refuted it. Yet if it was true—

How on earth could she have got it so wrong – for it was clearly so? How had she been made such a fool of?

The small white dressing room was a box, harshly lit, the trestle table heaped with coats and scarves, its only furniture apart from her chair, a butler's sink with a dripping black coat on it, cases of wine. She looked vaguely at these things, trying to remember exactly what Anders had said in the drive from the airport, why she had been so sure that he was not Carolina's father, and Gilver was.

Anders hadn't said much. He hadn't needed to, she had been so full of certainty, seeing Eugenia off. When Anders appeared by her car it wasn't even surprising: she knew who he was, he seemed to fit. He introduced himself, said he'd spotted her with his ex-wife, that he'd just flown in and caught sight of them. She offered a lift, gloating with pleasure. It was as if he had fallen into her lap.

Still looking aimlessly round the room Juliette remembered how she had studied him across the wide back seat; remembered Eugenia's words that evening in the hotel, splayed on Eugenia's bed. Eugenia had made it very clear that her dark-haired child didn't take after her father. Anders had dark hair, brown eyes. Carolina *couldn't* be his.

She recalled how, as they drove back to London, she worked painstakingly, sweetly, round to asking how he felt about someone else bringing up *his* child. For answer he gave a long look, lip downturned, his nose sharp. There was no mistaking that look: surely scornful, bitter. No leeway for error. God knows, he had certainly meant to imply that he was not the father—

He had meant to imply. That was what she missed. It was not her calculation he fitted, it was Eugenia's. Eugenia must have sent him to the airport to throw her off the scent, to mislead her. She thought she had been so clever, Eugenia so stupid: Eugenia wasn't stupid at all. But how had Eugenia found her out? How had she warned Anders, arranged for him to be at the airport? Surely it was impossible – unless Eugenia had known long before, mistrusted her from the word go?

The insulated silence of the room was broken by a sudden noise from the condenser on a steel ice-machine by the sink: a shaking rattle followed by a needling burr like the old telephone in her aunt's hall.

Hearing it, she understood. The afternoon she had spent at Gilver's studio, when he went downstairs to answer the phone and came back after such a long time, looking at her with strange eyes, and lied to her uncomfortably. Nothing would have kept him from her then unless it was important – he'd wanted her so much. She'd sensed something strange but put it aside in everything that followed. The person at the other end of the line hadn't been Alice at all: it could only have been Eugenia.

Fresh understanding came almost too fast for her to keep up: even when they were in London together, Eugenia had been playing a double game, tricking her. She thought she'd been so smart but Eugenia had fed Anders his lines and she, what a sap!, had swallowed them whole.

Gilver watched her calmly, thoughts he could not begin to reach flashing across her confused face. Incomprehension, gathering understanding, softened Juliette's bullish air.

Even though he only guessed what she had actually written against him, he knew the gist of it, the outline of her absurd allegation. Harry had made it clear that she had poured vitriol; and he knew, from the splendid scene he had just witnessed, that she had gone terribly wrong and was trying to work out where and how. But why had she done it at all? That was the thing.

Safe in his recently snatched success, the contemplation of her writhing fascinated him. She was muddled and enraged; not comprehending either, he knew full well the dramatic change in him. How his transformation must mock her.

Almost unaware of Gilver's proximity Juliette nursed her wrist. She had hurt it somehow, crashing into the gallery, struck her hand and its heavy trophy against the great bronze door-plate. Cradling the fingers of her left hand round the sore place, she held pieces of pink fractured stone and twisted gold clumsily together. One precious lump was missing. A thin trickle of blood had seeped from under the torn foil and somehow smeared high up on her bare leg.

Above and away from her, the wall cool against his back, Gilver felt something he couldn't describe. A sort of anger, a sort of pity, a scant handful of either: interest was what he felt for this unusual woman. Which way she would jump.

From his vantage-point he could see all the way up her thighs – the dress split so high. He saw the smear of blood too, a fascinating stigma. It was distracting. He leaned harder against the wall, put his hand into his pocket, found a soft-pack of cigarettes and tapped one out. 'Do you mind?'

Juliette shook her head imperceptibly. Gilver lit up, blowing a stream of smoke carefully to one side and looked hard at her. 'All right, I think it's time you explained what you've got against me.' He flung his arms wide in a poetic gesture. 'I'm in the dark. Help me out.'

On top of everything else, Juliette couldn't understand why he wasn't trying to strangle her. It was abnormal to be so equable; she still gave nothing. The whole thing was appalling. Where did you start?

'Look.' Gilver leaned forward, getting an unimpeded view down the top of her dress for good measure. She was in excellent shape. One good yank and the whole thing would come off. 'Anyone else might get really cross at what you've done.'

That's an understatement, Juliette thought. Seeing where his eyes were going she felt a faint gleam of hope.

'But I reckon you're too bright not to have a reason. So before I strangle you' – Juliette jumped, noticeably – 'I think you deserve a chance to explain.'

Gilver relaxed back and smiled down at her. His eyes shone with something. If she didn't know it was absurd, she might think it was laughter. Why, he almost seemed to think the evening was good fun! God, he was handsome. How on earth had he turned himself round like that? Lounging against the wall like some imperturbable dandy in a photograph she'd once seen – Oscar Wilde, wasn't it?, all studied elegance, by someone with an unpronounceable name. Why wasn't he boiling over with rage against her?

'We can't stay in here all night you know. People might talk.'

For Juliette, his smiling urbanity was intolerable. As if he was one step ahead in a game she did not even know she was playing. Reeling from everything that hadn't happened, still more from everything that had, she gave up. If he could take all that, he could take this. And he was welcome. She'd had enough of it. 'You want to know why?'

Gilver nodded brightly, as if she had asked if he wanted more tea. His face, tinged faintly with humour and mockery, his apparent ease, were all the goad she needed. The words came without preamble.

'You raped me when I was seventeen. That's why.' The dry word scythed the room.

Juliette glanced up briefly, drenched in overwhelming relief. Why on earth hadn't she said it before, when she'd had the chance, when they were alone that afternoon in his flat? It would have avoided all this. Instead she had made a complete fool of herself. The expressions she'd caught out there beyond the door proved it. Scorn. Contempt. But at her, not at him, as she'd planned. She had written her own death sentence. She couldn't think about that now, couldn't go out and face them. She was trapped in here.

Glancing at him for a second, she caught his shocked stare of disbelief. It was impossible to keep looking. Her feeling of relief faded as quickly as it had come: he had no idea what she was talking about.

Gilver didn't take his eyes from her downturned head but his smile was gone, humour stripped away under her accusation. He ground the cigarette with precision under his foot and regarded her without falter, her skin glowing against the whiteness of the room, the hard light. 'I don't know what you mean.'

After a moment she said something: a single word so faint he stretched forward and asked her to repeat it.

'Jules.'

There was a long pause.

291

'Jules . . . my God . . . but . . . seventeen . . .' In his confusion Gilver had no idea what he was saying. 'Surely you were older,' he managed finally, so low Juliette barely caught it. 'Then – then—' He passed a hand over his face.

Juliette looked down at the broken jewellery in her lap. She didn't feel so sure of herself any more.

There was complete silence between them. Gilver kept searching her; her bent head, her hands, the heavy crushed bracelet she still clamped to herself. Like a charm against injury, he thought, with a spark of something mixed with pity. That she could sound so calm after saying such a terrible thing.

Everything was altered by a single word, moved into a different place. Years were hurtling round him. He recognised her for the first time, remembered the whole thing. What she accused him of . . . Was that how she saw it? His own memory was completely different.

Withstanding an impulse to come closer, after a while he spoke to her downturned head. 'I looked for you, you know, when I – when you – but I didn't know where to find you. Christ, I'm so—'

'Don't.' She turned her head, very pure in profile. The movement was superb.

'But—'

'Don't.'

When Juliette spoke again her voice startled them both. 'What I've done is terrible.' She looked up and met his gaze at last.

Gilver considered it seriously. All his senses told him she had every right to strike out, if that was how she felt; so many things made sense in light of it. He felt no anger now

292

at what she had written, nothing. Admiration, almost; the wish to reach her. He tried to find some way through while the years still paced and roared. It was incredible, if anything, that she had held off so long. How could there be blame? You could not weigh one injustice against another. He shook out another cigarette clumsily, almost dropping it. Juliette noticed.

'I don't know how you feel about this . . .' Gilver started hesitantly, meaning it. 'It seems to me – of course, it's completely up to you – that we've both done enough. Maybe,' he cleared his throat before going on, wishing she would only stop looking at him, 'maybe we could call a truce . . . I'll understand if you don't want to.'

Juliette tilted her chin up. One of her earrings dazzled.

For a split second, a light showed in her eyes that Gilver found fascinating. A sideways flicker, of weighing up or holding back. She didn't answer his question. 'Someone's meeting me here.'

'Of course.' Gilver seemed to turn it over almost as if it amused him. But his face didn't quite say so. He unbraced himself from the wall and went towards her, shaking himself out like a coat. 'Shall we go and look for them?' He helped her up.

Hot, his hand over hers. She did not take it away. She spoke: 'A truce . . .' her hand was still under his, motionless '. . . sounds like we're still fighting?'

Gilver made a gesture that put something aside and held the door for her to pass.

The gallery was almost empty. They must have been talking for longer than he thought. A few people Gilver didn't know lingered near the street door, propped open to let in streams of cool air. The rain had stopped. On the far side of the room Jerry was standing in front of a painting with a well-dressed man in an expensive overcoat and scarf. No one had noticed them come softly out of the dressing room.

Juliette had moved a pace away from him and was looking round the room too. Keeping his distance he watched her covertly.

She took in the paintings one after the other, the red stickers here and there. Monumental figures in long garments; men and women speaking of another time, of grace. He watched her eyes stop at the painting she had reviled in his studio. She glanced at him, biting her lip. 'Susanna and the Elders,' he said sombrely, 'after my own fashion.'

Juliette nodded. Further along the same wall a canvas painted out of blackness in soft dark tones, umbers and ochres accented with creamy white holding the figure of an old man, stooped, held up by a stout stick. 'Abraham?' she guessed. He smiled.

Still apparently immersed in the paintings, Juliette turned back to Gilver, catching him watching her. 'They're not what I was expecting.'

'Neither are you.'

The man who had been talking to Jerry was coming towards them, looking with unbroken gravity at Juliette. At his approach Gilver felt rather than saw a change pass over her, the ripples on a skin of water, minute perturbations, suddenly stilled to leave the surface lifeless and glassy. Her expression changed, she made an almost imperceptible movement in the handsome stranger's direction.

Despite everything, looking at the tense face bent on

Juliette, the man he knew she was waiting for, Gilver felt a catch of disappointment. He inclined his head and spoke words too soft for the other man to hear. 'So, where do we go from here?'

'We? . . . We don't go anywhere.'

Without so much as a glance she walked away.

PART THREE

ALICE

I

Juliette went straight from the airport to the office, hurling her bag down by her desk with a thud that challenged anyone to so much as breathe for the next hour. Whatever fallout there was she wanted to tackle it at once. She felt she could handle anything now and was determined to get it over with as quickly as possible.

It already astonished her that Gilver had occupied her thoughts for so many years, that her obsession with revenge had been so consuming. Why, at the end of the day he was just another man she'd slept with – rather a handsome, talented one, she decided. Nothing to be ashamed about: on the contrary, you might even say he was a feather in her cap.

The nearly pleasant train of thought was broken by Daisy, carrying a pile of mail.

'*How* many times?'

'Three.'

Juliette thought she detected impertinence in the way Daisy held out the piece of paper with Alice's name on it. 'And what did you say?'

'I told her you'd call back.'

'Oh, you did, did you?'

Daisy, already regretting her words, took a step away from the desk.

'Let me tell *you* something. It's called Job Description. *I* tell, *you* ask.'

She couldn't believe Daisy was still standing in front of her.

'Oh, and the managing director wants to see you.'

*　*　*

In the cab back to her apartment that evening Juliette reckoned things could have gone very much worse. Marching
along the red-carpeted corridor to the managing director's
office on the top floor she tried to prepare herself. She had
only spent one day in New York after the evening of Gilver's
show; not enough time to make contingency plans in case she
got the sack, but plenty for trouble to start.

It was in her favour that Ben Harding, the MD, had backed
her appointment as editor of *Rogue* over another candidate,
saying the magazine needed someone young, with gumption.
With a background in marketing, he had been outspoken in
his support; he wanted some edge, to liven things up a bit.
Her brutal approach, he saw at once, met his own no-nonsense
methods more than half-way.

Juliette was ready to remind him of the remarks he had
made to the board. She had a copy of the memo folded up
in her pocket.

He didn't waste much time.

If he'd wanted a bull in a china shop he would have gone
to a livestock fair, he started, voice raised, ungating his
Yorkshire accent as he settled in. It was a damn good thing
she had chosen her words with at least a *modicum* of care.
No one appeared to be filing any charges against her or the
magazine – *yet* – astonishing in the circumstances. If anyone
had called *him* sadistic and depraved, the bugger's lawyers
wouldn't have had time to get their wigs on. That painter
was clearly a remarkable man, she should be down on her
knees thanking God that the result of her *handiwork* was
that his show was practically sold out. Maybe it had put
him in a good mood. Or he was wet. Either way she was

damn lucky. Wondering how he knew how many paintings had sold but thinking it better not to ask, Juliette hoped he'd finished.

'Now, about the other matter.' Her heart sank.

'Don't come that innocent look with me. I'm talking about the man you took it upon yourself to say wasn't the father of his own child, for crying out loud. What a load of twaddle.' Anders and he played squash together, he lambasted her, looking off out of the window; the Norwegian might be as slow as a mudslide but he had a long reach – there'd been a call from New York that morning. A personal call, he emphasised. Fortunately for Juliette – he lowered at her over the top of his mahogany trophies – the Countess thought the whole thing was funny, was prepared to laugh it off. The *gutter press* always *amused* her. But Anders demanded an apology: she might like to go and write it into her editorial before she got up to any more mischief. He raised his eyebrows, gauging her attempt at escape. 'One last thing.'

Juliette had thought it was over. She took her hand off the doorknob. 'Next time you pull a story off the presses in order to carry out a personal vendetta, clear it with me first. I'd sack you if it wasn't for the sales figures.'

She looked a question at him to cloak her loathing of Anders. 'Were they . . . ?'

'You're bloody lucky, Juliette. They were huge. Another stunt like that, though, and I won't budge, not even if they hit the ceiling. Not even to scrape you off it. Consider yourself warned.'

The cab was stuck in a jam crawling up Kingsway. Juliette leaned her head against the window. Grubby buildings moved past slowly, crumbling on the top of rows of coffee shops.

New York had seemed so clean compared with this. She watched an ageing prostitute hauling along the pavement on clumsy platform shoes, her battered coat, despite the April chill, open to tight silver shorts, bare legs. Neck and neck with the cab, she moved with confused slowness and peered inside, sensing someone watching. Juliette drew back from her gaze, glad the window was up.

Marcus had taken her out to dinner after the exhibition. He hadn't even kissed her in greeting or said hello to Gilver, deliberately ignoring him. He showed her out to where he had parked and left her to get in by herself.

On the way he hardly spoke, except to remark that she looked pale and ask what on earth she had done to her bracelet. She brooded until they arrived and were seated in a very smart restaurant, the sort he liked. It was noisy: Marcus obviously considered the table private enough to talk. He let his own wine be poured before saying that the piece she had written was extremely nasty and he couldn't understand what had made her do it. He had no idea she was capable of such a thing. He'd looked at the paintings while he was waiting for her to come out of the back – they'd been in there for ages, he complained, so Mr Grisher had taken him round to pass the time. She picked the seeds off a small bread roll while he went on getting increasingly agitated.

'What were you thinking?' He looked despairingly at her, his manicured hand round a second glass that he poured before the waiter got a chance. 'What in heaven's name was all that rubbish about him and his paintings? I saw him, I saw them – have you any idea what sort of people bought his work tonight? The chairman of the bank was there!'

Patiently Juliette started shredding the bald bread.

'He remembered Memmer from the last show, whenever that was: Mr Grisher told me all about it. He's probably going to acquire one for our collection, he's on the gallery's list.'

A small plate of something dark was put in front of them. Juliette, feeling nauseous, left hers untouched, watching Marcus fork himself into a frenzy.

'And Anders . . . I've had lunch with him, we've done business together. Have you gone completely insane?'

She looked at him: he seemed very young, she'd never noticed before. His life must be so ordered. Most of all he looked frightened. 'What are you really trying to say?'

Marcus took a large drink of water. 'That I can't . . . that it's too . . .'

Beyond his anger and embarrassment, Marcus saw that Juliette had turned completely white. After folding one end of her napkin into a ball she was crushing it in her fist. She let it go on the table. 'Will you excuse me for a moment?'

Leaving Marcus sitting staring she went and threw up in the cloakroom, and left.

The traffic was moving now, they were almost at her flat. It was a pity about Marcus, but she wasn't in the mood for explanations that probably wouldn't change the way he felt, at least not until he simmered down or things blew over, and possibly not then. Nor did she want to tell him everything, go over it again. If there was any hope of their starting afresh, raking over the past would be suicidal.

Juliette was more exhausted than she had ever been in her life. She didn't even know if she cared what he thought, if he came round; she was too tired to wonder about it. Two days ago she was certain he was going to propose. Before she messed everything up he had been in love with her, she was sure. He'd lick his wounds for however long that took and then he'd call.

She flicked on the answer-machine just in case. There were no messages, only beeps where someone had put the phone down. It might have been him already.

While the bath was running her phone rang. Alice's voice took her completely by surprise. 'I have to talk to you as soon as possible,' she announced, with an insistence Juliette had never heard. 'It's important.'

Too tired to argue, Juliette agreed to meet the following evening, and went to bed.

II

Alice never paid much attention to the clothes she wore as long as they were clean. With so many starving people, hemlines seemed neither here nor there. But this time she wanted to look right: in control from the word go. She'd had enough of being pushed around and had to know what had made Juliette do such an awful thing. She took a black jumper off again and threw it on the floor. Her favourite red cardigan looked far too lighthearted. She'd told Juliette she would meet her at the office at six, straight after work: Alice didn't intend to give her any excuse for cancelling.

On her clothes rail was a tailored jacket she hadn't worn since her job interview at the newspaper, very dark blue wool. The effect was businesslike. She caught her hair back with a black ribbon. It seemed about right, it would do. If Juliette had been capable of understanding the allusion she would have tied a red ribbon round her neck.

In the three days since she said goodbye to James at the airport, watching him set off to catch a plane she could have been on, Alice had been going mad with anxiety.

They had stayed almost two hours in the ersatz pub until the monitors said flights were running again. He got her a very large whisky, making her drink it down before fetching them both another. After an hour, relaxed by alcohol, she unrolled the magazine stuffed in her handbag and showed him.

He read it right through twice, sipping his drink. 'Extraordinary,' he said finally, rolling it up again thoughtfully and giving it back.

Accustomed to agonising over things in private, consternation made Alice want someone to tell her what to believe. This kind stranger, whom she would probably never see again, seemed as good as anyone. 'So, what do you think?'

'Well, she's got it in for him, that's for sure,' he observed frankly. 'Looks like a classic case of a woman scorned to me. It's hardly what you'd call objective journalism, is it? Where are the quotes? No one gets a chance to answer back. You said this woman, your friend, always had a thing about — what's his name? — Gilver. I'd say she had quite a thing about him. Why did they break it off?'

Alice looked shocked. 'They didn't — I mean, go out together . . . I wondered if they had a fling . . .' She looked at the rings on the table.

James leaned towards her seriously. 'How old are you, Alice?'

Mid-air her glass stopped.

'You're right, it's none of my business. But you're old enough to know the way the world works. Don't you think it's time to grow up?'

Kindly put, but it stung.

'Look,' he said, patting her arm, 'I feel horrible saying this, but you asked me. I'm an ordinary bloke and I've always taken people at their word. I suspect you have too, perhaps it's part of the problem. Or maybe you just don't want to see. It's difficult to say what I think without offending you. You say she's your best friend, although I can't really imagine you in this sort of world,' he flapped his hand expressively, 'and you're obviously in love with him.'

'Is it that obvious?' It was the whisky talking.

'It's written all over your face. I'd have to be blind. It doesn't matter, your secret's safe with me.'

He noticed her mouth twist at the slight levity.

'So naturally you want to protect him. You were going to rush over there, weren't you?, and defend him, and you find it hard to think the worst of either of them.'

At these words James saw a change come over Alice's expression.

'Oh . . .' Successfully he fought down a smile. 'It's all her doing and he hasn't provoked it in any way. Do you think that's really likely?'

Stricken by his accuracy she could hardly bear to listen.

'I'm sorry. Really. I didn't mean to upset you. I don't know when to stop. Finish your drink, it'll make you feel better.'

They sat in silence until the flight came up. James already knew she had decided not to go and thought it a pity to say goodbye, but he understood. It sounded as if she would probably get hurt all over again. 'Alice.' He took her hand lightly for a moment between his own. 'Look after yourself. May I call you when I'm back? I'd like to know you're all right, and take you somewhere decent to have a drink. May I?'

He rose from the cramped table. 'Chin up, I'll see you soon.' Nearing the ticket desks, James looked back at the pub with its cheap balustrading, but their seats were empty.

III

When her watch showed ten to six Alice went to *Rogue*'s offices to discover Juliette already coming out of the building.

On the broad stone step in a red leather coat and red lipstick, she was obviously on the offensive, making no attempt save a grimace in greeting. She went with Alice to a nearby café where they ordered coffee at the high melamine counter and sat down under overhead strip-lighting. Juliette perfunctorily rejected Alice's offer of something to eat; the first words she spoke.

If Alice had been in any doubt that she might lose her nerve, Juliette's curtness steeled her. She had had more than enough of it. There was no point wasting further time. 'I read that piece.'

'You and sixty thousand others,' Juliette interrupted, thinking of the fifty per cent rise in circulation. A bonus wasn't out of the question.

Alice ignored her. 'What on earth made you write it?'

'Oh, don't you start.' Juliette's voice was sharp. 'That's all I've heard the past few days, I'm sick of it.'

'It was horrible.' Alice refused to be diverted. 'I couldn't believe the things you said.'

Colour was seeping into Juliette's face. Now she knew the tack Alice was taking it shouldn't be so hard to waylay her. She drank her coffee noisily. 'That's your trouble, Alice. You've always had your head in the clouds – you wouldn't believe something unless it ran you over.'

'But I still don't believe it was true.'

Juliette was nettled by Alice's tenacity in bringing the conversation straight back to its original point. She'd always been able to run rings round her: this was a novelty. 'Which part didn't you believe?'

Alice had known before she came that Juliette would bully her. Despite the awfulness of Juliette's voice, the terrible sense that beneath her anger she was almost enjoying herself, Alice stuck to her guns. 'All of it. I've always known you could be – horrid,' she was going to say 'a bitch' but couldn't quite bring herself to it, 'but I thought even you had limits. I never really thought you'd do something so underhand.'

'Underhand? You don't call fraud underhand?'

Horrified, it took Alice a moment to work out what Juliette meant. She knew the article by heart. Her eyes brightened. 'But you admitted yourself that that wasn't proved. You just put it in to stir things up. It's exactly what I mean.'

The smile she got in return was ugly. 'Well, it's true. He got loads of insurance money on some engravings he sneaked

out of the fire, and then he sold them. If that isn't underhand I don't know what is.'

'How do you—'

'I just do. I had him followed. It's called a private detec-
tive, a child could do it.'

Her words didn't have the crushing effect she had intended.
'*You had him followed?* You'd sink so low after everything he'd
been through? He'd lost everything, but that wasn't good
enough for you, you had to do more damage?' Voice rising
despite herself, Alice hardly heard what Juliette said, enraged
in Gilver's defence. 'I've called you my best friend for years,
but you *knew* I liked him and you did that behind my back.
You've tried to take everyone I was ever interested in off me.
It's disgusting. Couldn't you have let me have one person I
liked, just one?'

Juliette folded her arms. That was what all this was about.
'Don't be so feeble, Alice,' she said levelly. 'Why should I, if
they preferred me? You've never fought for anything in your
life. I have. If I want something I take it. And if someone
gives it up without a fight, more fool them. Anyway, I told
you months ago that you could have him. I told you what I
thought about him. I don't see that you should pretend to be
so surprised . . . so, so – *noble* when I write it down instead.
It's no different.'

'Yes, it *is* different! What you said to me then was horrible enough, but writing it in a magazine! Accusations you
didn't back up, that can't all be true! So what if he managed
to save one thing? He was ruined! You would have done the
same if you had the chance.'

This was perfectly true. So would most people, in Juliette's estimation; she'd definitely been right not to put that bit in. Yet she'd traded on using Alice's scrupulous honesty to turn her against Gilver and it hadn't worked. The blindness of love, it was sickening. More fool Alice for not leaving well alone. She was riding for a hell of a fall.

'*And* you didn't even have the courage to put your name to it.'

Juliette sighed and examined her fingernails, how precisely they matched her coat. She knew that Alice, face peaked, hair pulled back, eyes not leaving hers for an instant, was lashing out all over the place. She didn't know how wrong the main thrust of the piece was and Juliette wasn't about to tell her, either. However uncaring Alice seemed about Gilver's cheating over the engravings, it must be making her less certain by the second, loyalty or no. She was probably doubting everything, and the retraction wouldn't come out for days. There was a chance Alice wouldn't ever read it. It was incredibly bad luck that she had read this.

Juliette knew Alice despised *Rogue*. If she'd minded her own business she would be much happier now. It was on the tip of her tongue to say so.

'Alice, I work on a gossip magazine. I write things to get people interested. It's all in the big picture. Do you think most people care? Do you know our ratings went into the stratosphere?' She let this sink in. 'Did you know he's sold most of the paintings from that bloody show because of me?'

Juliette observed Alice deflate, knocked back again. Thrown this unexpectedly flattering piece of information she was losing her sense of certainty. Juliette pursued the advantage. 'He should be thanking me. I've given him a comeback he doesn't deserve, which was bloody nice. And if you're so keen on him, if you think he's such a genius, why weren't you there? Didn't he invite you?' With satisfaction she observed Alice losing courage, losing her grip.

Alice rallied, aware that Juliette was doing it again, doing what she always did. The vanity of trying to hold together a friendship she had been afraid to admit was over left her so suddenly she took herself by surprise. 'You twist everything to suit yourself!' she exploded, not caring that she was shouting. 'You always have. Of course he invited me. That's not the point. I'm sick of this, I just want to know why you wrote it at all. Can't you give a straight answer once in your life? If it's the last time we ever speak to each other, can't you do that?'

'It means that much to you, doesn't it?' The teaspoon between Juliette's fingers flicked rapidly up and down, testing the wind.

'Yes,' Alice said, 'it does. I don't care if you try to hold it against me, it does matter. I really like him, I have ever since I first met him, and I can't stand it. I've known what you were capable of ever since you took that rower off me. God knows why I haven't learnt.'

Juliette dimly recalled the rower Alice was talking about: an indifferent evening, if she remembered correctly. That wasn't the important part of what Alice was saying. Curiosity got the better of her.

'Can't stand what?'

'Can't stand it that you've been having an affair with him.' Alice swiped away an angry tear that threatened to start. 'Why the hell couldn't you leave him alone?'

At a nearby table a couple looked over enquiringly at their raised voices.

'Haven't you got a television at home?' Juliette rose up like a cobra and they shrank over their drinks. She turned back to Alice. 'So that's what you think. All this anger, it's not really to do with what I wrote, is it? That's not what this is about. You don't even mind that he's a thieving bastard.'

Alice was mute.

'It's about whether I fucked him, isn't it?'

They could both be blunt, if that was what Juliette wanted.

'Yes, it's whether you fucked him,' Alice hissed back.

They stared at each other over the Formica table.

'No, I didn't.'

Juliette waited until Alice had taken it in, waited for the trickle of hope, of relief, to show. Nothing happened. Alice simply stared at her, her eyes full of hatred.

'*He fucked me.* You asked, so I'll tell you. Your Gilver Memmer, the man you doubtless dream about, your knight in shining armour, fucked me when I was seventeen, he fucked me when I said no, he fucked me and he made me pregnant. Happy now?'

'I don't believe you,' Alice breathed, shaking so hard her cup rattled.

'Believe what you like. It's the truth, take it or leave it. But grow up, Alice, the world isn't nice, people aren't nice. That's how it is. I had a score to settle and I settled it. Have him, he's yours.'

IV

Gilver watched Harry up a ladder in the studio with a thick blue pencil while a workman in a T-shirt held him steady. One hand on a side brace, the other, Gilver noted thoughtfully, on Harry's leg.

'Here, here and here.' Harry was authoritative, drawing rings round screwheads that needed sinking before the plastering started. He had been absorbed for over an hour, checking everything was done right.

'You've missed one.' Gilver indicated a spot just out of Harry's reach. He watched as both Harry and the man stretched to scan along the join.

Harry bent round and caught Gilver's grin. 'You bastard. I could have fallen off.'

'I'm sure Iannis would have caught you.'

Harry blushed and came down, letting Iannis go home for the night with what Gilver decided was a touch of regret.

'Handsome.' Gilver was just warming up. 'How old, do you think?'

'Give it a rest.' Harry snapped the ladder shut. 'I've had enough of your nonsense for one day.'

They were boarding over the once-gaping ceiling and putting in proper lighting. Gilver had only complained halfheartedly at Harry's suggestion on the flight home a fortnight earlier. After all, he could afford it now.

'You're becoming a tyrant, Hal, do you know that? All these grand clients are turning your head. Soon you'll be a monster and no one will be able to stop you doing anything you want.

Literally anything. You'll be swanning around with a harem and God knows what.'

Harry strolled about the almost bare studio, tutting at shavings of plasterboard and escaped screws that he put in the pockets of the chemist's coat he was wearing as an overall. 'You're a fine one to talk,' he countered. 'The biggest bully I ever met. Don't talk to me about harems either. The women who turned up for your show! I must have listened to at least ten telling me how much they'd been in love with you. They didn't care what Juliette wrote, I think it got them – well, you know. Some of them were going back *decades* as if it was yesterday. Leaping to your defence like lemmings.' Realising what he had just said was rather rude, Harry hurried on: 'You should have seen Jamie's face.'

'Well, I'm reformed. Lemmings or no lemmings. A new man. I'm going to padlock the front door, paint, and eat rusks. You know I've got a show at the beginning of next year. No time for any of that. *What are you doing?*'

Harry had picked up a small sketchbook that had been leaning against the wall under the windows. Turning the pages he came slowly towards Gilver.

'Give that to me.'

Harry ignored him. 'Hello!' He held up the leatherbound pad. 'So she's back?' He sank into the armchair, the book open in his lap, watching Gilver's face. 'It's Alice, I recognise her. When did you do this?' He turned the page, astonished. 'And this?'

'I don't know what you're talking about.'

'Oh, come off it.' Harry opened the book flat and pushed the first drawing up against his friend's nose. 'You're not that bad at catching a likeness. I'd know her anywhere.'

Gilver bridled. 'So kind. I take it you don't want a glass of wine?'

Harry bounced out of his seat, relinquishing the book. Gilver slid it quickly under the armchair with his foot.

'And while we're on the subject, what about this?' Harry had gone over to the only canvas left in the studio, propped against the easel out of harm's way. Without asking he turned it towards the light and lifted it on to the support. 'It's still not finished, is it? Why haven't you called her and got her to sit for you? You promised you would on the plane. Gave me your word.'

'I did. I've called several times, since you ask. I need to get that painting finished.'

'And?'

'She hasn't called back. I expect she's on holiday. People do go on holiday, you know,' he added defensively.

'So how do you account for . . .' Harry seemed to be searching for something. He frowned, catching sight of the drawing book clumsily thrust under his chair. '. . . those?'

'I saw her.'

Harry looked smug. 'Now the truth comes out.'

To his surprise, Gilver rubbed his hand uneasily through his hair, looking uncomfortable.

'I was in a café last week, I saw her through the window buying something on a market stall, standing looking at it, some sort of vegetable. She didn't see me, so I sketched her.' He was still fidgeting.

'OK, we'll come back to that. Pretty weird behaviour but I'll buy it. But the other one? Didn't she see you doing that? I mean, look at it.'

In the second sketch Alice sat at a table, writing. Her face was drawn in fine detail.

Harry had never seen Gilver so embarrassed, struggling with himself whether to speak or not. Indecision almost contorted his features.

Watching the discomfiture he had felt so often himself, what it looked like from the other side, Harry experienced the sense of power it brought. He sat again without leaving off staring, determined not to miss a second of whatever was going through Gilver's mind, full of wonder and curiosity. It was a revelation to see Gilver Memmer squirm.

'Good Lord, she didn't know you were there, did she?' he finally asked. 'How on earth—'

'Come on, have some wine, Harry, for God's sake.' Gilver poured for both of them and struck a light for his cigarette on a scrap of discarded sandpaper. He sighed. 'I told you, I rang every day just like I promised. I left messages asking her to call me. She hasn't. What more do you want?' It was a supplication that would once have made the other lose his thread. Relentless, Harry prodded a finger in the direction of the drawing book. 'You still haven't explained how you did that.'

'I used a camera.'

'You did *what*? Have you turned into a stalker?'

Now he had started Gilver found it a relief to explain. 'She didn't call back and it made me feel—'

'Rejected?' Harry interrupted deliciously.

'Thanks, Hal. Anyway, when I saw her from the café I was going to go out and say hello, and then I thought if I did it would seem—'

'Stupid?' Gilver's face made Harry stop teasing.

'So I thought, if I was quick, I could sketch her, you know, just rough, and if she saw me that would be fine, but she didn't, she went.'

'And then?' Every last ounce. Surely after all these years he deserved it.

'Then I realised that if I could just take a picture, maybe I could finish the painting from that . . . Oh, I don't know.'

'So how—'

'Through the hedge. There's a grotty sort of hedge at the front of her house, gappy. I took it through that when she was working. She was sitting at the window. She writes plays. I watched for a while and then I took it before she looked up.'

Harry relished the thought of Gilver crouching behind a hedge, peering through the branches. 'Exactly. You stalked her, like I said.' His triumph was almost complete. 'Let me get this straight.' He swung around the room again, bellowing out his white coat by the pockets. 'She doesn't answer your calls, for which I say, hurrah, the woman has more sense than even I gave her credit for. But that doesn't satisfy you. You've finally decided you're in love and a bulldozer won't stop you.'

Gilver started to protest.

'Don't insult me, of course you are.' Harry wheeled round again, tails flying. 'So you stalk her, photograph her through the hedge, finish the painting – my favourite, by the way – and then what? Go and leave it on her doorstep with a bunch of roses?' He stopped abruptly, flaps subsiding.

'Whatever,' Gilver muttered. 'I hadn't got that far.'

V

Badly wrapped in brown paper the large parcel, her name scrawled in enormous letters, was propped in the shared hall when Alice came home from work. Her upstairs neighbour must have brought it inside earlier, out of the drizzle. She tried knocking on the door to ask who had left it, but no one answered.

Alice bumped the unwieldy thing downstairs as carefully as she could and got it into her sitting room, where she tore off the wrapping.

She sat looking at the portrait of herself for an hour, staring out of the window from time to time to see if the downpour had stopped.

That it must go back at once was obvious. Her first thought was to march round there immediately, although it seemed a shame to let it get spoilt in the rain. Despite herself, Alice noticed the way he had painted her hair, almost as if it was living. She put her nose to the surface. A faint smell came off it, it was only just finished.

He had painted her reading at a table, holding an open book, light tumbling on to her hair and hands. Do I look like that? Alice wondered, inspecting herself in the bathroom mirror.

Three foot square, in her small room the canvas seemed bigger than it really was. It couldn't stay; where would she put it? How had he been able to do that when she had never sat for him? The thought of Gilver painting her, the hours he must have spent thinking about her, sped her breathing. Weakening, threatened into betrayal by the pounding of her heart as she studied what he had done, she reminded herself of how he had treated her and forced herself to remember Juliette's horrible claims.

Outside the rain strengthened, a gust spattering the window-panes, set to pour until morning. She couldn't sleep with the painting in the flat, wondering if Gilver might call as he had so often during the past three weeks. Each time he rang she knew she could put an end to it simply by picking up the phone. Instead she listened to his messages, always the same few polite words, asking her to call back. If she didn't answer his phone calls she would never have to know, never run the risk of hearing him lie about what Juliette had said. Surely it would be better that way. For once, she knew Juliette had been telling the truth.

The way he had painted the book, its pages every colour from white to dark ochre and violet, the way it cast shadow on the table and the pages almost fluttered in a light breeze that might come through a window, while coppery strands of her hair also seemed to flutter, was finely done.

Alice peered again at the face. It was hers, but didn't feel like her. Someone else trying to capture your soul. An involuntary shudder ran through her. Perhaps everyone who had ever had their portrait painted, even if they sat for it, felt that. And then, even if it looked like you at first, how did it seem as you changed and the painting did not? Was this how he saw her, her skin, her mouth? She mustn't think about it.

Entirely absorbing her attention, the painting undermined everything she had been convinced of. No ambassador could have pleaded so eloquently, argued so directly to her heart. If anything could be called a labour of love, surely this was it. Alice was so moved that she no longer knew what to think, except that her attempts to hate him were falling away beat by beat.

She went over the meeting with Juliette again, the rage in Juliette's voice. If there was the slightest doubt, the faintest chance of an explanation or of mitigation, she would have seized it. What if Juliette, bargaining on Alice's lack of courage, had made things seem worse than they really were, certain that Alice would never dare to find out for herself? So far Juliette would have been right: she had always shrunk from confrontation. Not answering Gilver's calls proved it.

Alice stared round the room, at her hands, at the portrait. How could the man who had done this—

With one movement she wrenched the covering off the sofa and bundled it round the painting, tied the thick fabric into the best knot she could and hauled the whole thing upstairs and out into the dismal street.

VI

'I can't stay.'

Drenched to the skin and panting from exertion Alice stood on the porch, just shielded from the rain. She moved down a step when he opened the door, preparing for flight. At the sight of him, whatever she had intended to say deserted her. She motioned towards the heavy package. 'I was going to leave it and ring the bell, only you might not be in.'

'That was thoughtful.' Guarded. Opening the door he had caught sight of the wrapped painting a fraction of a second before seeing her. He had not bargained on that, something was very wrong. Full of unease she balanced on the edge of the step, uncertain whether to stay or go.

'There's something I have to ask you.'

Water was dripping from her clothes, running from the hair flat on her head. She was almost black with rain against a sky needled silver like a hanging. Although the sky flared wide behind her she gave the impression of being trapped. Whatever it was obviously bothered her a great deal. Gilver couldn't begin to understand. 'Won't you come in?' he asked, making no reference to the sodden bundle leaning against a column, neither to touch nor look at it. It might not have existed. What mattered was that Alice was there, looking so strangely at him.

'No, thank you. There's something—'

'You said,' he reminded her gently. 'Please come in for a moment, Alice, you'll catch your death. You're wet to the bone.'

'No . . . thank you.' She couldn't stand there all night: looking at him, remembering him, was almost too much. She felt as if she might choke. Freezing from the wet she wiped rain from her eyes and thrust her hands into her soaking pockets. If she didn't speak now she never would.

Alice took a deep breath. 'Juliette and I—'

With his right hand Gilver suddenly gripped the painting, almost as if he intended to prop it better. When he finally spoke he couldn't recognise his own voice. 'I didn't know you knew each other.'

'Yes.' It was almost as if she threw down a challenge. 'I've known her since I was eighteen.'

Alice prayed he wouldn't understand her, would ask her to explain what she was talking about. At that moment, even if he lied she would have been glad. All she could see ahead was having to give him up, to lose him. It was all there was.

Staring out at the seething rain behind her, Gilver cast back to when Juliette visited him and saw the drawing of Alice, asking endless questions about it. *'Who's she?'* The memory of the words came so clearly Juliette might have stood between them. That they knew each other had never crossed his mind. It dawned horribly that Juliette must have told Alice the same dreadful things she had hurled at him. Which meant that these three weeks all the feeling, all the hope he had poured into the painting were a mockery. There wasn't any hope. Alice must hate him, too.

He had to find out. The way she stayed motionless on the step, rain beating at her, refusing to protect herself from it if it meant standing a millimetre nearer him, struck him as if she had struck him across the face.

'So she told you.'

'Yes, she told me. It's what I came to ask.'

Understanding the reason for her silence all these weeks hurt more than he believed possible. His attention bent on her, Gilver noticed a trace of something else: despair, pain even, matching his own.

'So . . .' Alice took another breath, reached out and patted the bundled painting, a valediction, readying herself to go.

'It's true,' he declared abruptly, determined to make one last attempt to keep her. 'She told me in New York.'

To Alice his words only half made sense. He watched her, waiting, still rooted. Behind her, its pavements running with wet, the street was silent except for the occasional *siss* of a passing car.

'Told you what in New York? I don't understand.'

322

They looked at each other, incomplete. Gilver broke the silence. 'Alice, I didn't know who Juliette was. I didn't know we—' He saw her agonised expression but had to go on. 'I didn't know you knew each other. What can I say? All these years, I haven't known how she felt. And, God, if I'd known she was so . . . so young . . . do you really think I would even have—'

She stared at him, trying to grip what he was telling her. 'You didn't?'

The seriousness of his face answered her.

'And you mean that all this time you didn't know who she was, either? You didn't remember her?' She still hadn't moved.

Gilver spoke, scarcely seeing Alice framed by the cold blackness behind her. 'It was just a night, a beautiful summer night, she was there with a friend. We went dancing, there were four of us, we thought they knew what they were doing. And afterwards I had no way of finding her . . . I tried.'

She didn't take her eyes off him, weighing him.

'It was half a lifetime ago. Then at my opening she told me . . . that.' He couldn't bring himself to use Juliette's word. 'That's it. There's nothing I can do to change it. I would if I could.'

Freezing, Alice scanned down the dark street as if tasting the air, first in one direction, then the other. 'Ah.' She still seemed to be searching for something, scenting it out.

He could feel her slipping away from him, disconnecting herself. 'Please don't go.' Gilver stood grasping the painting, hopelessly grasping the sodden bundle like a talisman as if it alone could make her stay. He had to say something to fill the silence. 'I did this for you. I've been trying to paint it

323

since Christmas, you have to believe me. I haven't stopped thinking about you.'

Vaguely, as if she wasn't sure where she was, Alice rubbed her hands together. 'I'm awfully cold,' she told him, as if noticing it for the first time.

He could see she was shaking and went towards her, where she was motionless on the step. 'For God's sake, Alice, please.'

'No.' Her voice had no strength in it; she still hadn't left. 'I have to go home.'

Gilver sighed. 'I shouldn't have tried to keep you, I'm sorry. Shall I walk you back? It's late.'

She smoothed the wet hair on her shoulder and looked round towards the pavement, the direction of home, before looking back at him. Her eyes were glistening. 'Can't you see it's all so . . .'

'I know.' Gilver hardly dared speak. 'It's a nightmare. It's not how it ought to be.' He moved a step towards her and put his hand on her sopping shoulder, knowing she might shake him off. 'Alice,' he said.

VII

Gilver Memmer sat on the blue chaise in his studio. Behind his back the eight-foot mirror Harry had fixed up reflected the back of his hair, half of which stuck up on end. Beyond him the foxed glass held captive the large room with its easel, a table and brushes set up next to it, and the row of windows beyond that, casting a good light.

He bent down yawning and pulled a shoe out from under the narrow sofa before thinking better of it. He shoved it back and went downstairs in socks, almost knocking over the painting where he had left it sticking out at the bottom of the flight.

Pushing his bedroom door open a few inches he looked in. Alice lay fast asleep across the bed, entirely clothed except for her coat. Her shoes were still on. One pillow was on the floor. Her coat sprawled on a pile of books. She had covered herself with the green cashmere shawl; her hair was mixed up with its tassels of dark green and gold, struck by a shaft of sun that had managed to get through crookedly drawn curtains.

For a while he stood looking at the way she slept, as if the Charge of the Light Brigade would not trouble her, and studied the way the shawl fell around her body, admiring its colours against the lit red of her hair. It would have made a great painting, if only Klimt hadn't got there first. On the other hand, Klimt's models were seldom fully dressed.

Mulling this over, Gilver went whistling down to get the newspaper.